BONE-A-FIED TROUBLE

Trouble Cat Mysteries #9

CAROLYN HAINES

KaliOka Press

Cover design by Cissy Hartley
Formatted by Priya Bhakta

ISBN-10: 0984700137
ISBN-13: 978-0984700134

For Cissy Hartley, an author's best friend and a great talent

CHAPTER ONE

I smell money! I've heard the expression all my life and thought it was an exaggeration of the rapacious American spirit of Manifest Destiny. Not true! I, quite literally, smell it. It's the odor of this rich Delta soil being turned over by the big machines plowing and planting. Another money crop is going into the Mississippi alluvial ground, and yes, now I understand what money smells like. Something to keep in mind as I learn my way around Sunflower County in Mississippi.

I'm here on a mission. A fellow feline, Pluto Delaney, has called me in to assist him in resolving a mystery. Pluto needs to find a missing female humanoid. Trudy Wells belongs to one sassy little marmalade kitty named Vesta, and Vesta is missing her human. Pluto has a thing for Vesta, and I'm here to help. Nothing flips my ascot as much as a mystery given to me by a black cat almost as eloquent and articulate as I—a mystery that also involves a missing person. If anyone can find the missing girl, I'm that bloke.

Pluto, who lives on a fine plantation in the Mississippi Delta, has issues of transportation. He's not savvy about hitching rides and public transit, which is in short supply in the land of King Cotton anyway.

When he heard I was in town with my biped, Tammy Lynn, he sent out an S.O.S. I responded, of course, and hence I'm currently sussing out the circumstances at the elegant Long Hall, home of Samuel and Charline Long. They're elders of the agricultural Long family—the place where Trudy Wells worked before she vanished off the face of the earth. While it's possible Trudy has simply moved on, Pluto suspects foul play.

Peeking out of the Long shrubbery, I'm getting an eyeful of a long-stemmed American beauty with a fiery mane.

The redhead in question has been snooping around Zinnia, Mississippi, the county seat of Sunflower County. She goes by Tabitha Kingsley and the locals say she has a pact with the devil. She's a psychic medium—or so she says—and can communicate with the dead. So what is she doing here at Long Hall?

I watch her exit a new Genesis G90 black sedan. She has all the physical attributes I normally find endearing, yet I have reason to be wary. Tabitha Kingsley has the look of a woman of money and privilege. It's in the way her long red curls swing when she walks, the perfect drape of her dress, the long, tapered legs and expensive heels—and I am a cat who knows my stilettos. Looks aside, she's likely a con artist. I have a healthy skepticism for such professions. My interest in Tabitha Kingsley concerns the nosey questions she's been asking about Trudy Wells. My mission—and I have accepted it—is to find out what she is after.

My immediate need is to make Tabitha think that I'm part of the Long family. I rush up to her, crying to be let into the house. Oh, my, her gaze is intensely green. She has very feline eyes that seem to pierce my soul! I hope she's not smarter than the average humanoid because she might see through my scheme to get into the house and eavesdrop on her conversation. She is knocking on the door just as I planned.

Long Hall is definitely a posh place—statuary along the drive, what looks like a topiary of...dear god, it's schnauzers. All poses of those high-energy, bouncing, and annoying dogs. When human taste goes wrong, it's deplorable! This is a perfect example of the old saying that big money doesn't mean good sense or taste. The topiary would be far more attractive if it were cats.

Lucky for me, Tabitha is too twitchy to pay much attention to me. She's shifting her slender weight from hip to hip, picking at her nails, settling her perfect dress, all the classic signs of impatience or nervousness. Could be both. I mean how is she faking those psychic readings she's conducting. But I, Sherlockian trained detective that I am, shall investigate. Trouble, the black cat detective, is far more adept at finding the diabolical machinations of the human heart than any mere biped.

Ah, the door is opening. I slide inside before anyone notices. There is a pleasant exchange of greetings and I have to say, I find Tabitha's voice to be polished and pleasing with a dollop of sincere kindness. If she's a fake, she's very good at the scam. Charline Long is seeking counsel from Tabitha. I must determine how Tabitha fits in with the missing Trudy Wells! The conversation is heating up.

Not to fear, all will be well. Trouble is on the case.

TABITHA KINGSLEY STEPPED into the foyer of the Long plantation and sighed. It was exactly what she'd been expecting. She walked to an antique sideboard that held a lovely arrangement of fresh camellias and stopped at a small sculpture of two figures holding hands. "That is a lovely bronze. An Erte?" she asked Charline Long, the slender woman with the very worried expression who'd greeted her at the door. Tabitha was proud of the hours she'd spent boning up on "culture" to be able to fit in with her clientele.

"Yes. My mother-in-law loved art deco. She collected quite a few pieces. This is one of my favorites. *The Kiss of Fire.* She was so excited when she purchased it." Charline turned away, her shoulders dropping. "I realize that many wives would be relieved that their live-in mother-in-law has passed, but I really loved her. I miss her."

"Keeping the bronze in the foyer is a lovely tribute to her taste and the things she appreciated." Tabitha looked around, catching a glimpse of the black cat who'd darted in the door. He was sitting on the staircase in deep shadow. Almost as if he were hiding. Perhaps he wasn't allowed in the house. Well, it wasn't her job to chase him out. She was sure the Long family had servants who could handle that. The Long plantation's immaculate upkeep spoke of lots of hired hands busy at work.

"You've called me here about your mother-in-law, haven't you? Her name is...I can't quite catch it because it's like two names. It begins with a...an S." Tabitha knew she was correct. Research did pay off.

"Yes, how did you...know? Her name is...was Suellen Long." Charline's eyes filled with tears. "Samuel believes that he senses his mother's spirit. I'm afraid he's going to snap and lose his mind. I sense her too, but I haven't seen her. I have to believe she's lingering here at Long Hall to tell us something we need to know." She looked down and away.

Tabitha read her body language—Charline was hiding something. "I see." Tabitha had anticipated this turn in the conversation. "Suellen Long loved this house." Tabitha walked down the foyer, looking at a lovely Van Gogh that had to be worth at least three hundred thousand dollars. "She liked sunshine and laughter. She wanted grandchildren, but she never blamed you, Charline."

Charline gasped and stepped back. "How do you know all of this?"

Tabitha shook her head. "I can't tell you *how* I know. I simply know. If a spirit wants to make a connection and can manifest the energy, all I have to do is open myself to what they're trying to tell me. Sometimes it's a symbol or a visual image. Sometimes a smell or even a song. Sometimes I see the spectral world. Here, with Suellen, it's much more subtle. She's sharing her feelings with me. I simply know how she feels, and I can relay that to you." What most people wanted to hear from a psychic medium was that their loved ones had made the transition and found serenity and happiness.

"That's so..."

"Invasive?" Tabitha filled in with a smile. "Yes, I suppose it is. But you'll be glad to know that by tomorrow morning I won't remember anything I've told you. As easily as the thoughts come into my head, they evaporate as quickly and completely. I'm merely a messenger. That's all. Nothing special or fancy, just someone delivering a message."

"Oh, you're so much more than that." Charline grasped her arm. "Come into the parlor and I'll have Nancy prepare some refreshments. I almost think we need a cocktail."

"Not for me," Tabitha said. "I don't want to cloud my abilities with alcohol, but you feel free. This is a difficult experience for many people. Relax as much as you can and just let it happen."

The two women moved into a beautiful parlor with lovely antique French furniture, a huge mirror over the mantle, and more art work. A silver service sat on a buffet, catching the afternoon light in the polished surface. "Your home is so lovely," Tabitha said. "I'm looking for a place to buy, but so far I haven't found anything that suits me. I'm forced to stay in a hotel, which makes me very unhappy. You know, people leave vibrations behind, psychic energy, so to speak. It's on the beds and dressers and all the furnishings in a hotel room. It confuses me at times. There is so much coming at me all at once. Here, I sense your touch, of course, and your husband's. And there are others. Maids, I presume. But also Suellen's and there's another, a woman? An unhappy woman?" She turned to look at Charline and knew she was playing her perfectly. "She isn't here often but she is vibrant—spilling energy."

"That's Samuel's step-sister, Hannah Sellers. She grew up here but after graduating from college she's only here for the occasional visit. She and Suellen weren't close, unfortunately. And Hannah isn't happy." She turned away to hide her emotion. "After Suellen passed, I thought I saw a change in Hannah. I thought maybe she regretted her hardness toward her step-mother. I could have sworn she was coming around, but recently..."

"And she doesn't get on with her brother or you, does she?" Tabitha asked.

"No, she doesn't. She and Samuel aren't...compatible. Oil and water." She sighed. "I was an only child and my parents died several years ago. I'd give anything for a sister. It seems such a shame that Samuel and Hannah can't bridge hard feelings to build a true relationship."

Tabitha felt a pang of pity. She'd had her ups and downs with Trudy, her notoriously hard-headed sister, who had suddenly gone missing. Trudy who'd fallen in with some unsavory characters before she up and abruptly moved to the Mississippi Delta. "Maybe things will improve."

Charline shook her head. "In the last month, Hannah has made her wishes clear that she'd prefer to sell Long Plantation. She wants the money, not the property. Samuel refuses to sell. This place was built by his great-great grandparents, and it's part of his identity. Now this sudden move on Hannah's part to force a sale. It's just incomprehensible." She laughed softly. "I'm from Memphis, so I'm not attached to the place the way he is, but I love it. Still, if it would make life easier for Samuel,

I'd be happy to move." She motioned Tabitha into a chair. "I'm not much of one for strife. As Samuel says, I'm No-drama Lina. That's his pet name for me."

"He's a lucky man." Tabitha took a wing chair where she soon spotted the black cat who'd followed them into the parlor. He was a watchful creature. If only he could speak, he might be a big help. But cats didn't talk, and Tabitha knew she was going to have to figure out a way to get a more permanent invite into the Long household. She had to be here—this was where Trudy's trail ended. If she meant to find her sister, she had to get an invitation to stay in the house.

"There's a lovely house for sale just north of Zinnia," Charline said. "I can arrange for you to see it. It isn't on the market yet, but I'm friends with the owners. Lovely people, and the house is exquisite. Not as large as Long Hall, but this place is far bigger than we need."

Tabitha's eyes widened. "Would you?" She did dream about a small farm with room for her, some horses, Trudy, and cats and dogs, but any real estate Charline Long was talking about was way, way out of Tabitha's league. The fine car was a rental, and the stay at the Prince Albert was stretching her budget.

"Yes, it comes with three thousand acres, but if you don't want to farm, I'm sure they'll cut the house out and sell it separately. As it is, the big agricultural companies don't really care about the old homes. They only want the dirt. They've bought a few old homes and razed them. I think the Bessmers would be glad to entertain an offer for just the house and say, ten or twenty acres?"

"That would be perfect. Really perfect." Tabitha smiled. Yes, that would be perfect. An old home, some acreage, it was her dream come true, but her bank account held no hope of purchasing such a place in the Delta. This was all just part of the set-up, her pretense of having money and a desire to own property in Sunflower County. She was acting on the principle that folks who owned the large farming plantations would trust someone closer to their economic status—hence the disguise. And she couldn't afford to stay at the Prince Albert or lease the new car for much longer.

"Why don't you stay with us for a week or so?" Charline offered. "It doesn't make sense that you're paying for a hotel room when we have so much unused room." She waved a hand around. "The house is simply too empty, now that Suellen has gone. I'd be glad for the company."

"What a generous offer." Tabitha bit her lip. "I don't know. I mean, I'm a stranger. Your husband might find it awkward."

"Everyone is a stranger until she's a friend," Charline said. "Please. If you find it uncomfortable, you can always move back into the hotel. And if you're here, you can more easily communicate with Suellen. She is here. I know it. And I don't care who calls me crazy."

"You're certainly not crazy, and it's true that being here, on site, would simplify things greatly." At last Tabitha smiled. "Deal! Once we finish our session, I'll go pack my things and come back. Are you sure your husband won't mind?"

"Samuel is very easy going. He'll be happy to see that I'm making an effort to be social. He's been concerned for me, because I've been so worried about him and the...ghost. Some might say I've been obsessed with it. I'm not. I worry that Suellen is here for a reason. There have been some strange... never mind. I just want her to go on and be happy. On to the next adventure. Samuel wants me to figure out what's going on and put it behind me. He'll be more than happy that you're here."

"You're a very generous woman, Mrs. Long."

"Call me Charline. If we're to be friends, we should use first names."

"Of course. Now let's get to the session." Tabitha reached into her handbag and brought out several small candles, a silver bell, and some cards. "These are all tools I use to help the spirits communicate. What say we give it a go?"

The sound of the doorbell chiming made Charline pause. "Excuse me. I'd hoped we wouldn't be interrupted." She rose and went to the front door.

"I won't let you get involved with a shyster." The male voice from the doorway came clearly to Tabitha, and she knew it was trouble for her. But who was the male? Not Samuel—she'd done her research and knew he was never that confrontational. Who was this brusque man? She didn't have long to wait.

A tall, well-muscled man in his late twenties stepped into the room. He glared at her. "You should leave now. My aunt is vulnerable, and you're nothing more than a vulture here to pick her bones."

"Raj!" Charline said. "Please stop. Tabitha is my guest. Please, you're embarrassing me."

"Aunt Charline, I won't have you made a fool of by someone claiming to see the future or talk to spirits or whatever her gimmick is."

"Tabitha Kingsley, this is my nephew, Roger Long. We call him Raj for short, and you can see why. He's a bit of a tyrant when he gets his dander up." She went to her nephew and stood on tiptoe to kiss his scowl. "Say hello to my guest."

"Ms. Kingsley." Raj nodded. "I apologize. I hope you understand I'm looking out for my aunt."

"Of course." Tabitha looked at Roger Long and thought of a panther. He was energy contained. And he was also at the top of her suspect list. Trudy had worked for him, and in the conversations Trudy had shared with her sister, Trudy had revealed that Roger Long was hot-tempered, volatile, aggressive, and generous to his employees. "We can have a session another time." Tabitha put a hand on Charline's shoulder. It was just bad luck that Roger had showed up so quickly.

"No, don't let me interrupt," Roger said. "In fact, I'm curious as to what brings you to Mississippi? I've heard the gossip in the local café that you're connecting all the best families with their dead relatives."

"Roger! Tabitha is here at my invitation," Charline said, stepping between the two. "And she'll be my houseguest for several days."

"I'm fascinated to see how Ms. Kingsley works," Roger said. "I'll stick to her like a burr to make sure she has everything she needs."

Tabitha wanted to stomp Roger Long's arrogant foot. She'd taken note of his expensive boots and oh-so-casually expensive polo shirt and jeans. Instead she smiled. "Mrs. Long is lucky to have someone who looks out for her...well-being."

He shot a curious look at her, reading between the lines as she'd intended him to do. "I hope you don't fill Aunt Charline's head with stories of ghosts lurking about. My grandmother was a wonderful lady who lived her life to the fullest. I don't believe regrets would keep her hanging around here."

"Then why do you suppose both your aunt and uncle sense her here? With some urgency, I might add." She waited.

"Because they miss her. We all miss her, but her spirit isn't lurking about. You can take that to the bank, along with whatever money you're bilking out of Charline and Samuel."

Tabitha forced a smile. "Oh, Suellen is here, Mr. Long. Never doubt that, but my sense is that she's here because she cares for this family. Perhaps there's some unfinished business, but certainly not out of regret." She decided to take a big risk. She touched her forehead lightly with her fingertips. "She wants me to tell you that the missing woman is okay. Not safe, but okay for the moment."

His reaction was everything and more. He pulled back from her as if he'd been shocked.

"See, Raj. You *were* worried about that young woman who didn't show up for work. She's okay. That should relieve your mind." Charline patted his arm. "Will you be here for dinner tonight? Samuel's grilling some Gulf shrimp."

"What time?"

"Six o'clock for cocktails, then dinner." Charline linked her arm with his. "Tabitha will also be our guest. As I mentioned, she's staying here until she finds a suitable property to buy." Her one cocked eyebrow brooked no disagreement.

Tabitha expected Roger to resist, but he only smiled. "How wonderful. I look forward to tonight and more revelations from the spirit world. Revelations anyone could know by spending three minutes in town." He shot her a sidelong glance. "Now I need to head up to the co-op to put in a fertilizer order and then return to the offices to finish up work."

"He's a lovely young man when he isn't being officious," Charline said, giving her nephew a hard look.

"He's only looking out for you." Tabitha supplied the expected response, though she wasn't sure at all that Roger had anyone's interest at heart except his own. She'd met his level steel gray gaze and could read nothing behind his eyes.

"Until tonight," he said and kissed his aunt's cheek before he left. The front door closed with a solid click.

"Let me get us some tea. The weather is a bit on the raw side, don't you think?" Charline asked.

"Yes, the wind is cold, blowing over this open land. The vista of the Delta is startling and a little unsettling." The land was so open, so windswept and free of houses.

"Have a seat. I'll be back in two shakes of a lamb's tail." Charline disappeared down a hallway and Tabitha examined the parlor. It was another stunning room with velvet drapes that puddled beside windows designed to open onto the front porch like doorways. The old plantation homes had been constructed to allow for air flow, the only relief from the terrible heat of the summers.

When Charline returned, she carried a formal tea service, beautiful china cups, and a basket of dried fruit scones. She placed the tray on the coffee table and poured the tea.

"I feel I should explain about my nephew. He comes across rather...harsh. But he's really a good guy. Raj earned his nickname because he's something of an autocrat, in the best sense of the word. He's taken over the running of the plantation, which is now all high-tech and crop futures, big equipment and high finance. It's very different from the farming that Samuel grew up doing. Raj worries about Samuel and me. He tells us all the time we have to keep up with cell phones and technology and computers. He doesn't want us to fall behind and be isolated. I agree, but it's just too much sometimes."

"Is he Hannah's son?" Tabitha needed to confirm all the family connections. She'd suspected that Roger Long had wrested control of the plantation from his uncle. He'd managed to put himself in charge of all business decisions. And very possibly all of the employees. Trudy had worked for Roger, and Tabitha was slightly heartened to know that Roger had at least mentioned a missing employee.

"It's a long story." Charline sighed. "Hannah is Samuel's half-sister and nearly twenty years younger. She was an unexpected child—Big Sam had an affair and Hannah was the result. Suellen and Big Samuel adopted her, but Hannah even refused to take the Long name when she was grown. She's a Sellers. They tried hard and doted on Hannah when she was young, but when she became a teenager, she refused to see them. She was spoiled rotten and never forced to face the consequences of her actions. Raj is Hannah's son, but I have no idea what kind of relationship they have. Let's just leave it there. Now, what can I do to help you with the reading?" She put her teacup aside and cleared a portion of the coffee table.

Tabitha pulled her focus back to the job at hand. She'd make this reading convincing. She'd already been invited into the bosom of the household, so she needed to cement her position with this first display of her ability.

"I'll do a tarot reading and see if we can make initial contact with Suellen," she said, shuffling the beautiful deck of dragon tarot cards and laying out a Celtic Cross spread. She'd learned the technique of reading the tarot months ago from the best card reader in New Orleans. Tabitha and Trudy had always had an interest in the tarot cards and the working of those who could touch the spiritual realm. Tabitha had explored her abilities, and Mama Bettite had told her she had real talent. She'd urged Tabitha to train to use her gift. Tabitha had never intended to read professionally, but she was glad now she'd gained enough skill to pass herself off as a psychic. At least until she found her sister.

"I'm nervous," Charline confessed.

Tabitha wondered if there was a reason, but she flipped over the first card, the Ace of Swords. "Someone definitely has a message for you. This is a card of communication, of secrets, and messages from the past," she said, pointing to a card. She placed another. "And this message is crossed by the knight of swords. There is someone, a physical person, who is in the way of this important message. It's about something that happened not long ago." She watched Charline closely. "Something involving...this can't be right, but it looks like a missing person. Suellen wants you to help find her."

Charline's eyebrows lifted quickly. "Really? If it's the young woman who stopped showing up for work, I can't see how that has anything to do with me. I can't even recall her name."

Tabitha frowned. "Was she somehow related to you or Samuel or this plantation?"

Charline sat back in her chair, her face going blank. "No, just one of the office workers." Her fingers pulled at the edge of the linen napkin she'd placed on her lap. "Young people today come and go. It isn't like it was when I was a young woman and a good job was something to hang onto. What does this have to do with Suellen? That's who I really want to connect with."

Tabitha checked herself. She'd tried to jump ten steps ahead, and in doing so, she'd rattled Charline. Patience. She had to learn patience. All of her work would be for nothing if she didn't take her time.

"Let me see." Tabitha bent to study the cards. "Suellen has tried to contact you in the past. There was a broken mirror?"

"Yes!" Charline gasped. "It fell right off the wall."

"That was Suellen, though she didn't mean to break it. She was trying to get Samuel's attention. She wants to tell him..." Tabitha put her hand over the Ace of Cups in the place of the past. "She loves him. He was always the source of her heart's love. She wants him to know she is safe and happy. She's showing me a picture of a field, green with a crop. It's not corn. Not soybeans." She hesitated, playing it out. "Maybe cotton. It's a different crop. She wants Samuel to look at a new crop for the land."

"That's incredible. Roger was just talking about a new crop." Charline stood up. "Suellen loved this farm. She knew as much, or more, about farming than any man in the Delta. Samuel will pay heed to her suggestions. Samuel isn't involved with the day-to-day operation now, but this is something he'll want to hear." She sighed. "He's missed having Suellen to consult with, and Roger will be delighted to have his proposal confirmed."

Tabitha felt a twinge of real remorse. Charline Long was a nice person, a decent person who loved her family and heritage. What Tabitha was doing, playing on that love and loss, was wrong. But she'd already crossed that line long ago. She was willing to do whatever it took to find her sister. The last place Trudy was seen was in the corporate offices of Long Agricultural Products, and Tabitha had a sneaking suspicion her sister had lied to her about her reasons for moving to the Delta. She'd been working in the front office as a receptionist, until she disappeared two weeks earlier. One way or the other, Tabitha meant to find out what had happened to her.

CHAPTER TWO

*T*he narrow road disappeared on the horizon, a straight path that cut east to west across the Long acreage. Roger pressed the gas pedal on the big v-8 dually he drove on farm business. He'd been to town and was loaded with a ton of fertilizer he had to deliver to a spreader truck in the north acreage. But first he headed to the office, driving through the back fields that he loved to tour and check out.

This year's crops were planted and the gamble on a new type of cotton had been taken. His grandmother, Suellen, would be proud of him for taking the risk. Farmers didn't need to go to a casino to scratch a gambling itch. Everyday life for a farmer was a huge gamble that depended on sun and rain, control of pests and fungi, and the ability to harvest when the crop was ready and not a day before or after. Timing, luck, and weather—a farmer controlled none of those, but lived or died by them.

He tried to focus his thoughts on the company budget, but every time he got one tangle squared away, he found himself thinking about the young woman who'd invaded his aunt's home. Something was up with Tabitha Kingsley, psychic medium. He'd heard about her at Millie's Café when he stopped by for breakfast and the morning gathering of local farmers. Stories of Tabitha were all over town. She spoke with dead people. She saw the future. Right. Just another blood-sucker preying on the desire of the living to have one more word with the dead to assuage some guilt they held.

Well, he'd about had it with people trying to take advantage of his kind-hearted aunt and uncle. Charline and Sam would give anyone the shirt off their backs, but they'd grown up in a time when folks were more trustworthy, more responsible for themselves.

He stopped at the business office of Long Agricultural Products, not half a mile from his uncle and aunt's home, and stepped into the warmth of the office. The empty desk where Trudy Wells had sat made his temper rise. The little butterfly in amber paperweight, the ceramic pig pen holder —it was all a reminder of Trudy. She hadn't worked for him for very long, but she'd been astute and smart. She'd had a bright future with Long Agricultural as a lot more than a receptionist. She'd seemed to be settling into the routine of Sunflower County and her work at the office. She'd eagerly taken on more tasks aimed at research and had done a fine job. The other employees had taken to her. So where had she gone?

Worry and aggravation made him sound gruff. "Ellie, start the search for a new receptionist."

"Yes, sir." Ellie, who was his personal assistant, swallowed. "Right away." She hesitated. "Any news from Trudy? I hate to hire someone else if—"

"She left without any word. Just find someone else."

"It's going to be hard. She was really smart about the plants and those new chemicals. I wonder why she'd just up and leave like that."

Roger realized that part of his anger was at that fact. "Yes, she was an asset. She had a future here, but she left. I've given her time, and I have to accept that she isn't coming back. Replace her."

"Yes, sir." Ellie turned on her heel and started to her office.

"And have Eddie bring the fork lift to the warehouse. More fertilizer will be delivered in an hour." He swept past her into his office and slammed the door. The first thing he did—before his curiosity about Tabitha Kingsley got in the way—was call the local sheriff's department to report that a bloodsucker had leeched onto his aunt and uncle. He wasn't surprised when Deputy DeWayne Dattilo explained that as long as Charline and Sam invited the woman into their home, there was nothing the law could do. The local sheriff, Coleman Peters, was out of town with his girlfriend, Sarah Booth Delaney. The two deputies, DeWayne and Budgie, were capable men, but they followed the letter of the law. Good enough. He'd handle it himself.

He went straight to the Internet and looked up Tabitha Kingsley, psychic to the suckers. He found a professional website that included a number of testimonials to her abilities to bring peace and solace to those grieving the loss of a loved one. It also said she'd worked with local law enforcement in New Orleans to solve cold cases. He stopped reading there and eased back into his chair. Zinnia already had one private detective agency—in fact he'd considered hiring Delaney Detective Agency when Trudy first went missing. But he hadn't. Now, though, he might need someone to look into both Tabitha's appearance and Trudy's disappearance. He wasn't psychic, but he definitely felt there was a link.

He stood up, the desk chair slamming backwards into the wall. Just another example of his bad temper for the office help to chew on and discuss. He grabbed his jacket and left again. He needed to check the new cotton crop. The weather had been good and the plants should be peeking out of the soil. A cold snap was forecast, and the wrong weather now could kill the tender young plants. This experimental crop was a real gamble—he'd paid a fortune for the seeds, even though Trudy had voiced concerns about the new crop. But the only way to stay afloat in farming was to risk and risk more.

He found peace out in the fields. He longed for the time when Samuel made the business decisions and he worked physical labor. Those days were clean, without the murkiness of money, employee needs, trying to balance his labor force, profit, and payroll in a way that proved fair to everyone. Everything was simply bigger than he'd expected.

Add Trudy's unexplained disappearance to the top of the pile. What in the world had she gotten herself involved in? He didn't want to believe her disappearance was somehow connected to his cotton, but a niggling worry in his gut told him he couldn't rule out that possibility. Of the many regrets he had in the past year, Trudy was at the top of his list. There had been inconsistencies in her story. He should have sent her packing the day she showed up asking for work and pretending she knew anything about being a receptionist. But she'd jumped at the job and worked so willingly, throwing herself into Long Agricultural. Water under the bridge. He couldn't undo what he'd done. Now he had to work.

So, Tabitha Kingsley has ingratiated herself into the Long household. Just as Pluto suspected would occur. One thing you should know—

Pluto claims his residence called Dahlia House is haunted. Excuse me while I scoff. Pluto has been sippin' the mint juleps! Perhaps everyone in Sunflower County is a bit barmy. Both owners of Long Hall are seeing things. I wonder if they're hearing voices. Nonetheless, Pluto does have a mystery to resolve, and he thinks someone here in Long Hall has information about what has happened to Trudy.

Trudy's behavior isn't consistent with her love for the little marmalade cat. Pluto tells me that Vesta is insistent that Trudy would never dump her. Trudy's absence can only be attributed to foul play.

I've seen Vesta—a foxy little fluff tail—and I have to agree. No one in her right mind would abandon such a magnificent feline. Some evil is afoot. I must act quickly, too. My humanoid, Tammy Lynn, brought me over to Zinnia while she's attending an indie bookseller conference. We're staying at the Prince Albert, but around this little burg, it's easy enough to catch a ride, especially when there are vehicles that proclaim Long Agricultural Products on their doors. I am, after all, trained in logical deduction.

My logic tells me that I've learned all I can here in Long Hall. Tabitha has gone to get her belongings to move in. Charline is in the kitchen, supervising the menu for dinner. I'm going to try for something to eat. If I get booted out, then I'll walk to the agriculture offices about a half mile away. I should go back to the hotel. Tammy will be out of her meeting soon and she'll let me pick from room service. A small sample of warm sole in a light cream sauce would give me renewed energy for the work. How to convey that to Charline Long?

She's taken aback to see me in her kitchen, but she isn't angry. More like curious. Yes, she is stroking my fine black fur. And she is asking me if I'm hungry. I'll give my most pitiful yowl and it is working like a charm. She's raiding the fridge for some...chicken parmesan? Yes, that will do nicely. One thing about these Southern ladies--they know fine dining, or at least they hire a cook who does. This is delicious and will sustain me in my quest.

Before I skedaddle from the "big house" and head back to the hotel, I need to stop off at Long Ag offices. That's where Vesta said Trudy worked. That's the last place she was seen. A good detective knows to pick up the trail where it ended. If there's anything to be deduced, I shall discover it and thus begin the journey of finding the missing Trudy.

And I also intend to poke around a bit in the business of one Tabitha Kingsley. It's a mighty big coincidence she shows up to speak with the dead when a Long employee has gone missing. Like my father, Familiar, and my hero, Sherlock Holmes, I do not believe in coincidences!

TABITHA THREW her clothes into the two suitcases and then carefully searched the hotel room to be sure nothing was left behind. This had worked out even better than she'd anticipated. Gaining entry to the Long house might have taken a week instead of one day. A week of hotel bills that were draining her meager savings account. So far, very good.

She checked out of the hotel as the afternoon was waning. True spring wasn't far away, but the days were still short and chilly. It was during the gloaming that she found it most difficult to control her anxiety and worry about her sister. Trudy was headstrong and impractical—and not always truthful. She went off half-cocked on a regular basis, involving herself in madcap plots. Her trip to the Mississippi Delta was one such ill-advised scheme. According to Trudy, she'd gone on some dating website, met a man who claimed to be a gentleman farmer, and he'd invited her to move to Zinnia. But there was more to the story of Trudy's sudden interest in cotton and Sunflower County—and if Tabitha could figure it out, maybe she could find her sister. Tabitha had found brochures about cotton crops, pesticides, GMO seeds in Trudy's suitcase. Trudy may have come to the Delta to date a man, but there was a lot more to it, and all roads led to Long Agricultural. But how or why? That's what she didn't know.

Things had gone swimmingly when Trudy first arrived in Sunflower County. She'd called regularly, talking about her work at Long Agricultural and the mystery man that she refused to name. But Trudy had been happy. Truly Happy. And then Tabitha had gotten the call. Trudy was scared. Someone had been following her. Tabitha had offered to drive to Zinnia to get her sister, but Trudy had said to wait a few days.

Tabitha had urged Trudy to abandon her wild plans and to move back to New Orleans, but her sister wouldn't hear of it. She liked the little Delta town. She liked her job and the people. She was staying. She said she was involved in something really important at her work. And that was the last time they'd talked. Now no one answered Trudy's cell phone.

Tabitha was torn between calling in the local law or hunting herself. She'd taken on the job of finding Trudy because she had no evidence that a lawman would believe. And, in truth, she wasn't sure what Trudy had gotten herself involved in. There had been a few past incidents where Trudy had fallen in with unsavory people up to no good. Rather than rely on the law, in desperation, Tabitha had developed her own cover story to pry into the family where Trudy had been working.

She couldn't help but wonder if Roger Long was the man Trudy had fallen for. He was handsome enough, and Trudy did like the bad boys. Domineering, a shade on the side of rude. That would crank Trudy's motor; she was always up for the challenge to tame a man or bring him to heel. It never worked, but Trudy bit for the lure every single time. Trudy should have learned this lesson from her mother, who'd had a series of bad boy boyfriends after their father had been killed overseas. Larry Kingsley had been a great soldier but a terrible father. Even though he'd forgiven his wife for the affair that resulted in his second daughter, he'd failed to give Trudy his last name. Perhaps he would have come around to adopting Trudy in time, but an IED had taken his life in Kabul, leaving Shelly with two kids and no source of support except the small pittance from the government.

Shelly Kingsley had been a distracted mom. In the end, Tabitha had mothered Trudy. When Shelly died of a bad heart, Tabitha had naturally stepped into the full-time role of mother. She'd done her best with her wayward and headstrong sister, but now she was worried about Trudy.

As she drove through the open brown fields with the first hint of green sprouting up, Tabitha almost turned around to go to the local sheriff and report Trudy missing. Something stopped her. Something in the last phone call she'd had with Trudy. Her sister had made a comment to the effect that everyone in the rural county knew each other and they stuck together no matter what. Trudy was the outsider. A big city girl, Tabitha was wary of small town politics and the desire to close ranks against an outsider. If Trudy was involved with a married man, which wasn't beyond possibility, she might have gotten herself into real danger from a romantic triangle instead of issues with new agricultural products.

There was also the possibility that Trudy had involved herself in something illegal. It wouldn't be the first time. She'd always been on the fringes of mad schemes to make quick money. She'd been an unwitting accessory to one plot to bilk insurance companies. Trudy had seen it as a victimless crime. Tabitha had other opinions. Cheating was wrong—no matter what the reasoning behind it. A fact that applied to her subterfuge to get close to Charline Long. Tabitha wasn't trying to steal from the Longs, but she was being deceptive. And she would continue to be. She couldn't risk calling in the law until she found out exactly what Trudy was doing.

Tabitha continued to the Long estate, determined to find her sister on her own.

She decided to try her sister's cell phone one last time just as she turned down the shell drive to Long Hall. On the third ring, someone answered.

"Hello, Trudy?" She was so relieved. "Where the hell are you? I've been searching everywhere."

There was only the sound of breathing on the other end.

"Trudy?" Tabitha couldn't keep the panic out of her voice. "Say something, dammit."

The reply was the click of the call ending.

Tabitha stopped the car and fought back tears. She only cried when she was angry or afraid. Now she was very afraid. If that had been Trudy, she would have said something, given some sign that she was safe. The only logical conclusion was that someone else had Trudy's phone.

She was hyperventilating when a big dually pulled up behind her and hit the high beams. It startled her out of her panic attack, and she eased down on the gas and continued to the house, the truck lumbering behind her. She pulled over, trying to park inconspicuously. The truck drew abreast and the passenger window rolled down.

No surprise, Roger Long stared down at her. "The help parks in the back," he said.

It took all of her restraint not to lift her middle finger in his face, but she didn't. She just rolled up her window and killed the engine. If Charline and Samuel wanted her to park in the back, she'd be glad to do so. After the actual property owners told her.

She got out of her vehicle and grabbed her bags, still fuming. Her anger was just a way to avoid the sheer panic that wanted to rise up and suffocate her. Who the hell had Trudy's phone and why wouldn't they speak to her?

Charline met her at the door and ushered her inside and upstairs to a lovely suite. Tabitha was glad for the kindness and sense of welcome. Her feelings were raw, and it took all she could do not to confess her scheme to Charline.

"Dinner is at seven," Charline said. "Samuel is home and happy that you'll be staying with us. He's serving cocktails at six in the parlor if you'd like to relax with a drink. If you're tired, we understand. I know you need time alone to...connect with the spirits."

"Thank you." Tabitha was really grateful—and also ashamed of taking advantage of this kind woman. Perhaps Roger Long had good reason to behave so brutishly to her. After all, she was little more than a flimflam man in the Long home under false pretenses. She didn't see another option. If the facts supported her suppositions, then someone in the Long family could end up in jail for abducting her sister. All she had to do was prove it—and find Trudy.

As much as she wanted to hide out in the lovely suite, Tabitha freshened her makeup and went downstairs for cocktails. Within two minutes of entering the parlor, she had an old-fashioned in her hand and a warm greeting from Samuel Long, who seemed delighted to have a house guest. He was a trim older man, the perfect mate for Charline in temperament and graciousness.

"I do believe my mother's spirit is here," Samuel said. "Little things. Knickknacks that are moved, a recipe that's fallen out of a book and just happens to be one of my favorites, the clock in the hall chiming the wrong number of hours."

A little chill rushed up Tabitha's body at Samuel's recounting of events. She wasn't a psychic medium, but she did believe that the ghosts of the past often lingered with their loved ones, sometimes to protect or warn and sometimes to extract revenge. She'd had no sense that Trudy's ghost was around, which she was taking as an omen that Trudy was alive. She had to cling to that.

"So, Tabitha, tell us how you became interested in the occult," Samuel asked her.

His question held no censure, only open curiosity. She was about to answer when she sensed a darker presence in the room and turned to find Roger standing behind her, his signature scowl in place.

"Yes, tell us," he said with a contemptuous smile.

"I grew up in New Orleans and wrote a music column for a local website for several years. I'd make it a point to listen to the new bands or gatherings of musicians, and I met some tarot readers and psychics. They were open and willing to tell me about what they do and why they do it." So far she was telling the absolute truth. She paused for a few seconds to be sure Roger was listening to her. "Surprisingly, the psychics I know want to help people. Yes, some of them are pretenders, but the truly gifted readers and psychics have a talent. Often they can bring comfort to a grieving child or parents. That's their gift."

"Even if it's a pack of lies?" Roger asked.

Charline walked up to her nephew. "Raj, I love you, but you're being rude and ugly. Stop it now or leave my house, and it is still my house. Keep that in mind."

"I'm sorry, Aunt Charline." What looked to be true

remorse passed over Roger's face, until he looked at Tabitha, and then his features hardened.

"Ms. Kingsley is our guest. I invited her because she does bring me comfort. I don't care if you don't understand or don't believe. This is for me and Samuel, and you'll respect our wishes or leave."

"Of course. My apologies, Aunt Charline, Uncle Samuel." He turned to Tabitha. "May I freshen your drink?"

"No, thank you." She wasn't big on alcohol and certainly not in a situation fraught with emotion.

"Tell us about your family," Roger said in the most civilized tone.

"My parents are dead, so there isn't much family left."

"I'm sorry to hear that," he said with what sounded like sincerity.

"Yes," Charline said. "No wonder you're so attuned to the other side."

"My interest in connecting with the departed is partially a result of my losses." This was also true, and she wanted to stay as close to the truth as possible.

"I'm surprised a woman as lovely as yourself hasn't married and started a family," Samuel said.

Tabitha forced a smile. "I haven't focused on building a new family, I suppose." No, she'd spent too much time trying to corral her wayward sister and work on her writing career to worry about dating and marrying. In truth, she couldn't risk caring for another. When a person opened her heart to others, she was asking for pain.

"What have you focused on?" Roger asked.

"Developing my skills."

"As a psychic?"

"And a writer and musician. I write lyrics for some of the local bands."

"How interesting." Charline was genuinely impressed. "I always wanted to paint, but I ended up collecting work by other artists. There are those who do and those who collect, I suppose."

"And both are necessary," Samuel said, putting his arm around Charline's shoulders. "You've helped me run a big business and this house. That's creative aplenty."

Tabitha jumped at the opening. "How many employees do you have in your agricultural business?"

Roger was quick to respond. "Fifteen in the office, and up to a hundred during harvest, which is almost year-round now because of the crop rotation. Skilled workers. Equipment operators, crop analysts. Farming isn't hoeing and picking cotton anymore."

"The vista here is so beautiful. The openness of the fields that stretch forever." She did her best to build rapport with Roger since he'd given her the tiniest opening.

"So you grew up in New Orleans? I think I'd suffocate in those neighborhoods where the houses are so close together."

She smiled, ignoring the barb. "When I was a child, I loved it. I had a dozen playmates all within half a mile. We could bike to each other's house, gather after school for games, and then be home in time for...supper." She almost said for her to cook supper. "I live in the Quarter now."

"What an interesting life," Charline said. "The Quarter is filled with characters."

"Music, laughter, and a lot of sadness," she agreed. "But it's home. I'll be glad to return there." She caught herself just in time. "If I don't find the property here that I'm looking for."

"Whether you move here or not, you always have a place

with us. We do appreciate you staying here until we resolve the visits from Suellen," Charline said, getting a nod of agreement from Samuel.

"I'm happy to help. Would it be possible for me to see the farm operation? I've been working on this song, kind of bluesy, and for some reason, I feel like knowing a little about farming might help me finish it up. After all, this land is the heartbeat of the blues."

Roger started to object, but Samuel stepped in. "Raj would be happy to show you around, wouldn't you?"

"Sure, Uncle Sam. I'd be delighted. Meet me in the kitchen at six o'clock in the morning."

"Great. I'm an early riser." She matched his challenge.

"I'll see that Nancy has something warm ready for breakfast," Charline said, a knowing smile on her face. "Maybe you can picnic along the way."

Tabitha had to struggle not to laugh out loud. Charline Long had gotten her nephew's goat in the most effective way. With kindness.

"I believe dinner is served." Raj dodged the subject of a picnic. "Now let's enjoy the food that Nancy prepared for us."

They went to the dining room and Tabitha was impressed with the simple goodness of the food. She hadn't expected soul food at Long Hall but the peas, cornbread, and pork loin were all delicious. She noticed a pretty yellow cat sitting in the dining room window. "Is that your kitty?"

Roger frowned. "No, it belongs to one of our employees. It would seem she's abandoned the poor creature."

"May I take it some food?" Tabitha had plenty of left over pork roast.

"Of course. I suppose I should bring her inside. The nights can be cold." Charline went to the window and opened it wide for the cat to come inside. The little marmalade didn't hesitate. She hopped right into the room and went for the dish of food Tabitha put on the floor. "I love cats," Charline said. She looked at her husband. "It seems she's chosen us."

Samuel started to shake his head, but he sighed instead. "If she chooses to stay, keep her. My grandmother loved schnauzers. They're wonderful dogs but so active. She installed the topiary. Suellen was more of a cat person. Charline loves all animals."

"We haven't had a cat since Suellen's pet passed away several years ago," Charline said. "She adored that cat, Sheba. We all did." She walked behind her husband and put her hands on his shoulders, leaning down to kiss his cheek. "Thank you. I miss not having a pet."

"What about the black cat that was here when I arrived?" Tabitha asked.

"Black cat?" Everyone but Charline looked blank.

"There's no black cat living here," Samuel said. He turned to Charline. "Is there?"

"Maybe," Charline said with a secret smile.

"He was sitting on the stairs. I saw him clear as day," Tabitha insisted.

"Grandmother's cat, Sheba, was black." Roger said, bemused. "Could it be the spirit of Grandmother's cat?"

Tabitha was caught off guard. She was positive the cat had been flesh and blood, but she couldn't say so, repudiating her skills as a psychic and medium. "Of course, it could be a spirit cat. Just another sign she's here and wants you to know it."

"He's one spirit cat with a good appetite," Charline finally said. "I fed him in the kitchen earlier. I do believe he's flesh and blood."

"Maybe the cats are an omen," Samuel said.

Tabitha had other thoughts. Maybe the orange feline was Trudy's pet cat that she'd adopted. Trudy had sent a photo of the little female she'd found at a dumpster on a back street in Zinnia, and this kitty looked exactly like Trudy's Vesta. But what was the cat doing at the Long plantation? Logically the cat would be in the rental where Trudy lived. There was no cat there—Tabitha had looked for the animal, knowing it would be confused and scared at Trudy's absence. But then, two weeks was a long time to be on her own. Maybe she had sought solace and shelter in a place that was familiar.

"Perhaps the cat has a message," Roger said, barely able to contain his smirk.

"Tomorrow I'll see if I can summon the spirit of Sheba. I have a very special talent with pets," Tabitha said, knowing she was digging herself deeper and deeper into a hole. She was pretty good at selling her abilities as a communicator with the dead, but soon she'd have too many balls in the air to keep up.

"Would anyone care for coffee or an after-dinner drink?" Charline asked.

"No, thank you." Tabitha eased her chair back from the table. "Everything was delicious. I think I'll take a walk. I need to stretch my legs and let some of that wonderful food settle." More than anything she wanted a chance to snoop around Long Hall.

Trudy had written eloquently of the lovely estate and the grounds. And she'd been strangely content working in the agricultural business office. Trudy had a talent for numbers and charts, comparing and contrasting, and she'd found a niche. Perhaps she could pick up her sister's trail. She was still disturbed by the fact someone answered Trudy's phone, and this was the best place she could think of to start looking for who it might have been.

"The driveway can be very dark," Charline said, a pinch of worry between her eyebrows. "Maybe Roger should--"

"Thank you but I'll be fine. I have a flashlight and I just need to move around so I can sleep." Tabitha was firm. Roger Long was poor company in a roomful of other people. Alone he would be intolerable. Besides, she couldn't snoop if he dogged her footsteps. The strange call to Trudy's phone made the situation even more urgent. "I won't be out long."

It looked as if Charline might protest, so Tabitha quickly made her escape out the front door into the darkness. The night was cool, bordering on cold, but she set out down the driveway at a brisk pace. She could smell the land, and it relaxed her. Growing up in Nola, she'd dreamed of having a horse with pastures surrounded by wood fences, a patch of a garden, of living in a place where she couldn't hear the neighbors argue. Long Hall was like one of her childhood Cinderella fantasies. Even in her wildest dreams, though, she'd never envisioned the graciousness and beauty of the Long home.

Perfection would describe it—if only Trudy were there to share the place with her.

Where in the hell had her sister gotten off to? Why had she left without alerting anyone to her plans? And why would someone be following Trudy?

CHAPTER THREE

*T*hank goodness the glamourous kitty Vesta is residing in Long Hall and being cared for. Pluto helped her make it out to Long Hall to look for Trudy, but he's been worried about her, out alone in the night. There are coyotes and wild dogs roaming the Delta and no kitty should be out roaming at night. Now she's in the house—and being spoiled rotten by the lady of Long Hall. As part of the Long household, Vesta will do her share of sleuthing and report back to me in the morning. Now, I'm cutting across the fields for a little recon work at the business office. Desk drawers and computers must be searched. If push comes to shove, I can hole up in the business offices for the night and catch some shut-eye. I'm savvy to the dangers of the night, and I don't want to end up as catfish and chips for a coyote either.

Because I'm svelte and athletic and have the feline ability to compress and lengthen my body, I can gain entrance through the bathroom window that was left open...just enough for me to squeeze through. Yes, it is twelve feet off the ground—nothing for a cat who can climb a nearby tree and jump five feet to the window ledge.

After this escapade I'd like to settle into a nice English pub for some Scotch eggs with curry mayo. Ah, there is no such culinary fare in the *village of Zinnia, but Vesta assures me the grub at Millie's Café is quite excellent. No bangers and mash, but perhaps some fresh local fish. I don't indulge in the fried delights of the South too often, but I dearly love them. Pluto tells me that the proprietress of this diner often cooks especially for him and that...hound, who is his companion. Sweetie Pie. Lord save me from the charming names some people give their pets.*

Now I'm inside, let's see what's what.

There's the desk Trudy worked at. The nameplate says Trudy Wells, Receptionist. And on the desk is a photo of Trudy and the traveling psychic medium currently forking down her food in Long Hall. Even I can see the resemblance between the two. It's so strange that the Longs haven't put this together. Ah, the bipeds—not so skilled at observation. And this resolves a big mystery for me and also relieves my heart a little. I'm glad to know what Tabitha is up to and that she's worried about her sibling. I believe she'll prove to be a valuable asset to me. While I'm more than competent in most matters, it's always good to have a biped on the case to do such things as drive, stroke my fur while I'm cogitating, and prepare the gourmet delicacies that sustain me.

Methinks I should get rid of this photo. If Roger were to look too closely...Obviously Tabitha Kingsley is here undercover. Based on this discovery I'm inclined to think the whole psychic medium thing is a ruse, so I needs must do what I can to preserve Tabitha's cover. It's just a matter of pulling off the back of the frame, sliding out the photo, and secreting it in a desk drawer. Now it's out of the way but not destroyed. On to more productive snooping. Good girl, Trudy kept an old-fashioned calendar that doesn't require a computer password to read.

Here it is, Wednesday from two weeks ago. "Meet Lisa East at six." Lisa East. This is a new name in the investigation. And there's no location. A very interesting note is also on the calendar—"send Tabitha the files." And there is something else. A symbol with a question mark. It looks like something from ancient times, but my exposure to symbolic history is limited.

What files does this reference? ...Intriguing. And now the calendar has to go also. The name Tabitha is a dead giveaway. If Roger Long reads this, the jig will be up for our pretend psychic. So I'll flick it off the desk and slide this under the bookcase.

Now I have two leads. Lisa East and files. I'll have to have human assistance in accessing the computer. I'm quite clever, but passwords defy me. When my dad was building his clientele, he had a real knack for guessing human passwords. He was brilliant at it. But that was in the day when people used the names of their children or birthdates or maiden names. Now passwords require those stupid nonsensical characters, plus capitals, and numbers. My feline brain balks!

I've taken note of the desk set up and I suppose I'll somehow have to drag Tabitha down here to help me. We do share the same goal, I believe—finding her sister. Wait a minute. Someone is coming. I can hide in the shadows, but if the intruder turns on the light, I'm toast.

It sounds like they're picking the lock on the door. Using a cell phone for a flashlight—good. They're also breaking and entering. This could be very good or very bad for me.

Ah, so the psychic lass is here. I call that proactive in finding her sister. Uh oh, what she doesn't realize is that someone else is headed this way, creeping along in a big black dually truck. And I can guess who that is.

Tabitha has picked the lock and is coming through the door, and I have one play! I launch myself at her with all of my fifteen pounds.

"What the—"

No time for explanations. I head butt the office door shut and hear the lock click back into place. I give her thigh a nice nip to move her into the shrubbery. She wants to curse, but I shush her with a low growl and deep hiss.

She's about to lay into me—or as Sherlock would say, berate me-- when she hears the same thing I heard moments ago. A vehicle is approaching. She inhales and calms instantly, pulling me into her arms. We huddle in the hedge around the office building and wait.

The truck rumbles toward the building and stops. The door opens and a tall man steps out. Tabitha tenses and folds down more tightly around me, whispering for me to be still and quiet. She's wasting her breath. That's Roger Long and I somehow think he would be very, very upset at finding either Tabitha or me here. He tries the door and finds it locked. For a moment he stands at the door, then returns to his truck. He drives away slowly. When he is truly gone, Tabitha sets me free and stands. She is trembling.

I rub against her legs and give her a few of my delightful little trills.

"Well, that was close. We were almost in a lot of trouble."

"Me-ow!" I nip her lightly to let her know she got my name correct. She looks at me. "Trouble?"

"Me-ow!" I am adamant. And she understands that is my name. Now I only have to convince her to take me to town so I can meet Tammy at the Prince Albert. My humanoid is going to be worried at my strange absence.

ROGER SURVEYED the open fields as he drove back to Long Hall. Tabitha Kingsley had vanished. Completely. She'd walked down the driveway and by the time he'd extricated himself from his well-meaning aunt and uncle, Tabitha was gone. He'd been certain he'd find her poking around the ag office. Even though he'd failed to apprehend her doing something questionable, he still believed she'd been there. Why would a psychic be interested in agriculture? He didn't for a minute believe her cover story of writing lyrics for a blues song. But why? What was Tabitha Kingsley up to? If that was really her name. Psychic to the stars, ha.

His cell phone buzzed in his pocket and he slowed to pull it out. He answered immediately. "Have you found anything?"

"She has a website and it's professional, but it appears to be very new. Like a few weeks ago," a woman answered in a drawl even thicker than Roger's. "As far as I can tell, Tabitha Kingsley has never been a fortune teller in New Orleans."

"Thanks, Ellie." Roger put his phone away. Just another layer of mystery around Tabitha Kingsley and her hokum story about being a New Orleans psychic medium. Roger had come to one clear understanding—Tabitha Kingsley was at Long Hall because she, too, was involved in the disappearance of Trudy Wells. What Roger had to determine was how Trudy and Tabitha were involved together. And he was beginning to come to a conclusion based on visual evidence. There was a photo on Trudy's desk in the ag office. Two women, arms around each other. One was Trudy, the other...he'd never bothered to ask. Now he didn't have to because he knew the second woman was Tabitha Kingsley. But what interest did they have in his uncle's plantation?

He drove past Long Hall and toward town. The night was young. There was time to check out a few more leads he had regarding Trudy Wells' disappearance. She'd seemed happy at work, involved in the farming business, eager to learn. Perfect for research. Farmers were bombarded with new crops, new fertilizers, new "opportunities." A lot of it was bull crap. But some of the information that poured into his office was valuable and required evaluation. Trudy had demonstrated an interest in that work and a mind that was more than capable of analyzing facts and culling out false promises. She'd completed several assignments, and Roger had been impressed with her work ethic and intelligence. Then one day she left at five o'clock and never returned.

The little orange cat that had strayed up at Long Hall looked a lot like the cat Trudy was always showing photos of on her phone. She'd named the cat Vesta and talked about her all the time. But how had Vesta gotten from Trudy's apartment in town to Long Hall? It didn't make sense.

A lot of things didn't make sense.

TABITHA LOOKED south toward the lights of Long Hall. She should head back to the "big house." Charline and Samuel would wonder where she'd gone. Her brush with Roger had left her unnerved.

"Come on, Trouble." She motioned the cat toward the road. Instead of following her, the cat snatched at the hem of her dress, pulling her toward the door of the office. When she urged him to follow her to the house, he resisted. He obviously wanted her to go inside the office.

She summoned her courage and picked the lock—a skill she'd learned from the days when her mother had failed to leave a key--again, opening the door. The cat shot inside. In a moment the feline clawed at the desk drawer and meowed. She couldn't believe what was happening, but she used the light on her phone to examine the contents of the desk drawer. The first thing she saw was the photograph of her and Trudy.

"Holy cow," she murmured. If Roger recalled that photo, her goose would be cooked. She pulled it from the drawer and tucked it into her jacket.

When the cat went to the bookshelves and began digging under them, she helped him pull out the calendar. Trudy's calendar. Lisa East. The last appointment listed for her sister on the day she disappeared. Who the hell was Lisa East? And what files had Trudy meant to send her? And the symbol—what did it mean?

"What gives with you?" she asked the cat. "What's your interest in my sister?"

"Meow."

It was almost as if he wanted to tell her. First Vesta, and now this cat who liked the name Trouble. The felines were all over Trudy's disappearance. Was it possible Trudy had adopted more than one cat? Again, how had both felines made their way from town to the ag offices? It was a good four miles at the very least.

It was probably desperation, because Tabitha had never felt so alone, but she was glad for the cat's company. When he hopped on the desk and patted the keyboard for Trudy's computer, Tabitha sat down and turned the machine on. After ten tries of passwords that failed, she had to accept defeat—at least for the moment.

"I'll come back tomorrow," she promised the cat.

Trouble grabbed at her hand, his claws sheathed.

"What?"

The cat looked up at her with green eyes that seemed to comprehend her worries and fears. He jumped to the floor and headed to the door. He was smart—it was definitely time to leave before they were caught. And thank goodness she'd retrieved the photo. It had never occurred to her that Trudy would have put a framed copy of a picture of them together on her desk. If Roger recalled that photo, she would have a lot of explaining to do. Now she had to hurry back to the Long plantation house, and the cat was certainly eager to push her down the road.

. . .

GETTING *Tabitha to head to her car is like herding geese. Honestly, what's a black cat to do? She keeps trying to go inside the house. What she doesn't understand is that I need a ride. At least she's passing her car, but she keeps dodging left toward Long Hall. I can't allow that. I have to get back to the Prince Albert right this red-hot minute.*

Too bad Tabitha isn't wearing pants. I hate to do it, but a little snag of her skin at the back of the knee—oh so tender and she is swatting at me. And cursing. Now that I have her attention, I'll get her back to her super fancy ride. I would prefer an old farm pickup for surveillance but I get that Tabitha is playing the part of a very successful psychic medium. Which she is not. I still don't know exactly what she is, but I'm going to find out.

Okay, she's looking at me batting the car door. She is catching on. Yes, she's opening the car and letting me in. And she's asking me where to—as if I could simply tell her. I'll have to help her steer. Man, if I had thumbs and longer legs, this would be a piece of cake. As it is, trying to program a biped to do my bidding is a herculean task.

At the end of the driveway, I sit up in the passenger seat and meow as I stare out the window toward town. Tabitha obliges. She's catching on, quicker than the normal biped. And now we're on the road to town. Thank goodness the Prince Albert is on Main Street. Not a lot of turns. I could have walked it, but why when there's this fine new car to ride in. Still smells new!

She's turning into the front of the hotel. While a valet tries to park her, I'll make my escape and head inside through the revolving door. There's loud chatter and laughter in the bar and I spy my beloved Tammy, having a martini with Jamey and Kelley Kornegay from Turn Row Books. They seem to be having a good time. I'm heading to the room. I will lounge for a while, and perhaps do some midnight sleuthing. A detective's work is never done.

CHAPTER FOUR

*R*oger was loaded for bear when he strolled into the kitchen at Long Plantation at six in the morning. He wasn't prepared to see Tabitha sipping coffee, waiting for him. He was early, and so was she.

"I love to watch the day break," she explained, nodding out the window. "I've never visited the Delta. This is an incredible place. It's like...the horizon goes on forever."

"Those fields seem like forever when you're planting or harvesting." The morning light caught the auburn highlights in her hair and set them on fire. Her pale skin took on a rosy glow as the sun began to clear the distant tree tops.

"Thank you for agreeing to show me your business. I'm ready whenever you are."

"Oh, I need some coffee. And we need to talk."

His tone made her swivel to face him. She was good, but not good enough to hide the alarm on her features. And a pinch of guilt, if he was reading her correctly.

"Talk about what? I swear to you I'm not trying to bilk

your aunt and uncle out of money. I really want to bring them peace."

"It's not Samuel's money I'm worried about. It's my agriculture business." He realized she knew then that he was on to her. Was she smart enough to own it or would she lie?

"Trudy is my sister." She brushed a few strands of hair from her face, obviously trying to decide what to reveal. "I'm trying to find her."

Her direct words were like a kick to his gut. Deep down, he'd hoped Trudy had gone home. Now he knew that wasn't the case.

"So this whole 'talk to the dead' thing is a ruse?"

She nodded. "Pretty much. I needed access to the wealthier planters' homes. I needed a reason to be invited in. I have to find my sister—and people will talk to a psychic medium when they won't talk to anyone else. Just so you know, I haven't taken a penny in fees."

"That's a pretty nice car for someone who has no way to make a living."

She sighed. "I know. I'm a writer and songwriter. I rented the car. I had to play the part." She shook her head but not before he saw the tears welling in her eyes. "I was desperate and I came up with the best plan I could."

"Maybe you should have simply asked me."

She met his gaze. "I couldn't. I suspected you."

Man, she wasn't one to pull her punches. And he liked that. He completely understood her lack of trust. He'd been Trudy's boss. The last place she'd been seen, to his knowledge, was her desk at Long Agricultural Products. No wonder he was high on the suspect list of people who might be involved in foul play.

"Do you still suspect me?"

"Yes." She didn't blink.

"Yet you were willing to get in a vehicle with me?" He was growing more and more amused. And impressed.

"I studied martial arts."

That statement made him step back. "Really?"

"Yes. I've studied for years. I practice with some musician friends who are also in law enforcement."

He sat down at the table to study her more closely. "So what do you think happened to your sister?"

"I don't really know. She came to Sunflower County to date some man she met on a dating website. He *said* he owned 'a vast tract of property' that he planted in cotton and other crops. Or at least that's the story she gave me. I should have been suspicious, but Trudy sometimes gets herself into scrapes where it's better for me to handle it than call the law."

"She never told you his name?"

Tabitha bit her lip. "No. She knew I'd get my cop friends to check him out. I raised Trudy, and I made her toe the line. She still acts like I'm her mother and she's trying to escape me."

"She's how old? Twenty-four?"

Tabitha nodded. "Yes, twenty-four going on fourteen when it comes to her rebellious streak."

"Did she send a photo of this guy, the name of his farm, anything? I know all the farmers who run large tracts of land. There are two who are single, but this guy may have lied about his marital status."

"I've thought of all of that too. I could wring Trudy's neck. Being so secretive and determined to make her own decisions —now look what's happened. Can you tell me about her last day at work?"

"You think her disappearance is linked to Long Agricultural?"

"Trudy had fallen in with a group of people in New

Orleans. They were young, radical looking, and reeked of secrets. Trudy always stopped talking on the phone when I walked up, but I did overhear Trudy say something about finances and farming."

"So she came to the Delta with an interest in farming?" Roger had to think back. As far as he could remember, it had been a normal early spring day. "We'd planted some of the fields with a new type of cotton." His eyebrows lifted. "Trudy had helped with the research on the new plants. She'd been skeptical about the crop. She said it looked like trouble down the road."

"Meaning what?"

"The company that produced the strain of cotton could come back and demand a lot more money for seeds in future years. The claims that the cotton was resistant to certain pests might result in an overgrowth of fungus or root rot or a lot of other complications. Trudy had done her research. These new crops—they sound great in the beginning—can develop a long list of issues. Trudy was very astute at pinpointing problems with certain seeds and companies. She could see through the lies and P.R. She was very smart."

"She has a great bullshit detector," Tabitha said, and Roger was surprised again at her willingness to speak the truth.

"Surely if this man she was dating was full of it, she'd have figured it out." Roger pointed out the obvious.

"Which could be the very thing that got her in a pinch."

Roger hadn't thought of it that way. "Okay, so how do you want to approach this?"

Tabitha took a deep breath.

IT WENT against Tabitha's nature to trust a man, but sitting across the kitchen table from Roger Long, she realized she needed help and Roger was offering it. She didn't have to trust him a hundred percent, but she had to let him help her. Time was slipping away, and it wasn't like she had a choice. He'd busted her red-handed. The only thing she could do was come clean and hope he was the employer he seemed to be—and not some sicko.

"I broke into your offices last night and found Trudy's calendar. She was meeting a woman named Lisa East on the day she disappeared."

"Lisa East?" Roger stood abruptly.

"Do you know her?"

Now it was his turn to look away, clearly deciding how much he should reveal. He faced her. "I dated her for a while. We broke it off about two months ago. I didn't realize she and Trudy had become friendly."

"Maybe they weren't friends. Could there be another reason they were meeting?"

Roger swallowed. "Yes. It could be the strain of cotton. Lisa works for a chemical company that created the new cotton I planted. As I said, Trudy wasn't a fan of that particular strain. She thought I'd regret trying it."

"What about this Lisa? Is she...dangerous?" Tabitha felt the pressure squeezing her lungs, a sure sign that her worries had grounding in reality.

"She's a beautiful woman, but..."

"But what?"

"She's volatile. And she's really devoted to DayZ Seed and Chemicals. She was furious with me when I didn't instantly agree to plant all of my fields with their newly developed strain of cotton. That's one of the reasons we broke up. She was just too pushy about it."

"How volatile?" Tabitha tried to keep her voice from shaking.

"Enough that I stopped seeing her. She was terribly angry with me. When she finally calmed down, I'd had enough of the drama."

"Did she do anything...dangerous?"

Roger didn't look away. "Someone slashed my truck tires while I was in a local blues club. I can't prove it was her."

"But you think she did it."

"I do."

"Did you report it to the police?"

"No, I didn't." He shrugged. "I've known the sheriff, Coleman Peters, my whole life. I didn't want to go tattling to the sheriff like a school boy who got pushed down on the playground. I realize now, I should have reported it, just so there was a record of it. If Lisa did this thing, people should be aware of it. If she didn't, I shouldn't feel that she did."

"Okay, I think we need to talk to Lisa. Or I do. This may be something I should do on my own."

"I agree." He found a pen and paper and wrote down an address. "That's her home address and the address of DayZ Seed. She's one of their top salespeople so she travels around Mississippi and Arkansas selling their products."

"Do you have any idea who my sister was dating?"

"She never said in front of me, but we can ask around the office. Trudy was friendly. People liked her. It's possible she mentioned her beau to some of the other employees. There are several young women working there she might have palled up with. We can go there now."

"Thank you, Roger."

"I've been worried about Trudy. I should have reported her missing, but you know, she'd only been with me a few months.

I was planning on promoting her, but she disappeared. I was disappointed and I suppose a little angry."

"Oh, you and me both," Tabitha said. "I'd like to skin her hide, and I may when I get my hands on her."

Roger finally smiled, and Tabitha realized it changed his entire demeanor. He was a handsome man when he wasn't scowling. He'd proven to be unexpectedly helpful. She could only hope she wasn't making a bone-headed mistake, a la Trudy, by allowing him to help her.

GETTING *outside the Prince Albert is a snap. The staff doesn't even seem to notice me, and if they do, they smile. No one is interested in reporting a black cat on the loose. And that revolving door. It's a death trap, but convenient! Now I'm on the street and just in time for my rendezvous with my mirror image, Pluto. I must be accurate and admit that Pluto has about four pounds on me because he is "the beloved pet" at the local café. In fact, that's where we're meeting. He swears the owner of the café will provide delicacies fit for a king.*

In my regular work day I accompany Tammy to the Book Basket in Wetumpka and indulge in a few yum-yums her customers bring to tempt my appetite. I also find myself involved in cases all around the country. My skills as a detective are growing, and I do like to stay busy. Mental acuity comes from use of the brain. Or as Tammy's romantic other, Aiden Waters, would say—use it or lose it. Rather catchy, don't you think?

Millie's Café is not far from the Sweetheart Drive-thru and I spy a fine black kitty hanging around the back of the café. It's Pluto, and he yowls a greeting. We have much to catch up on.

He is true to his word, and the attractive Millie, lover of movie gossip and scandal as Pluto describes her, takes us into the office of her business and gives us two plates of tempting tuna in a delicate broth.

She is quite the cook. I need this recipe for Tammy. The whole time she is stroking our fur and running on about how Sarah Booth would be very upset to see Pluto so far from Dahlia House and gamboling around town by himself. She asks about the dog—who I hope is not lurking about. Millie warns Pluto that she will drive him home herself and make sure he stays there. Really? Humans always underestimate us. Pluto stays at Dahlia House because it makes Sarah Booth happy and because he wants to. Otherwise, he'd be on the lam. Cats have certain expectations...and they are met, or else.

Now that Millie has returned to her duties in the café, Pluto and I can catch up. I fill him in on Vesta's appearance at Long Hall and he is greatly relieved the little marmalade feline has been taken in and is okay. I assure him she is living large while we find her human.

I also bring him up to speed on the arrival of Trudy's sister who is also investigating her disappearance. Lisa East is our best lead. Pluto is not familiar with her, but he suggests a trip to the local courthouse where he claims a law officer will assist us. Really? I'm not holding my breath, and if I end up in some pound because of this, I will exact revenge. But we do need biped help to find Lisa East's address. That much I agree with, so it's off to the courthouse we go.

We both hate to upset Millie, who will be worried, but there's no help for it. When the door to the office opens, we shoot out and through the dining area to the front door. A helpful human holds it open just as Millie comes after us crying for us to stop. There will be hell to pay for Pluto when his humans return. I am a stranger in this burg, and today, that's a good thing. I must admit that if Tammy were calling my name I would think twice before ignoring her. There are some things that really set a human's hair on fire!

As Pluto promised, we're welcomed into the sheriff's office by a deputy with the name Budgie. Pluto has told me how the two deputies help Sarah Booth and her partner Tinkie solve their cases. And how accommodating the law officers are to cats. They have been made *aware of our superior skills. This is a promising beginning. He treats Pluto as his equal and he seems willing to pay attention when we play charades with him. He has guessed the East part of her name. Now for the Lisa. This is a bit harder. Pluto's approach is...unique. He is rolling on the desk moaning. Then tapping the computer keyboard. I'm fascinated. I know what he's trying to say, but will this Budgie creature? Yes, he's getting it...*

Budgie has made it to moaning and Mona—now to get to Lisa. This truly is an exercise in teaching humans to communicate on a higher level.

"Mona!" *Budgie shouts! And Pluto and I jump about and praise him with our antics.*

"Mona East?" *Budgie guesses.*

The door opens and a tall, lanky deputy comes into the room and questions our behavior. The minute Budgie tells him Mona East, Deputy DeWayne Dattilo corrects him.

"You're thinking Lisa East. She's a sales rep for DayZ Seed and Chemicals."

Pluto and I dance around DeWayne's shins, giving him rubs and lots of purring trills. When he asks what we want with Lisa, we know we have him hooked. When he suggests to Budgie that he drive us out to Lisa's house, we are beside ourselves with glee. If only all bipeds were as eager to learn as these two, my work would be greatly simplified.

Budgie is amused at the suggestion, but willing to take us, and we are off.

One advantage to working with the local law is that they have access to addresses, criminal histories, cell phones, and best of all, sirens. Pluto flips the switch for the siren and Budgie gives him a roll of his eyes, but lets it sing.

Lisa East lives at a small cottage on a side street of Zinnia. It's a lovely little place, shaded by a huge magnolia. I sense danger. The front door is ajar. It could be Lisa forgot to shut it firmly on her way to work, but this doesn't bode well.

Budgie lets us out of the car while he walks to the porch and raps on the door. No answer. And something is smelling a lot like decomp. Terrible for humans but even worse for the keen olfactory senses of a cat.

Budgie asks us to stay back and we oblige. We are savvy detectives, but we are also furry and we could contaminate a crime scene. We don't have long to wait. Budgie puts in a call to the sheriff's office and the coroner. Someone is dead, and I'm pretty sure it's Lisa East. This puts a dire spin on the whole disappearance of Trudy.

And here comes a big dually pickup driven by that officious human male Roger Long with Tabitha as a passenger. Strange that they would end up here. Tabitha spots me right off and does a double take at Pluto. I'll never be able to convey Pluto's name to her. Thank goodness Budgie steps in and takes care of such things—and holds Tabitha and Roger back from the crime scene. Tabitha is very upset. Pluto goes to comfort her, and that's a good thing. I want to snoop around the back of the cottage. See what's what.

CHAPTER FIVE

*R*oger was at a total loss what to say to Tabitha when it was clear that Lisa East was dead, and not from natural causes. He didn't try to exclude Tabitha from the conversation he had with Budgie, a man he'd known for most of his life, but he found he wanted to soften the details—a strange feeling for him.

"How was she killed?" Roger asked the deputy.

"Pretty sure she was shot, but Doc Sawyer will tell me more."

"Can you tell how long she's been dead? I have an employee who's missing. Trudy Wells. She hasn't shown up for work in two weeks. She was meeting Lisa the day she disappeared."

Budgie shook his head. "You might have said something before now, Roger."

"Yeah, I should have." Roger didn't even want to defend his lack of action. "She was new. I just thought...young people today move around a lot."

"They do," Budgie conceded.

"This is Trudy's sister, Tabitha. She's worried about her."

Budgie studied the tall, slender redhead and nodded. "I've heard talk around town that you communicate with the dead."

"It's a gift," Tabitha said, but Roger was aware of the slight flush that touched the delicate skin of her slender throat.

Budgie looked skeptical. "Look, unless you two have something to add to this scene, why don't you go over to the courthouse and wait for us?"

"What are those cats doing here?" Tabitha asked. "That black one, the thinner one, was out at Long Hall last night. He's...not a normal cat. He jumped out of my car at the Prince Albert."

"This one here is Pluto, and he's a pretty special cat. He belongs to Sarah Booth Delaney, a local private investigator. She sets a store by him and claims he helps solve cases, but she's out of town at the moment." He pointed to Trouble. "I have no idea who this black devil is, but he's smart."

"His name is Trouble," Tabitha offered. "Don't ask how I know."

Roger turned to Budgie. "Do you have any idea who might have...harmed Lisa? I knew her. She was in the Long offices not so long ago talking up a new strain of cotton she wanted me to try."

"Is that where she met Trudy?" Budgie asked.

"I think so." Roger thought about it. "I have four or five young women in that age range working for me and they seemed to socialize together. They talk about going to Playin' the Bones to dance or driving up to Memphis for fun." He held up his hands. "I never thought about how they knew each other."

"My sister was dating a man who farmed a lot of acreage," Tabitha said. "In the week before she disappeared, things weren't great with them."

"Do you have a name?" Budgie asked.

"I'm sorry, no. Trudy is my younger sister. She was so headstrong about her independence."

"I taught teens for a while," Budgie said. "I'd rather deal with convicted killers than teenagers. Some never outgrow it."

"Amen," Tabitha said softly. "My sister is smart but willful. She's always poking her nose where it doesn't belong."

"Trudy is smart," Roger agreed. "And the more I think about it, the more I agree with Tabitha. She was too interested in this new strain of cotton. She and Lisa--"

"Let's not jump the gun and assume the worst," Budgie said. "Here's DeWayne and Doc Sawyer. How about you leave and take those two cats with you? We've got some forensic work to do and I don't need cats or humans tromping through it. When I have some answers, I'll be in touch."

"Thanks," Roger said. He put a hand on Tabitha's shoulder for support as he turned her away from the cottage. She didn't need to see what was inside. Her imagination was probably already working overtime.

"Hey, can you really communicate with the dead?" Budgie asked. "If we run short on leads, maybe you could get in touch with Lisa East."

Tabitha turned and inhaled. "The spirit has to want to communicate, and just so you know, I haven't charged anyone for my services."

Budgie only grinned. "I'll let you know if we need your help."

"Yes, that would be a logical move," Tabitha said before she started toward the truck. Roger had to admire the way she held her shoulders back and didn't give anything away. He hadn't found his missing employee, but he had learned something valuable about Tabitha Kingsley. She had come into his aunt's home under false pretenses. He'd initially thought she was a con artist trying to fleece his relatives out of hefty fees for "psychic" contact with his grandmother, but that didn't appear to be the case. No, it was a lot more serious than just a con. A woman was dead and Trudy was missing. Even more worrisome, Trudy appeared to be caught up in serious business —serious enough for murder. He'd wanted to believe that Trudy was simply footloose and fancy free, a young woman who'd moved on to greener pastures. But with each passing hour, he had to consider that Trudy Wells might be the victim of a kidnapping. Or worse. But since no body had been found he was going to hope for abduction. He'd worry about how Tabitha's betrayal affected his aunt and uncle later. Right now something far more dangerous was going on around the Long family.

At the truck, Tabitha glanced back at the cottage as if to examine it one more time. There were clearly tears shimmering in her eyes, but they didn't spill. She lifted her chin. "Let me grab that Pluto cat and see where Trouble got off to," she said.

"What are we going to do with the cats?" Roger asked.

"We'll take Pluto to his home, and Trouble can come with us. They're involved in this somehow. Think about it. We've had three cats show up, and they all seem involved in this case. The orange one your aunt let in—that's my sister's cat, Vesta. I'm sure of it and I have no idea how she got from Trudy's house to Long Hall. I don't know what's going on, but until I find my sister, I'm going to follow every lead I get."

"Round up the cats," Roger said, because he knew it would be pointless to argue.

. . .

TABITHA PUT a docile Pluto in the truck and went after Trouble. He was aptly named. She went behind the cottage. She knew he wouldn't answer to kitty, kitty. He wasn't that kind of cat. He was somehow distinctly...British? It didn't make a lick of sense, and she wondered if the stress of Trudy's disappearance was making her thinking loopy.

She caught sight of the feline on top of two garbage cans where he was frantically digging to get inside them. He didn't strike her as a cat that enjoyed rank food so she went to help him. Two minutes later he had dug some papers out of the trash. She brushed off a few stray coffee grounds and examined the report from what looked like a laboratory. It was an analysis on some plants, but it was way above her pay grade.

Holding only the edge of the page, she scooped Trouble up in her arms and hurried back to the truck. When she was inside with the door closed, Roger arched one eyebrow.

"What's that?"

"You'll have to tell me. I should give it to the cops but not before we have a chance to figure out if it gives us a clue to Trudy."

"Garbage is a clue?"

"More than that, it may impact your business. It's an analysis of something. Since Lisa worked for a chemical company, my guess it would be one of their products. "

Roger took the pages from her hand and studied them, his frown deepening. "This is soil analysis. And it was submitted by Trudy—that's her initials, which means it probably has something to do with Long Agricultural Products. But look, there's that strange symbol that was on Trudy's calendar. I've never seen it before, and to be honest, I've never seen a report like this. It's from...a company I've never heard of. Bitner Labs."

Tabitha felt her dread grow. Trudy was involved in something. Crop analysis, soil samples—all things that were out of her normal wheelhouse of interests. Once again she wondered what her sister had gotten involved in. "We can check on this report, right?"

"We can and we will. Now let's get out of here."

They pulled away and headed out the road to Dahlia House, a place Roger knew of but had never had reason to visit. At the intersection, Trouble once again tried to take control of the steering wheel.

"He wants to go the other direction." Tabitha knew because he'd done the same to her.

Roger was dubious. "You've got to be kidding me."

"Try the other way."

He took up the challenge. As soon as he turned in the direction the cat favored, Trouble settled back in Tabitha's lap.

She didn't say a word but she couldn't hide her smile.

"Where do the cats want to go?" Roger asked. "You're the psychic, maybe you can tell me. Or maybe you're also a cat in disguise."

"Me-ow!" Trouble answered. Pluto slipped under Roger's arm and nudged his right hand. When he turned in that direction, Pluto settled back onto the seat.

"Trudy's place," Tabitha guessed.

"Meow!" the cats chorused.

"This is not happening. I'm going to wake up any minute and realize this is a nightmare. Cats do not know how to tell people where they want to go."

"Dream on," Tabitha said. "The cats are now in control and let's hope they know how to find my sister."

They turned down the driveway to Trudy's place and parked beside the front porch. Tabitha was aware the little house had taken on a sad and abandoned air even in the brief time Trudy had been gone. Dead leaves had collected at the front door, and pots containing plants had been knocked over. The wind? Roaming dogs? Or an intruder? Trudy had mentioned someone following her.

Tabitha shared a look with Roger.

"Let me go in first," Roger said. "Just in case—"

"Trudy isn't here. I checked when I first got to town."

Roger sighed. "Thank goodness. But nonetheless I think I should go in. So what are we looking for?"

"Her car is missing. I'd like to find her personal computer, which I didn't see when I looked, but I didn't search thoroughly. And I couldn't find her spare car keys. She always used to leave them in the drawer with the spoons. It was something we both did for emergencies." Tabitha took a breath. "I'd like to find some indication of the man she was dating or the website she met him on. And we need evidence of a connection to Lisa East."

"Okay." He opened the truck door and the cats were out. They made a beeline for the front steps. Roger was right behind them.

Tabitha went around the house to the back. Two lawn chairs were beside a fire pit that had been used in the recent past. There was evidence of some burned papers, but they were too charred to be of any use. She did notice that a screen on a back window sat on the ground below. Wind damage or an intruder? She examined the window and had her answer— someone had broken into the house.

She heard Roger call her and she returned to the front and went inside. The house was just as she'd seen it.

"Looks like her clothes and suitcase are here," Roger said. "There's no sign of a struggle. Since her car is gone and there's no sign she was taken against her will, maybe she left on her own."

"Yeah." Tabitha's hope was taking a heck of a beating. "It's possible she found out that Lisa was killed and ran."

"Wouldn't she call you?" Roger asked.

"If she's afraid, maybe not." Tabitha knew she was grasping at straws. Trudy was headstrong, rebellious, and often jumped before she thought things through. But she would never deliberately worry her sister. "Maybe she doesn't want to involve me in this. She might have been at Lisa's place since they were going to meet up. Maybe she saw what happened to Lisa and..." She couldn't finish her thought.

"Don't jump to the worst conclusion," Roger said. He put a comforting hand on her back. "I'm sorry, Tabitha. Do you know where she kept her computer?"

"The logical place would be the kitchen table. It wasn't there when I looked before."

"Then we should look for thumb drives or something she could have hidden. If Trudy was on to something, she's smart enough to have hidden the evidence."

Roger was right. They began a systematic search of drawers and other places of concealment. Tabitha went to the closet, remembering Trudy's love of shoes. She upended numerous pairs until she saw the cowboy boots they'd bought on a trip to Dallas. Trudy loved them. She tipped one over and a bright green thumb drive fell to the floor. The relief was intense. At least they had something.

"Look at this." Roger came into the bedroom holding a disk marked 'Interview Delta Dating.' This may be the dating site Trudy was using."

"Do you know it?" Tabitha asked.

He nodded. "The address is not far from here. We can

check it out while we're so close. One of us should go apply. That's the quickest way to get inside."

"You," Tabitha quickly said. "That way you can show interest in Trudy. But won't they know you? Everyone around here knows everyone it seems."

"That's true. So it has to be you. We have the video here so maybe we can see what Trudy put on her page."

"And what about that report on the plants?"

"Another good lead that I'll pursue. I can ask questions without arousing suspicions. We should photograph that and give it to the deputies. We don't want to withhold information."

"You're right. Thank you." Tabitha stopped in her headlong pursuit of finding Trudy long enough to appreciate how much Roger had gotten involved. He didn't have to help yet he was doing so willingly.

"Young women don't go missing in Sunflower County. We look out for each other here." It was as if he could read her thoughts.

"Let's find a computer and check that disk. Someone took Trudy's laptop."

"Tabitha, if we involve the law, maybe they could track her cell phone. There's a GPS. It's possible--"

"Someone else has her phone. I've called her a million times and yesterday someone answered but wouldn't say anything. If Trudy had it, she would talk to me because she'd know how worried I am. She may be undercover or..." She decided to be honest. "Or she might be caught up in this. Trudy hasn't always used the best judgment. I'm afraid if the cops show up, she'll get hurt. If she isn't hurt already. Let's see what we can find out on our own. Let's give it twenty-four hours and then I'll agree to turn everything over to the law. I have this sense that Trudy was searching for something."

"The law is already involved." Roger's expression was worried. "We have a dead woman."

"True, but I have to believe Trudy is alive. And I think we have tools now to find her."

Roger blew out a breath. "It's your call, but only for the short term."

Tabitha held up the disk. "Let's check this out."

They found the cats ready beside the truck and Roger didn't suggest taking Pluto home to Dahlia House. He'd accepted that the cats were part of the investigation. The leaner black one rode with his front paws on the dash as if he were scouting the terrain for bad guys. When they arrived at Long Hall they were greeted by the little yellow cat who made straight for Pluto. She licked his head and purred.

"Looks like Trudy wasn't the only one looking for a date," Roger said as he opened the door for Tabitha. "Those cats seem to care about each other."

CHAPTER SIX

*W*hen Tabitha saw Charline Long in the kitchen, she was struck by the look of relief on her face. "Has something happened?"

"I was just a little worried. You were gone longer than I anticipated." Charline looked past her at Roger. "I was a bit concerned that my nephew might have driven you away."

Roger only laughed. "Aunt Charline, you've said many times I can be charming."

Her smile was tinged with relief. "And you certainly can. You can also be an arrogant ass. I know both faces you wear."

Tabitha laughed, and for the first time in several weeks, she enjoyed the sensation. "Roger has been very kind to me," she said. "We have some common interests. In fact, he's going to show me some work on his computer. I'll see if I can get any positive feelings about his proposed plans." She didn't turn around to see how Roger was taking her explanation.

"Wonderful. When can I plan on a session?"

"After lunch?"

"That would be lovely. Cook is making salmon croquettes,

which I think these cats will love." She looked pointedly at Roger. "You brought home more stray cats?"

"I don't think they're actually strays," Tabitha stepped in. She didn't want Charline to get too attached to Vesta because when Trudy came home, she would want her kitty back. "The plumper black one belongs to Sarah Booth Delaney."

"The private investigator? What's he doing here?"

"Visiting Trouble and," Tabitha pointed to the yellow cat, "Vesta. It seems they're all...friends."

"Are you pulling my leg?" Charline asked.

"She wouldn't think of it," Roger said, swooping his aunt up in a hug. "Vesta belongs to the young woman who hasn't shown up for work lately."

"How did the cat get here from town?"

"I'm looking into that," Roger said. "Just enjoy them while they're here and when they're returned to their owners, we can go to the shelter and get you half a dozen cats if that's what you'd like."

Charline frowned at Roger and gave him a sidelong look. "What drugs are you taking? I've never seen you so agreeable. And cats! Who would ever have thought a cat could turn your head."

"I am learning many things, especially about cats," Roger said with a grin. "I may be mellowing."

"Nancy, Nancy!" Charline called to the cook. "Put some champagne in the refrigerator to chill. Raj is mellowing. We must celebrate while we can. He's liable to revert back any minute."

Tabitha burst into laughter, and even Roger chuckled. "Am I that much a tyrant?"

"Yes, you are," Charline said, "but I love you anyway." She faced Tabitha. "I'm glad you've gotten to see the side of Roger we love. Perhaps he won't have to spend the rest of his life alone if he shows more of that side."

Tabitha couldn't stop the shock. Charline Long was match-making between her and her nephew. Roger's response was a long, loud laugh. "You are something else, Aunt Charline. About as subtle as a ton of rocks. I do believe I can manage my romantic future without any help."

"Then get busy and do it," Charline said, completely unper-turbed. "Let's see some of that famous Roger Long action." She stepped closer to him and whispered very loudly, "Or else I'll think you're a coward."

Roger turned to Tabitha. "Run for the hills. Aunt Charline is looking to add you to the family."

"I think I can handle myself," Tabitha said archly. She knew she was flirting but she couldn't resist. "Now, Roger, the ques-tion is, can you?"

Charline applauded. "Oh, yes, she can hold her own. Now you two go finish whatever you had planned. Lunch is served at noon." She shooed them out the back door with the three cats following.

"I should apologize. I was caught up in the moment," Tabitha said. The moment she was alone with Roger, she felt self-conscious.

"No apology necessary. A bit of harmless banter makes the day go faster. How about we head to my office so we can look at that recording?"

"A wise plan." Tabitha tried to keep her gaze from following Roger's back as they both got in the truck, the cats leaping in after her. She was more acutely aware of his good looks and physicality with each passing hour. And also more aware of his kindness in helping her find her sister. That was where her focus had to be. They drove to the agriculture offices in silence.

ROGER CALLED the fourteen office workers into the reception area. They were a diverse group of men and women of all ages and they stood silently as Roger introduced Tabitha.

"This is a serious matter and I need your help," Roger told them. "As you know, Trudy hasn't been to work for two weeks. We fear something has happened to her, that she's fallen into the wrong hands." He motioned to Tabitha. "This is Trudy's sister. She's looking for some clue where Trudy might have gone. I'm asking you all to cooperate. If you know something, even something that may seem insignificant, please tell us. Did Trudy mention to anyone where she might be going?"

A young woman who worked in filing came forward. "She said she'd found a problem with some of the orders. She was talking on the phone about it just before she went home the evening she...disappeared. She was upset. Maybe even angry."

"What kind of problem?" Tabitha asked.

The girl, Felicity Montgomery, shook her head. "Trudy was too smart. She caught on to things very quickly. She'd been studying those new seeds and plants you told her to research and she found some things she was concerned about. She was meeting that seed and chemical representative, Lisa East. They were going to look into some tests or something of that nature."

Roger felt a surge of hope and deeper worry. Many of the chemical companies and seed developers had been under fire from environmental protesters. The claims against the companies were more than troubling, and Roger had only reluctantly agreed to try the new strain of cotton. A cotton plant resistant to pests and fungus that wouldn't require mass chemical spraying would be a godsend to farmers, but not at the cost of environmental damage or repercussions to humans and animals. The stakes were high, and if Trudy and her friend had found something damaging to DayZSeed, he could easily assume why Lisa East was now dead.

"Where were they meeting up?" Roger asked.

"At some field to take pictures of the plants that were coming up. They said something about soil samples too."

"Did they give any hint about where this field might be?" Tabitha asked.

Felicity teared up. "I'm sorry. I was trying not to snoop into Trudy's business. She was always super nice to me but she made it clear she didn't like people prying into her business."

"That's my sister," Tabitha said, but not unkindly.

Roger thought back over the other farmers who'd been approached to try the new cotton. Only one other had agreed. What field had Trudy been investigating? Was that where she'd disappeared from? Was her car still parked in a brake between fields?

"Do you know what happened at Lisa's house?" an older woman asked. "I heard on the radio that the police were there."

Roger wasn't the kind to sugarcoat bad news. "Someone murdered Lisa."

"Oh, my, god," Felicity said. "What about Trudy? Is she okay?"

"We don't know. There's no indication that she's been... harmed." Tabitha inhaled sharply. "Right now she's just missing. And please don't mention this to anyone. The fewer people who know, the better our chances of getting her back safely. If this becomes town gossip, and if she is being held hostage, the talk might provoke her captors to kill her." Her voice broke but she managed not to cry. Roger knew how hard that was for her, and he almost went to comfort her. But he barely knew her—and had no idea if she'd welcome any solace he could offer. His aunt was right—he was becoming soft, and all for a woman he hardly knew.

"Felicity, you're positive they didn't meet at Lisa's place?" Tabitha clarified. This was good news only because it meant Trudy probably wasn't there when Lisa was killed. "Do you know which field? Whose property?"

"I can't say for sure because I didn't go with them," Felicity said. "But I think it was some field planted with G9-14. I think that's what they were talking about."

"Did Trudy ever say what was wrong with the plants?" Tabitha asked.

"Only that she was concerned about devastating the entire cotton crop if what she suspected was true."

"Anyone else know anything that could help us?" Roger asked the whole group. Folks shook their heads.

Roger motioned to include everyone in the room. "Please keep this to yourself. Trudy's life could depend on your ability to stay quiet. We've always been like a family here, and I hope you care enough about each other to do as I ask. And if you think of anything or hear anything, please come forward."

Felicity made fists of her hands, but then spoke. "Trudy was dating some guy she was afraid of. She was secretive about it, but I overheard her. She said she thought someone was stalking her. She was afraid."

"How afraid?" Roger asked. He grasped Tabitha's hand and held it, signaling her to let him ask the questions. The gentle squeeze he gave her fingers was meant to comfort her.

Felicity looked like she wanted to cry. "Trudy said he

manhandled her once. She was mad about it. She stood up for herself, but she saw him parked across the street from her place, watching her. She mentioned that the day before she disappeared and she didn't like it."

Roger saw Tabitha's reaction, the look of fear and the blanched face. "Who was she dating? Did she say?"

Felicity sighed. "She never said his name. She did say he owned a lot of land in Sunflower County." Felicity threw an apologetic glance at Tabitha. "Trudy liked nice things. Cars, clothes, going out. She wasn't interested in dating an average guy who owned a local furniture store or anything like that. She and this man liked to take his private plane to Memphis for dinner. That kind of thing. A lot of the big land owners have planes and their own landing strips."

Tabitha wanted to deny it, but she couldn't. Trudy had always loved the finer things in life. She was willing to work for them and earn them, but she also liked men who could bring those things into the equation.

"Thank you all," Roger said. "Please don't hesitate to come to me if you think of anything else."

One of the male staffers cleared his throat. "I heard Trudy was having a hard time with some guy and I offered to help her, but she said she had it under control. I got the sense she was afraid of him, but that she felt confident she could keep herself safe. I should have insisted."

"Trudy didn't care for people poking around in her business," Roger said. "You offered. You did the right thing. Thank you." He opened his inner office door and swept Tabitha inside.

CHAPTER SEVEN

*I*t's clear to me Trudy has gotten herself into a fine pickle. She's up to her ears in alum and almost puckered to death, or as the Brits would say, she's reached maximum sixes and sevens. I'm going to have to figure out how this lissome bird got herself in such a predicament. And after that, I have to save her. Vesta is beside herself with worry, which means Pluto is anxious and upset. Both are smart cats, but they haven't been exposed to the crime-solving techniques of Sherlock Holmes or my dad, Familiar. I have to take the lead, and fast. I'm annoyed that Roger and Tabitha shut me out of the office. Me and Pluto and Vesta. Really? They're keeping their best investigators in the dark. I will not be outdone.

I need to move the cat conclave to the back window of Roger's office. We can see what's on that dating DVD. Sometimes the humans simply don't think. Wait! The door is opening, and Tabitha is signaling us inside. She's as smart as she is pretty, and she's redeemed herself in my eyes.

Roger has the DVD cued up and ready to go. I take a seat on his desk with Vesta and Pluto. These humans never fail to slay me with their ridiculous romantic endeavors. They dress and strut and perform *for each other like prairie grouse. They seem to forget that to engage in the act of love, they must shed those feathers of finery. Make-up will be smeared. The mating rituals of humans are worthy of a book. Cats, on the other hand, are always dressed to perfection and while a little fur may fly in a romantic encounter, by half an hour later we return to our natural state of elegance!*

I give a little hiss to Pluto to let him know to keep his mind on the missing person and not Vesta's magnificent body. She is attractive, no doubt about it. A fine bird, as we Brits would say. There'll be plenty of time for romance at a later date, when her person is safe and Tabitha is relieved of her burden of fear.

I do have to make mention that I've watched Roger cast more than one assessing look at my glamorous little fake psychic medium. Roger went from zero to sixty in twenty seconds. He was calling her a shill and leech this morning. Now, I detect a glimmer of arousal in his grey eyes whenever he looks at her. Yes, he's definitely interested in a romantic kind of way. And she reciprocates, if I know my long-legged beauties, and I do. They are besotted with each other but haven't figured it out yet. Good. Solve the mystery, then dive under the quilts! But first things first. Get the sister girl home safely.

Ah, dim the lights, where's the popcorn, the film is about to begin.

TABITHA REALIZED she was holding her breath as the image of her sister came up on the computer screen. This was a Trudy she'd seen before, but not one she felt was true to her sister. With her hair swept up in a coiffed 'do' and make-up heavy with smoky eyes and dark lipstick, Trudy looked like a Hollywood celebrity.

"That's Trudy?" Roger asked.

Clearly this was not her normal look at work. Tabitha nodded. "Trudy always loved playing dress up."

Tabitha took in the diamond earrings that dangled from her sister's ears, the Rolex on her wrist, and diamond pendant that hung provocatively between her cleavage. "I don't know where she got that jewelry," she added. "Trudy doesn't own that kind of expensive stuff. This is like...Trudy doppelganger in an alternate world."

"She was always neat and professional at work, but nothing like that," Roger said.

On the video Trudy began to talk about herself, and everything that came out of her mouth was a lie. Tabitha couldn't believe it. Her sister portrayed herself as some New Orleans belle whose family had fallen on hard times. She talked about parties and dancing and Tulane—all things Trudy had never done. Sure, they'd had fun in Nola, but not posh parties at Commander's Palace and lawn parties in the Garden District hobnobbing with the social elite. Certainly not college at Tulane. That had never been their world—more like community college--but that was what Trudy was selling. No wonder she was in so much trouble. Tabitha felt the first tear slide down her cheek and she didn't even bother brushing it away. Her sister was in danger, and partly because she was pretending to be someone she'd never been. Even if her stalker boyfriend wasn't involved in the cotton or Lisa East's murder, Trudy was in deep trouble, and now Tabitha could no longer pretend otherwise.

They watched the entire interview before Roger turned off the computer and sighed. "It looks to me like she was playing someone," he said. "She came here to hook a fish, but what she intended to do with the fish is the question."

"What do you mean?" Tabitha tried to hide her tears, but it was pointless. When Roger came to her and pulled her into his arms, she didn't resist. She was so upset and worried she couldn't stop herself from crying, and it had been a long time since she felt protected in someone's arms.

He merely held her, patting her back gently, until she'd gotten past the worst of it. When she drew in a deep breath and squared her shoulders, she stepped back and he offered her a box of tissues from his desk.

"I'm sorry," she said. "It's just the shock of her behavior, the way she looked, the coy and flirtatious way she behaved. That isn't my sister."

"At least not the way I know her," Roger agreed. "It would seem you and Trudy have something in common."

"What?" Tabitha looked confused.

"You're both very good actresses. She sold me on the whole Cinderella story of her life in New Orleans. You sold my whole family on your psychic medium tale."

Tabitha felt the blood rise up in her cheeks. Shame was never a comfortable feeling, but Roger was right. She'd lied about who and what she was. She, like Trudy, had come to Sunflower County under false pretenses and he had every right to call her out on it.

"Looking at this, I can only say I'm worried sick about Trudy and I'm sorry for pretending to be a psychic medium. I was desperate to get a lead on Trudy, and it just never occurred to me that anyone would help me. I swear to you I haven't done anything harmful to anyone and I haven't scammed anyone."

Roger touched her cheek and lifted her face to his. "I didn't mean that the way it came out. Think about this. You came here with the goal of finding your sister. You were willing to pretend to be someone you aren't to get answers. Give Trudy the same benefit of the doubt. What was your sister trying to find out? Why would she pretend to be a socialite fallen on hard times on a dating site?"

Roger was absolutely right! Tabitha stood up. Trudy was playing a role and not necessarily to victimize anyone. "She came here because she was looking for something and it wasn't a date."

Standing up too, Roger nodded. "I believe that. Trudy was undercover, just like you were. But why? Let's take a look at that thumb drive. There's obviously something on it worth hiding."

Tabitha was unprepared for her sister's face on the computer screen. She'd obviously made the recording at her desk in Long Agricultural. "Tabitha, if you've found this, I'm in trouble. I haven't been honest with you, but not because I didn't want to. I'm a member of Green World, a group of environmental activists. You're not going to like this, because you believe in doing things exactly the legal way, but sometimes we don't have time to wait for the law. The planet is under assault by these chemical companies. We have to fight. I'm sorry, because I know this will worry you. I'm helping Green World find out who's behind the release of new crops that could devastate the agricultural world. I know you didn't like my friends, but that's because they didn't want you to like them. To keep you safe. This is dangerous business, but I knew that before I agreed to move to the Delta. Please don't ever blame yourself. Or anyone else. I wanted to do this. I wanted to make a difference. I love you."

The screen went blank. Tabitha felt as if someone had jabbed a knife in her chest. "What the hell was Trudy up to?" she said, focusing on holding back her tears.

"I knew Trudy was smart, but I had no idea what she was

involved in," Roger said. "I'd say call the police, but if Trudy is being held captive, that could really put her life at risk."

Roger's words were a revelation, and one that had Tabitha wondering how much about her little sister she really didn't know. Trudy was smart and had loved science and math, growing things, seeds, the rudiments of farming. But her knowledge of agriculture was a true surprise. Now, it was like a bell gonged in Tabitha's brain. Yes! Of course. Trudy was playing a pretend role, but to what end? Roger had asked the most important question of the day—what did Trudy know that was worth kidnapping and murder. "Then if that's true, it would mean Trudy came to Sunflower County to find out something. This whole move wasn't some wild hair to date a farmer or see the Delta or hang out in blues clubs like she said. She came here because she was investigating something!"

"The cotton." Roger pushed his fine, dark hair back from his forehead. "Dammit. I should have paid more attention. It's all clear now. She was always hanging around, asking questions about this, that, and the other, but all of it had to do with the new crops, with research, with the pesticides and their effect on the environment."

Tabitha sank into a chair. "What was Trudy involved in?"

"I don't know, but we have to find out if we hope to find her."

"She's smart, Roger."

"And that may be the thing that saves her skin." Roger was pensive.

"We need to find out who she was dating. And if he is somehow connected to this cotton issue."

"Yes. It's time to pay a visit to that dating service. You're going to have to sell yourself the same way Trudy did. You won't be at risk—we can simply screen the applicants. See if we can pull up some suspects. After you have your session with Aunt Charline today, we'll get you ready for your video."

"What do you mean?" Tabitha asked.

"We'll borrow some of my aunt's finery and set you up as the same kind of woman Trudy portrayed. If that's the shark she was fishing for, maybe we can lure him in."

Tabitha swallowed. This was not what she'd anticipated, but Roger was correct. If Trudy had come to Sunflower County to dig into crops and seeds and fertilizers, and she'd used a dating service to gain access to someone, the quickest way to find her was to follow in her footsteps.

"I can't believe my sister didn't confide in me."

"She didn't want to put you at risk, and be truthful, you would have been in the middle of this with her."

Tabitha nodded. "That's true, and yet here I am, in the middle of it. And I've dragged you along to boot."

"If something is going on with cotton or the crops, it's my business. This land is my heritage, it's in my blood. I won't sit back and let someone poison it or destroy it."

There were unexpected levels to Roger that Tabitha hadn't anticipated. He made his living from the land, but the passion in his words went deeper. He was connected to the Delta soil in a visceral way. Tabitha understood. Her love for New Orleans was in her bones.

"I know you're worried, but let's have lunch and then talk with my aunt. While you're doing that, I'll find the wardrobe and accessories for you to wear in your video, and I'll check out that report you found. The car you're leasing is the perfect touch. While you're working with the dating service, I'll see if I can get into the office and find out if there's a way to access the computer files to see who Trudy may have been dating."

"That's dangerous." Tabitha could see a lot of trouble headed Roger's way if he was caught.

"This whole thing is dangerous."

Doubt assailed Tabitha, and she bit her lip to control her emotions. "What if Trudy is dead?"

Roger picked up both her hands and held them. His hands were so much larger and roughened from outside work. "You can't think that. She isn't dead. We would have found the body. A better question is, who may have found out what she was up to?"

Tabitha shook her head as she truly pondered the question. "I don't know. It's clear that the sister I thought I knew so well had depths that I never even looked at. What about this special cotton? Is it something people would kill for?"

"There's a lot of money tied up in research, and now it's in production. It's a big deal."

"Big enough to kill two young women?"

Roger firmly held her hand. "Trudy isn't dead or we would have found her body. They didn't bother to try to hide Lisa East's corpse. They just left it for someone to find. They would have done the same to Trudy. Whatever she's doing or saying, they're keeping her alive.

"But for how much longer?"

Roger chafed her hands to warm them. "You're freezing. Look, all that matters is right now we can assume she's alive and uninjured. It's up to us to find her before that changes. Now talk to Aunt Charline. Make up whatever you need to say to bring her and Uncle Sam some peace."

"I don't always make everything up," Tabitha confessed. "I'm not a psychic or a medium, but I do get a sense of dead people, and your grandmother is there at Long Hall. She's there because she's watching over your family."

Roger's hand cupped her face. "That's what you need to tell Aunt Charline."

A knock at the door interrupted them. Roger shut down the computer and motioned Felicity into the room. "I forgot to tell you but Dirk Cotwell was here early this morning. He was upset. He asked you to call him."

"Did he say what he wanted?"

Felicity shrugged. "I shouldn't speak out of school, but he was going out with Trudy. It seemed really casual, but..." She sighed. "I tried to warn her about Lily Kennedy and the engagement. Trudy swore she was just having fun and had no intention of interfering in anyone's life or career."

"That's an odd phrasing. Career?"

"Trudy was always focused on work. I overhead a few conversations with Dirk and it was more about cotton than romantic feelings. She liked a good time, but who doesn't?"

Roger took the phone slip from her hand. "Thanks. Anything else?"

"Trudy did say something the last morning she came in. She was laughing, so I didn't take her seriously, she said that people would kill to keep a secret."

"Which people?" Tabitha asked.

Felicity shook her head. "She was talking about visiting some of the cotton fields with Lisa East. She didn't say a name. That's all I know."

Roger patted her shoulder. "Thanks. That's a help."

CHAPTER EIGHT

*R*oger stopped the pickup at the front steps of Long Hall. He and Tabitha had been silent on the short ride, but her tension was palpable. Even the cats were subdued, though Trouble once again watched the horizon as if he expected Satan to pop out of the dirt. Roger opened the truck door, but Tabitha caught his sleeve.

"If there's anything you can tell me about your grandmother...I didn't set out to trick anyone. I do want to bring Charline and Samuel comfort."

"Aunt Charline and Suellen were best friends. Most people shudder at the idea of living with an in-law, but the three of them had a loving family, and they always included me. They would have welcomed my mother, Hannah, if she'd let them."

"Where is your mom?" Tabitha asked.

"Last I heard she was dating a lord or marquis or something of that nature in Europe. She has a man for each season, depending on where the weather is best. Monaco is a favorite spot. Venice, maybe." He shrugged. "I don't begrudge her a good life. I just don't want her upsetting Charline and Samuel. Or meddling in the business of the farm."

"Charline told me Hannah would prefer the family sold the plantation and agricultural business."

"She'd go through the money like sh--, well like food through a goose." He grinned. "Sorry. Mother gets a huge allowance and is always borrowing from me or hitting Samuel up. He seldom says no." He paused for a moment as if he were thinking. "Lately, though, she's been asking about the crops. What she doesn't realize is that if the farm were sold, there'd be no steady income. For someone who loves money, she has no grasp of how to make it or use it. And she's had every opportunity to come home and learn the business. My mother isn't stupid but she is lazy and she's made a career out of being the victim in the Long family, the poor little cast-aside—which was never the case. Charline and Samuel have done everything to include her."

"Family does seem to mean a lot to Charline. She mentioned how much she wanted to be close to your mother."

Roger got out of the truck and came around to open the door for Tabitha. "My mother is her own worst enemy. I've given up that she'll ever find anything that satisfies her in a way that is more than just material gratification."

"That's too bad. I had a pretty rough upbringing. I would have given anything to be included in a family where love was in abundance."

"My mother is...she's selfish. She always felt like she'd been pushed to the outside. Not because Suellen or Roger and Charline treated her that way. She put herself outside and then punished everyone else because that was where she stood. I saw that long ago and refused to support her negative delusions. My uncle and aunt have been very good to me. That's when she lumped me in with Samuel and Charline as a traitor."

Tabitha put a hand on his chest. "I'm so sorry."

"Hey, I've been lucky. I had plenty of love here at Long Hall. I'm sorry for my mother, but I also accept that I can't change her. By the way, she's coming for a visit. You'll get to meet her."

He saw the surprise and then dread cross her face. "I should move back to the hotel. This sounds like a family time and a stranger shouldn't interfere."

"Not so fast." Roger grasped the hand that had touched his chest. Her fingers were long and tapered, her hands delicate. "You have to stay. You can prevent World War III. Besides, I need you to send my mother a message from the great beyond."

"What?"

Roger laughed at her shock. "I mean you're here. You're relaying messages for Charline and Samuel. Couldn't you send one to my mother?" The look on her face was priceless. She was truly shocked that he would manipulate his own mother.

"What kind of message?"

"Just tell her Micah Malone still loves her and wishes for her happiness every day. That he's watching over her."

The relief on her face was palpable. "That's a sweet message. Who is Micah Malone?"

"The only person, other than herself, that she's ever really loved. My mother can be a real b...witch, but the pain she inflicts on others is nothing compared to what she does to herself. I have a theory that she has never allowed herself to feel love, except with Micah. He was a troubadour, a singer song-writer California surfer. He drifted into her life and because he had no expectations and didn't understand the concept of pressure, she didn't have any defenses against him. He slipped beneath her armor. She loved him deeply." He could see that Tabitha was clearly caught up in the story.

"What happened to him?"

"Something went wrong when he was surfing. He ended up in a place that was dangerous, and a wave crashed him into some rocks. He died." He shook his head. "The one time she didn't bully someone to get her way, she should have. Can you believe it?"

"I can," Tabitha said, and she turned away. "I had a terrible feeling when Trudy said she was moving here. I should have stopped her."

"You can say that," Roger said. "You can even believe it, intellectually. But emotionally you know there was no way to dissuade Trudy from a damn thing. You might as well try to capture the wind." He put his arm around her shoulders. "Blaming yourself is wrong and gets you nowhere."

She looked up at him, "Thank you. I needed to hear that."

But he could see she wasn't ready to forgive herself yet. He recognized that need to hang onto responsibility. He was like that about his mother. He couldn't control her yet he constantly felt responsible for her actions.

"When will your mother arrive?" Tabitha asked, looking up at the massive dwelling.

Roger checked his watch. "She should be here this afternoon." He took her arm as they walked to the front door. "You may charm her. You're unique."

He liked the tinge of a flush that touched her cheeks. "After my reading with Charline, I'll ask her if I should leave."

"She knew Mother was coming," Roger said. "She invited you anyway. The house has two dozen bedrooms. There's no shortage of space. The only awkwardness could be meals, and if that happens, I'll invite you to dine in town with me. Mother won't miss me."

He opened the front door and ushered her inside before she could protest. Lunch was ready to be served, and he made sure there was no time for her to back out. He wanted to find Trudy, but he also wanted to find out more about Tabitha Kingsley. She'd intrigued him, and he didn't mind admitting it.

WHEN THEY APPEARED in the kitchen with three cats, Charline only lifted an eyebrow. She prepared three bowls of fresh Gulf shrimp that Nancy had steamed and shelled. When she put the bowls on the floor, the cats ate with relish.

"The orange kitty belongs to one of my employees," Roger reminded his aunt. He could see how attached she was becoming. "The two black ones..." He laughed nervously, "As I told you, one belongs to Sarah Booth Delaney and the other lives at the Prince Albert hotel."

Charline nodded. "Yes, one is a detective and the other a traveling salesman. They're from the planet Catnip and they're here to study how humans grow cotton."

The black cat called Trouble polished off his shrimp and made a great show of rubbing against Charline's legs.

"That cat knows who to butter up," Roger said. "Next thing he'll be sleeping in bed with you and Sam."

Tabitha burst into a laugh, and the issue of the cats passed. Samuel had gone to Memphis to run some errands, so they gathered in the dining room. The conversation was easy and casual, and Tabitha was aware that Charline kept glancing from her to Roger and back.

Lunch was a delicious squash soup with a fresh avocado salad. When the meal was done, Roger excused himself and

Charline motioned for Tabitha to follow her into the parlor. "Is this a good time? Are you refreshed?"

"It's a perfect time," Tabitha said, feeling like someone had starched her jeans. Guilt scratched and pricked her skin. She was playing Charline, and she didn't like it. She couldn't back out now. She'd set this whole thing in motion and she had to see it through. The only comfort she had was that she honestly hoped to bring relief and closure.

They settled at a small table in a sunny corner. It was a perfect early spring day with warm sunlight filtering in. The window gave a view of a vast, flat expanse of cropland. The house was surrounded by magnolia and cedar trees, but the fields were immaculate except for the brakes that allowed protection from wind erosion and drainage. There trees were allowed to grow thick and lush, a windbreak and also a refuge for the wildlife that was once plentiful but now on the decline. Tabitha took in her surroundings as she centered herself as Mama Bettite had taught her.

She looked down at her hands lightly holding Charline's hands on the small table. Closing her eyes, she focused on her breathing, on letting everything negative out with her breath and drawing in healing and energy with each inhale, opening to the sensations that sometimes spoke to her or left her with images or symbols.

"Suellen Long," she said softly, "please come to us. Charline misses you. She wants you to know that she and Samuel both miss you."

She heard Charline's sniffles but she didn't open her eyes. There was no guarantee that she would get any message but if she didn't, she'd have to fabricate something. She'd practiced a spiel, but that was before she'd come to see Charline's deep loneliness and Roger's regard for his aunt and uncle. They'd been a theoretical couple she needed to get close to if she meant to find her sister's trail. Now she really wanted to make a connection with the departed Suellen, if she could.

She'd done fine with the other couples she'd held séances for in Sunflower County. Well, there'd only been two of them, but word traveled fast—and grew with embellishments—in a small town. She'd counted on that and it had certainly worked. Now, dealing with a woman she genuinely liked, she couldn't let her emotions get in the way of her job, and her job was finding Trudy.

She tried to clear her mind of the anxiety and the minute she calmed, a damp, cold chill touched her skin. It was so unpleasant, she almost reacted by pulling her hands away from Charline and standing up. The bright sun still warmed the table, but she was so cold her teeth almost started to chatter.

She sensed rather than felt something behind her left shoulder. Someone. Even if it was just her imagination, she had to come forth with something for Charline. "Suellen, do you have a message for Charline? She'd love to hear from you. She wants to know that you're happy and okay."

The energy she felt was male rather than female, and with it came the sound of waves kissing a shoreline and the smell of the ocean. She could almost see a manifestation in a corner of the room, but it didn't form. There was only the echo of a thought. "Hannah." The word whispered around the corners of the room. "The truth lies beneath layers." And then the entity was gone, replaced by the light smell of magnolias and Suellen's lighter energy.

"Suellen, Charline is here, waiting for you."

"Find her. Quickly." The words entered her mind on a voice that was feminine and refined, though Tabitha knew no one had really spoken. This was exactly as Mama Bettite had told her connecting with spirit would be. More sensation than fact, but Tabitha couldn't deny the urgency conveyed to her.

"Find who?" Tabitha asked, but she knew. This wasn't a message for Charline, it was for her. Either her subconscious was in overdrive or some spirit had made contact.

"Too trusting." The words came on a sigh, like a breeze teasing spring flowers.

Tabitha inhaled sharply. "Where is she?"

Before the spirit could answer, a beautiful painting across the room fell to the floor. The clatter made Charline stand up so quickly her chair fell over. "What is going on?" she asked, distressed. "Is Suellen angry? Why would she do that? She loved that painting. She loved telling the story of how the Long family came to own it."

Tabitha used all her reserve to pull herself out of the cold realm and back to the present. "No, no, Suellen is fine," she said. "She had a message, that's all."

"For me?" Charline's eagerness made Tabitha feel guilty all over again.

"For you and one for me too. I've been looking for someone and she was trying to help me."

"By knocking a painting to the floor?" Charline had two high spots of color on her cheeks and her eyes were still wide. Tabitha realized that she had to take quick action.

"Maybe it's a clue," she said. "Let's look at the painting and see. Would you tell me the story you mentioned?" She went to the heavy painting that had not been damaged in the fall and lifted it up. The hook holding it had come loose from the wall.

Charline had regained her composure and she looked at the hook and then the empty hole in the wall. "I've never seen anything like that happen here. It took me by surprise. I didn't mean to sound so...upset."

"Please don't worry." Tabitha examined the painting. It was a lovely landscape of the Delta. The flat land extended to a horizon where a bank of clouds that could be a cavalry charge was highlighted by shafts of golden light and the colors of sunset. "The vistas here in the Delta are so beautiful. Was this painted here at Long Hall?"

"It was something Suellen acquired. It's the Delta but it was painted probably seventy years ago." Charline was happy to talk about the Long family's history. "Suellen said that back in the Depression, there was an artist traveling through the area. He'd stay in some of the plantations and would paint for his room and board. His name was Redmond, Asa Redmond. He stayed here at Long Hall for nearly a year, and that was one of his paintings. If you go up to the third floor and look off the back balcony, you can see the exact same vista."

"I've heard of traveling artists like that." Tabitha was glad the conversation had turned to a more neutral topic. "During the period before the Civil War, a lot of the wealthier homes opened their doors to painters and musicians who would then entertain at soirees and gatherings. I always thought what a gracious and inspiring life that would have been."

"Yes, if you were part of the social elite," Charline said. "Farming is a hard life, but once it's in your blood, there's no happiness anywhere but on the land."

Tabitha studied the painting, the way the artist had created almost sensual curves with the green land, the mist, the clouds in the sky. "It is lovely. I hadn't realized that flat land could be so awe inspiring." Tabitha was reluctant to leave the painting.

"I'll have Roger rehang it when he's finished with his work for the day." Charline's tone had returned to her normal calm. "It seems Roger has taken a special interest in you." She smiled. "He needs a woman in his life. One who can share him with this land."

"I'm hardly what he needs." Tabitha felt the heat rise in her own face. She couldn't deny that she found Roger attractive. He was a handsome man with confidence and certainly a degree of kindness she hadn't expected. The sensation of his arms around her, comforting, came back to her. He had a lot of qualities she liked, even admired, but their paths had crossed because of Trudy's disappearance. Once Trudy was safely found, Tabitha and her sister would return to New Orleans where they belonged. Roger's life was in the Delta, growing crops, harvesting, working the land. They had little in common except the missing woman.

Tabitha took a long, slow breath and resettled at the small table. She took Charline's hands again and closed her eyes. The scent of wisteria came to her, strong and sweet. It was a summer day and she suddenly stood outside Long Hall in a garden.

The same refined voice came to her again, and Tabitha caught snatches of summer, a beautiful garden, and the sweet lemony scent of magnolias. Tabitha was filled with a sense of serenity, an ease. She understood she was to convey that to Charline.

"I will." Tabitha spoke the words aloud, though she knew Charline could hear only one end of the conversation.

For a brief second, an older woman in an elegant lavender suit stepped out of the garden shadows. Tabitha felt the moment slip away from her. She found herself sitting in the sunshine in the parlor.

"Did Suellen wear a scent, something light, like magnolias?"

"She did." Charline sat forward. "What did she say? You were talking to her?"

"She's grateful to you and Samuel for the upkeep on Long Hall and the way you love this place like she did. She is happy and safe. She doesn't want you to worry about her or waste your time missing her. She wants you to live your life to the fullest. She'll always be around here if you have need of her. She takes great comfort in the love you have for her grandson and for Long Hall. She is happy, Charline. She wants the same for you and Samuel."

It wasn't exactly the message Tabitha had received, but close enough, and it would bring the Longs real comfort.

"I knew she was right here with us," Charline said, squeezing Tabitha's hands. "Thank you."

The front door opened and closed, and Tabitha was relieved when Roger stepped into the parlor. "If you've finished with my aunt, I'd like to show you those processing plants I told you about," Roger said to Tabitha.

"Oh, by all means, show her the farm," Charline said with a mischievous smile. "Nothing like an education in farming to give a woman an appetite. I'll make sure we have something hearty and delicious for dinner. You two have become quite the team."

Roger blushed, and Tabitha found it charming. He was a confident man, but his aunt knew exactly what buttons to push.

"Aunt Charline, I'm borrowing some of your jewelry for a photo shoot. Long story, but I'll return it later today. I helped myself in the safe."

"Photo shoot?" She raised an eyebrow. "You're always up to something, Roger. As Samuel says, you're a marketing genius. Help yourself to whatever you need."

"Aunt Charline, did you ever meet Trudy Wells, my missing employee?"

Charline frowned. "I did meet her. I went down to the office one day and she was the receptionist. She seemed... sweet." She hesitated. "She did ask me something very strange."

"What was that?" Roger asked.

"She wanted to know if I had any relatives in the Delta other than you."

Roger cast a quick look at Tabitha. "That is interesting. There are no more relatives. We're the last of the line."

"That's exactly what I told her." She looked at Tabitha. "Which is why Roger needs to marry and have children," Charline said without a whit of shame. "It's Roger's place to do that."

There was the sound of the front door closing again and a lovely brunette woman in her late forties came into the parlor. She wore expensive clothes and shoes with at least a five-inch heel. "It's Roger's obligation to do what?" she asked, walking up to Roger and kissing his cheek though he didn't look all that pleased to see her. "What is it you're trying to wrangle my son into doing?"

"Reproducing, Mother," Roger said without a shred of affection in his tone. "Aunt Charline and Uncle Roger are thinking of selling me off to the highest bidder to keep the Long line going."

"An innovative use for you." Hannah Long raised her eyebrows. Her eyes moved over Roger as if she were memorizing each plane. She turned to Charline. "Charline, you're looking good. And this is?" She stopped in front of Tabitha.

"Tabitha Kingsley, psychic medium," Roger said with a quirk of his lips. "Play nice, Mother. I heard you were coming for a visit, but may I ask, what brings you to Long Hall?"

"Money, what else. I'm here to check in so my adoring

brother keeps up my allowance. It would be better for us both if he simply turned the money over to me, but he refuses. There's some awful kind of rumor that I'm not competent with my inheritance. I wonder who promoted that concept."

Tabitha wanted to escape the room, but there wasn't an easy out. This was family business and Hannah had no place airing it in front of a stranger, but that wasn't going to stop her. Tabitha stood up and made for the door to the kitchen.

"Not so fast." Hannah's hand snaked out and caught her wrist. "What are you up to?"

A warning shot through Roger's eyes, but it was too late. He started to intervene, but Charline was quicker.

"Tabitha is my guest," Charline said. "She's been relaying messages from Suellen."

"Oh? Suellen is still with us? I always knew the grave couldn't contain her."

"Hannah!" Charline was truly shocked. "I don't care that you act like a brat but you won't speak about Suellen in that way. I loved her, even if you didn't."

"It's hard to love someone to whom you're a bitter disappointment every single day of your life." Hannah flipped her hair back. "I'm just so unlike Samuel, the devoted son. You know, the only thing I could do that Samuel couldn't was reproduce." She linked her arm through Roger's. "And what a fine son I have, even if he is a bastard."

CHAPTER NINE

*M*y, oh, my, that woman is a harridan of the highest order. She's little better than a fishmonger strolling the streets of old London town. And what a wicked tongue she has! I do believe she needs a bit of a lesson in manners, and I'm just the cat to deliver it. I'll slink into the room making sure that no one notices. Pluto and Vesta are hanging out in the foyer watching me with wide kitty eyes. One yowl and they'll come to my rescue, I'm sure. Cats are loyal like that.

Let's see if I can sneak behind the old scold. Yes, and she's wearing that short skirt—perhaps too short for her age--which leaves a perfect target, the back of the knee. I'll just tickle her a little with my fine black tail and goodness. She has the shriek of a banshee. But Roger appreciates my maneuver. He is laughing and not doing a thing to conceal his amusement. Even Charline is laughing. The only person not amused is Hannah. And she's aiming a kick at my head.

Uh-oh, Pluto saw it too, and now he's tickling the back of her other knee. Down she goes. Those high heels aren't meant for trying to kick a cat. She's toppled over. And she is hornet mad! She's crawling after Pluto. And she just banged her head on the side of the table.

*When Roger reached down to help her, she lashed out at him,
which only resulted in the teapot falling on her head. Now she has hot
tea all over her. And she is howling mad, so mad she is actually
foaming at the mouth. A proper British lady would never find herself
in such a shabby display! Poor Charline is trying not to laugh but can't
help herself.*

"HANNAH, LET ME HELP YOU UP," Charline offered.

"You're trying to kill me, aren't you?" Hannah jerked away
from Charline's outstretched hand.

Roger felt the blood pounding in his temple, a sure sign his
temper was about to get the better of him. Because of the
numerous scenes he'd grown up witnessing, Roger hated to
lose control, but no one could push him to the edge like
Hannah Long. "Mother, no one did a thing to you. You did
every bit of this yourself with your awful temper. You want to
know why Samuel doesn't trust you with money, look at yourself, crawling around the floor and wrecking furniture." Roger
had no tolerance in his face or voice. "You are an embarrassment. I hope Uncle Samuel gives you your check and you
leave. Tonight."

"Just as soon as I get my monthly allotment," Hannah said.
She used a chair to gain her feet. Tea dripped from her hair all
over her expensive outfit. "I came here with the best of inten-
tions, and then this...this happens. You all hate me, I know it.
You control my money and you and Samuel have stolen my son
from me." Hannah rounded on Charline like she was the
enemy. "There is a price to pay for what you've done to me."

Roger grasped his mother's arm none too gently. "You are a
fool, Mother. Charline and Samuel gave me the only stability
I've ever known. They gave me a job and a career. They've

loved me without demanding a price for their love. Now clean yourself up before Samuel gets here or I swear, I'll tell him how horrible you behaved. I'll ask him to take legal action to freeze your money." He thrust her arm away from him and turned his back on her.

"I am your mother," she said. For a split second, her fury was mixed with sadness. "You will not turn your back on me." She picked up a leaded crystal candy dish from the coffee table and drew back to throw it. Before she could, Tabitha grabbed her arm.

"Don't do that," Tabitha said softly. "You'll only regret it."

"Take your hands off me."

Tabitha released her arm, but the moment to strike Roger in the back with the dish was past. He was facing his mother, eyeing the dish in her hand and clearly reading what she'd intended to do.

"Mother, understand this. If you ever raise a hand to me again, I'll have you arrested. I put up with your abuse when I was a kid, but no longer. And don't test me on this." He swallowed. "Aunt Charline, if you'll excuse me and Tabitha, I've promised to show her the plant."

"I'll make some more tea for your mother and once she's changed, we'll have a chat until Samuel gets here."

"I don't want tea. But I've brought a guest of my own." She went to the front door and threw it open. "Antoine, please come inside."

A tall, well-dressed, middle-aged man had obviously been waiting on the porch. He stepped into the foyer and then made a slight bow in the direction of Charline and Roger. "Antoine Lafitte," he said, walking forward and extending his hand. He shook Roger's, kissed Charline's, and made to kiss Tabitha's, but she backed away.

"Antoine is my...fiancé." Hannah smirked. "Darling, wait for me upstairs. My suite is on the second floor to the right at the end of the hall."

"Shall I gather the bags?" Antoine asked.

"That would be lovely."

He gave the room a little bow and went back outside. In ten minutes he was back with two bags. He carried them upstairs.

"I'm glad you've found someone to care about," Charline said to Hannah. "He's very handsome."

Roger could only marvel at his aunt's compassion and kindness. She should have made Hannah wait on the steps. He kissed his aunt's cheek and motioned for Tabitha to precede him from the house. When they gained the yard and the cool breeze, he leaned against his truck. "I'm sorry you witnessed that."

"Family." Tabitha shrugged. "I've seen worse. My mother didn't have the best taste in men, and trust me, none were as well dressed as Antoine." She smiled. "Trudy and I have been on our own for a long time. You're lucky to have Charline and Samuel."

"Tell me about it."

They saw the front door open and the three cats ran out into the sunshine.

"Can you believe those black cats?" Roger was smiling. "It's as if they sensed the ill will that is my mother."

"It looked calculated to me," Tabitha said.

Roger chuckled. "The psychic and her familiars."

"That's witches and their familiars," Tabitha teased.

Roger opened the truck door for the cats to load up. "Psychics, witches, cats, or toads. If they can help us find your sister, that's where we should focus our energy. Mother will be gone as soon as she gets her money, and good riddance to her."

"What's the story with Antoine?" Tabitha asked. "He's very smooth and courtly."

Roger glanced at her. It seemed that Tabitha had sensed something amiss with the polished gigolo. His mother had a talent for attracting men who enjoyed helping her spend her "allowance."

"One in a long line of parasites," he said with resignation. "My mother is lonely, but she never ends up with a man who cares about her. They care about her inheritance, the family wealth. She's home to try to force Samuel and Charline to give her a lump sum payout instead of an allowance. Old story, repeated again and again."

Tabitha's hand grasped his arm and squeezed. "Let's check out the cotton."

TABITHA SETTLED into the truck seat with the cats sprawled across her lap and the seat as Roger drove. They both had a lot on their minds. Tabitha knew what it felt like to be embarrassed by the behavior of family, and Hannah Long had certainly shown her posterior. How could Hannah have such anger at Charline and Samuel, who were two of the kindest people she'd ever met? But Hannah had been a late in life child and one that always felt like an intruder. That was hard, too. The Longs had plenty of money but the same troubles that everyone else had.

Roger drove past the business and kept going. "Let's get that dating DVD made. It's a local company and our best clue. I'll drop you off to submit your profile and I need to give Dirk

Cotwell a call. He's another farmer that used the G9-14 cotton. I'll be curious to see what he called about."

"Sounds like a plan."

"I hadn't given this a lot of thought, but you should know, Dirk had an interest in Trudy."

Tabitha was instantly alert. "What kind of interest?"

"He asked me if she was single. He thought she was pretty. I didn't put much stock in it because Dirk's engaged to Martin Kennedy's daughter, Lily. They're to be married in the fall. The Kennedys are the wealthiest family in the region, and Lily is a beautiful woman. Dirk isn't stupid enough to mess that up."

There was something in Roger's voice that caught Tabitha's attention. "Lily is wealthy and beautiful. Sounds perfect. Why would Dirk be interested in my sister?"

"Dirk is a womanizer. Always has been. And Lily is the perfect Southern belle cliché. Iron fist in the velvet glove. Dirk may be the head of the Kennedy lands, but only in title. Lily will always have the final say. That can wear on a man."

Tabitha sat forward in the truck seat, dislodging the cats. "You think he might have been seeing Trudy on the side? Could he be Trudy's mystery man?"

Roger sighed. "Felicity said something about the two of them having fun together. I wouldn't have thought it. Dirk's always been a flirt. Even as a kid, he could turn that charm on and make young girls and old ladies feel special. But he and Lily are serious. He really seems to care about her. And there's a huge inheritance riding on his appropriate behavior. He's not a stupid man. In this world, you don't get your cake and eat it too."

"Do you think he might know anything about Trudy's disappearance?"

"I'll find out. That's a promise."

. . .

PLUTO AND I AGREE. *Dirk Cotwell is a lead that must be followed. Strange that Roger didn't mention Dirk's interest in Trudy before now. And he's tense. I attributed that to his crazy Mama's behavior. Drama Queen of the highest order. But I detect there is something else going on. And Pluto agrees. Which is why we'll split up. I'll stick with Tabitha, and Pluto is going to hang with Roger. It's a good thing Sarah Booth Delaney is out of town with the sheriff, which gives Pluto a little more latitude. But he is something of a celebrity in town and his movements are more restricted than mine.*

He was delighted to spend a bit of time with his ladylove, Vesta. She's safe and being well treated in Long Hall, and that's the best he can hope for until Trudy is found. Now the game is truly afoot. I hope soon to be able to say, "Elementary, my dear Watson," and find the trail to the missing Trudy Wells.

CHAPTER TEN

$\mathcal{R}$oger dropped Tabitha at the dating service and headed to DayzSeed and Chemical, Pluto the cat riding shotgun in his truck. He'd pay his condolences about Lisa and see if he could glean any information about what she was up to. On the way, he called Dirk Cotwell.

"You left a message to call. What's up, Dirk?" he asked.

"I was hoping you could tell me where Trudy Wells has disappeared to," Dirk said. "We were supposed to meet for dinner a couple of weeks ago. She never showed. I've left calls and messages for her at home and at Long Ag, but she doesn't respond. I called your offices today and they said she hadn't been into work for two weeks. Any idea what's going on with her?"

"She did quit coming to work." Roger tried to keep the details to a minimum without lying. If Dirk was somehow involved, Roger didn't want to arouse his suspicions. It was probably a silly precaution, but since he didn't know what had really happened to Trudy, he was playing his cards close to his vest.

"Why'd she quit?" Dirk asked.

"I don't know. She didn't say. She just stopped showing up."

"Do you know where she went?"

Dirk's question could truly be that of a man who had a romantic interest in Trudy—or it could be something more sinister. "I'm at a loss," Roger said. "Did she mention anything to you? Any troubles with anyone? I heard you'd taken her to dinner a couple of times." He couldn't hide the disapproval in his voice.

"Yeah, we went to Memphis for some barbecue and then dancing at the local blues club a couple of times. She's a fun girl. I'd hoped to spend a little more time with her."

"Maybe she had a family illness or something," Roger said. "Did she mention any family to you? I'd really like to know she's okay and put that worry out of my head. She was showing real promise at her job, but if she isn't coming back, I need to replace her."

"She never said a word about family. All I know is that she was from a good New Orleans family that fell on hard times. Degree from Tulane. She was smart, but kind of a tumbleweed. She liked the finer things in life, but she was willing to work to have them. I mean she wasn't spoiled, like some debutantes."

Roger realized two things--that Dirk's knowledge of Trudy came from her dating video and that Lily Kennedy, for all of her assets was wearing thin. Dirk Cotwell was, *technically*, single. And he did farm a vast track of land, though it was a combination of the Cotwell land and the Kennedy property— belonging to the family of his fiancée. Everyone in the Delta knew Dirk had asked Lily Kennedy to marry him, and that he was "marrying up" in Delta society. "Dirk, I have to ask. Why were you dating Trudy when you're obligated to Lily?"

Dirk laughed. "Lily knows I'm not the kind of man to

settle down. Besides, I'm just sowing a few wild oats before the bracelets are slapped on me." He paused, then continued. "Lily's family wants the marriage, and I'm happy to oblige. I'm not going to change who I am. I've been honest about that."

"Were you honest with Trudy?" Roger drove down the straight Delta farm roads that cut through the fields. Corn, soybeans, cotton—it was all coming up. So far the perfect weather had worked in favor of all farmers. How long would that last? No one knew.

"I never led her to expect more than an evening's pleasure." Dirk was beginning to sound a little testy. "I like my fun but I'm not a cad."

Reading between the lines, Roger knew exactly how Dirk had played his hand. He'd wowed Trudy with fun dates but never intimated that he was interested in more than momentary fun. He'd never pressure her for more than she would willingly offer. To give the devil his due, Dirk had never pretended to be other than what he was—a hardworking farmer with a broad streak of partying. Roger didn't judge Dirk's choices, but there was more on the line than how Dirk led his life. A young woman was missing, and Roger had to admit—if only to himself—that he cared that Tabitha wasn't hurt. "Did you tell Trudy you were engaged?"

"Didn't have to. The gossips in Sunflower County were happy to oblige. She knew. Trust me, she knew and she didn't care anymore than I did."

"So, Trudy knew." But Roger was willing to bet Lily didn't. Delta society closed around young women to protect them from "the harsh realities of life." While people might tell Trudy the score about Dirk's playboy ways, it was probable they'd held their tongues around Lily Kennedy and her family.

"Is it possible Trudy felt she was getting too emotionally involved with you and decided to leave on her own?"

"I know you don't approve of my behavior, Roger, but the girl knew the score. I never led her on. If she took off for greener pastures, it wasn't because she understood our relationship wasn't going anywhere. What we had was casual and fun. A few bands and bars, some dinners...nothing more. Trudy came across as...easy, but that wasn't the case. She wasn't a floozy and we only had fun, not an intimate relationship. Hell, she wanted to talk about cotton all the time. So don't start building scenarios in your head where I harmed that girl for any reason."

Roger knew he'd pushed as hard as he could. For the moment. And he'd learned something valuable. Trudy was working Dirk. Maybe she liked him, but she was interested in his cotton crop. Because she was working under cover for an environmental group. It wasn't Dirk the group was after, but the seed and chemical companies. "Any idea if she was seeing anyone else?"

"Never came up. Like I said, I didn't have a claim on her or her time. Hey, are you pleased with the new cotton? That G9-14? It's coming up like gangbusters."

Roger had a hunch. "I need to check the fields. I've been busy with family, and I've fallen behind. To be honest, Trudy was keeping up with all of that for me. Which fields did you plant with it?"

"The Thornbrush field. I should have planted more. Lisa East knew what she was talking about when she talked up the seed."

Roger couldn't avoid telling Dirk the truth that he was bound to hear about at any hour. "When was the last time you talked to Lisa?" Roger was almost at DayZSeed, and he slowed to a crawl on the empty road. The cat had curled into a black ball on the seat, but he sat up and looked out the window when Roger slowed.

"Couple of weeks, why? Don't tell me she's missing too. Those girls were friends, though. I didn't think of that. Could be off somewhere partying."

"Lisa was murdered, Dirk. They found her body yesterday."

"Murdered? What the hell is going on?" Dirk scoffed. "So this is why all the concern for Trudy. Lisa is dead and Trudy is missing. And I have connections to both of them."

"That's true, Dirk. But so do I," Roger said. "Every farmer around here links to Lisa."

"I may like my good times, but I don't hurt women," Dirk said. "You can take that to the bank."

Roger turned down the narrow road that led to the seed company. Dirk Cotwell—if he was telling the complete truth—had been a fountain of information. "I never meant to imply anything. Just keeping you apprised, and I am worried about Trudy. She and Lisa were friends, as you pointed out. Should you hear from Trudy, ask her to please call me."

"I just remembered something. There was a sales rep from the Grundle Seed Company asking questions about Trudy. That's the parent company of the G9-14, isn't it?"

Roger pulled into the parking lot of DayZSeed and stopped his truck. "Who was it? Do you remember his name?" He fought to keep his question casual and easy. Pluto put his paws on the dash of the truck and flicked his tail back and forth, his gaze focused on the building.

Dirk kept talking. "Didn't know the guy. He wasn't local. Came in for the G9-14 presentation last fall. More of a salesman than a farmer, I'd say. He showed back up in the area a month or so back. He seemed to have a big interest in Trudy. At first, I assumed it was romantic in nature."

"How'd he run up on Trudy?" It seemed that Dirk knew a lot more about his employee than Roger did.

"They met up in some field. I thought it might be your property off the Hollow Road. Apparently Trudy got under his skin with some questions. That's the talk I heard."

"Do you mind telling me who was talking?"

"No can do. Sorry. I gotta live around here too, and Martin Kennedy is not a man who likes a troublemaker. Lily and I set the date for the wedding and I'm not going to mess in my own nest. Folks think I have it made, but you know Lily. She's...difficult."

Roger had dated her for a brief period, and he knew. "Difficult and demanding. I know. Thanks," Roger said.

"Check your fields and let me know what you think about that new cotton. So far it's looking great. If it's resistant to pests like they advertise, we may have a real winner."

"Sure thing." Roger clicked the phone off and sat in the truck, motor running. Instead of going into the seed company, he whipped the truck around and drove toward his own fields. He was about to turn off the main road when a cute blue sports car came toward him, horn blaring. Speak of the devil. He recognized Lily Kennedy.

She whipped to a halt in front of his truck and got out. The sun struck her honey-blond hair as she came toward him. She was truly a beautiful woman.

"Roger!" She rushed up as he got out of the truck and hugged him. "You're a hard man to track down." She looked past him at the cat on the front seat. "Most farmers travel with a dog. I applaud your originality."

He chuckled. Lily was a live wire. Dirk might think she

couldn't tame him, but Roger was putting his money on Lily.
"Why are you looking for me?"

"I'm throwing a surprise party for Dirk, and I need you to
help me get him there without giving away the surprise."

"That could be a challenge. What are the particulars?"

"Saturday, 8 o'clock at The Club. It's a cocktail party to
celebrate our engagement."

"Wouldn't it be simpler to just tell Dirk?"

"But not nearly as much fun." Lily laughed out loud. "He
might as well get used to the fact that smart women manipulate their men."

"So I've heard." Roger had never bought into that particular method of building a relationship, but he saw plenty of it.
"I'll do my best, Lily. I do wish you both all the happiness.
Dirk is a handful, but he's got a good heart. I believe you
do too."

"Thanks, Roger. I know Daddy is relieved to have a man to
take over the farming so I 'don't have to worry my pretty little
head.'" She put a hand on his chest. "Daddy says you're the
smartest farmer in the Delta. He's eager to see how that new
cotton seed produces. He goes on and on about that kind of
thing, but it just goes in one ear and out the other. He says
you're going to beat all the other farmers because you
innovate."

"Farmers always have to complain about something," Roger
said. "Tell him thanks. He's got a good farmer in Dirk. He
knows that too."

"Of course. So you'll have him at The Club? I can count
on you?"

"I'll give it my best shot."

"Tell your aunt and uncle I send my love! They're invited,
too, of course. The invitations will be hand delivered."

"It's on my calendar." Roger got back in his truck. Lily was lovely, and smart. And determined to have her way. Thank goodness she hadn't set her sights on him.

He headed toward the fields, his mind back on the cotton. He'd planted a few hundred acres in the new seed. It wasn't a huge tract, but if it was bust, it would hurt him financially. Trudy hadn't been enthusiastic about the new seed. She'd studied the statistics on the G9-14 and had urged him to go slowly.

"These modified seeds have a good showing. At first," she'd said. He could see her standing in front of his desk, hands tucked in the pockets of her jeans. "It'll be September, near harvest, before we know the yield. What really concerns me is if there's any residual effect in the soil from this. No one has really studied that aspect of these GMO crops."

Instead of really listening to her, he'd answered, "We have to try new things, Trudy. This land has been farmed for nearly two hundred years now. New crops offer replenishment to the soil as well as resistance to pests."

"Perhaps." Trudy had met his gaze with a level one of her own. "Science is wonderful, Roger. Sometimes. If something sounds too good to be true, maybe it's best to believe it isn't true."

The image of Trudy faded, and he cut through the local roads that were the grid for farmers and ended up in the field where the new cotton had jumped up in the last week. It was twice as tall as the other cotton he'd planted, and the leaves were lush and green. Any farmer would be crazy not to be excited about the new seed. "*If it looks too good to be true, it probably is.*" He could hear Trudy's voice.

The cotton was more than any farmer could ask for, and he drove slowly around the field, taking a look from all angles.

The crop looked better than he had any reason to expect. When he came to an equipment trail that wound around the field and disappeared into a thick brake, he hesitated. The ground was rutted. A vehicle had been through there. And as far as Roger knew, none of his employees had cause to be in that part of the farm. He shifted down for traction and started along the farm road when his phone rang.

"Roger!" Charline was breathless. "Please come home. I hate to interrupt your day but Hannah and Samuel are at each other's throats. Antoine has decided he wants to control Hannah's share of the farm. He claims he's an expert at cotton, and he's gotten Samuel very upset."

"Antoine is a farmer?" The more likely word applied to the man would be gigolo or fraud. Or at the kindest, dandy. He looked more the type to be at an opera or fashion show rather than a field. Antoine was all polish—from his cufflinks and ascot to his high-gloss wingtips. Roger couldn't imagine him driving a combine or tractor or even stepping foot into a field.

"He says he's an expert." Charline sounded way too stressed. "Roger, Hannah is going to give Samuel a fit. It's like she wants to drive us away from her. Can you come?"

"I'm on the way. Aunt Charline, would you mind calling the ag office and asking Felicity to pick up Tabitha? She's running an errand for me. Just give her Tabitha's cell phone so they can rendezvous." He didn't want to reveal the dating site unless he had to.

"I'll do it."

"I'm on my way. Tell Mother to pack her bags. And why don't you book two tickets to Monaco for her and Antoine. I'll send one of the men to drive them to the Memphis airport if I have to."

"They have a rental. They can drive themselves," Charline

said. "And you should know, Roger, they've been in the area for several weeks, snooping around and prying into the family's business. They were staying at the Peabody in Memphis and Antoine said something about dining at the Prince Albert and how good the food was for such "a provincial little burg.""

"Maybe Samuel should buy out Mother's share." Roger couldn't help the anger he felt. He'd devoted his life to protecting the farm—the source of income for all of them and particularly his mother who did nothing to help. Now she was bringing a strange man into the family business and trying to wrest control of the land. "This is just another one of her ploys to force us to sell out."

"Samuel says he's going to talk to Mac about our legal rights. No one ever anticipated that Hannah would want to farm."

Mac MacKinney was their lawyer and long-time friend. "It's good Samuel is checking the legal aspects. I'll deal with Mother." Oh, and he meant to do it none too gently.

"She is an heir, Roger, whether we like it or not." Charline's reminder was gentle.

A new plan hit Roger almost like a clap on the back. "Don't worry, Aunt Charline. I think I can take care of this and make everyone feel good about it."

"What do you have up your sleeve?" Charline asked.

"Just a little séance. Tonight. Tabitha can conduct it. We'll see what our ancestors have to say about this business." Roger wasn't discounting the impact that a visit from Micah Malone might have on his mother. After all, Micah might be the only person Hannah had loved unselfishly. Maybe the arrival of Tabitha Kingsley into his life had been orchestrated by his guardian angels. If so, he owed them a big thank you. It was the perfect opportunity to push back against Hannah's manipulations—but it was a lot more than that. In a very unexpected way, Roger found that Tabitha had gotten under his skin. She'd come to the Delta under false pretenses, true enough, but she wasn't a con artist or flimflam woman; she was searching for her sister. And Roger had a bad feeling about what had happened to Trudy Wells.

CHAPTER ELEVEN

*T*abitha found it extremely awkward to sit on a stool, face a camera, and talk about herself. Especially in an animated tone, as the "love consultant" had advised. Candy —so appropriately named—had helped her fill out the paperwork to join the dating site, and was now advising her to sit up taller, lean forward, and *sell* herself. The truth was, Tabitha hated the whole idea of listing herself on-line for men to check out. It was just...creepy. And dripping in the jewels that belonged to Charline Long was even creepier. But Trudy had done it, and Tabitha was willing to follow her sister's footsteps if it might develop a possible lead to Trudy's whereabouts.

She held a list of things she should cover—hobbies, habits, fantasies, as well as the biographical basics of who, what, when, where, and why. She'd listed her local address as the Prince Albert hotel "until she found a suitable small property to buy." All lies. But she didn't mention her front as a psychic medium. Best to be quiet about that.

"Tabitha, just relax. You're a hot woman, let the steam

show." Candy stood behind the camera and coached her. "You sure that cat is going to sit in the lobby and not tear anything up?"

"He's very well behaved." Tabitha felt foolish even saying the words for a cat she'd known less than twenty-four hours. In that time, though, Trouble had demonstrated an amazing ability to think and act. He was smarter than a lot of people she knew.

"If he claws the furniture or does anything destructive, you're liable for it."

"Absolutely."

"Okay, let's roll with this." Candy reached to turn the camera back on.

Tabitha's phone buzzed and she felt a whoosh of relief. She stepped away from the camera and took the call, even though Candy tapped her foot with impatience. It was Roger.

"Hey, I have an emergency with my mother. I'm sending Felicity to pick you up—is there anywhere away from the dating service you can meet her?"

"Sure, there's a service station across the street. I'll wait there."

"Perfect, and I have news on Dirk and the cotton, but no leads on Trudy yet. I do need you to read for my mother this evening, if you're still up for that."

"Sure. Did Dirk say he was dating Trudy?"

"I'll tell you all about it at Long Hall. Just have Felicity drop you off. And remember the name, Micah Malone. If you happen to have a moment with Mother, plant a little seed that Micah has a message for her. How's the dating profile coming?"

"Done soon. I'll be waiting across the street for Felicity."

She hung up before he could ask any more questions. She was ready to finish the dating site profile and escape. The digital dating center left her feeling unsettled. The idea just bothered her, even though thousands of women and men were finding companionship and romance on internet dating sites with matchmaker companies.

"Tabitha, are you ready to finish?" Candy was still tapping her toe. "You're going to get a lot of date invitations from this video. If we ever get it posted. You know, you kind of remind me of another young woman who came in here. She found the love of her life."

Tabitha fought to remain calm. "That sounds like a fairy tale story. Tell me about it."

Candy motioned Tabitha to the tall stool. She fiddled with the video camera as she talked. "The girl was a natural beauty and she came from a great background. We put her profile up and the phones were ringing off the hook. Men from Memphis, Arkansas, all over the Delta and down to Jackson, Mississippi were interested. She was like honey to bears."

"Did she pick one and find true love?" Tabitha forced a smile.

"She didn't cancel her profile, so I'm not sure. But there was one guy who really pursued her."

"Wow. Would you know his name?" Tabitha knew the moment the words left her mouth she'd pushed too hard.

"Client confidentiality." Candy motioned to her to get ready. "Now let's get this done."

Tabitha was surprised to find that the remainder of the "interview" went smoothly and she was finished in fifteen minutes. She paid the fee, and checked around to see how the office was set up. If there were files with information that could lead to Trudy, she'd do what she had to do. When she was ready to leave, she found the sleek, black cat sitting on Candy's desk in her office, purring up a storm.

"Trouble," she said. "How did you get into the office?" She'd left the feline prowling around the lobby of the business.

"I don't know how he got in here, but he's sitting *on* my desk," Candy said. "He hasn't messed anything up, but just so you know, the office manager isn't a cat person, so it would be best if he was gone before she gets back."

"Sure thing," Tabitha said. "Let me get him." She reached across the desk for the cat, but he nimbly hopped to the floor. He looked from one to the other with his dazzling green eyes and the hint of a Cheshire grin crossed his face before he darted away, evading both of them.

"Trouble!" Tabitha was shocked. "He's never like this. Kitty, kitty." But Trouble made it clear he had no intention of being captured by any mere mortal. He jumped and danced around the office, until finally Tabitha and Candy stopped to catch their breath and to laugh.

"He's a real devil," Candy said. "But he's going to get me fired."

"Trouble." Tabitha turned to him. The cat came over to her and rubbed against her shins. She stooped down and picked him up. The cat was definitely up to something. "I should take him outside before he gets loose again."

"That would be best." Candy was looking out the window to the empty parking lot. "If my boss or other customers come in, they're going to be upset with a feline in the business."

Tabitha started toward the front door. She'd completed the video, paid her fees, filled out all the paperwork, checked out the layout of the business--and possibly tipped her hand about her interest in Trudy. She had no reason to stay longer.

The cat obviously had other plans. He leaped from her arms and landed on Candy's desk. Skidding across the slick surface, he took out file folders, stacks of mail, a vase of fresh cut zinnias, and a computer screen, which only tipped over and didn't break.

"Trouble!" Tabitha was scandalized. She'd seen the cat maneuver with extreme agility. This was almost...deliberate. She ran forward and began soaking up the spilled water from the flowers with some tissues she found on the desk.

"I'll get a towel," Candy said, rushing toward the back of the business.

Trouble jumped up on the desk and went straight for the keyboard. To Tabitha's amazement, the menu of files popped up. Trudy's name was close to the top and she clicked on it. She only had a few seconds, and she focused on the names of men who'd shown an interest in her sister. Dirk Cotwell was one. And another was Alan Dotsun. She heard Candy returning and closed out the computer screen and just in time. The office door started to open. In two bold leaps, the cat was across the room and at the front door, which he nudged open. Then he was gone.

Candy returned with clean towels and began cleaning up the mess.

"I'm so sorry," Tabitha said as she began blotting too. "I've never seen Trouble freak out like that. He's normally very quiet and...coordinated."

"Something startled him." Candy was doing her best not to be aggravated. "Nothing was damaged. It's just a little bit of tidying up."

When the desk was dry and all of the files back in place, Tabitha took her leave. She wasn't surprised when Trouble came out of the shrubbery.

"Let's walk over to the station where we're catching a ride." She made sure Charline's diamond necklace and earrings were in her pocket. She'd return the jewels at Long Hall and then go down to the ag offices to use a computer. Then she'd figure out what the black cat was trying to show her about Dirk and Alan Dotsun.

As she was about to cross the street to the service station, she saw the pickup with Long Agricultural on the side. Felicity was behind the wheel, but she was busily engaged in talking with a young blonde in a convertible. She started forward, but the cat caught the hem of her dress and stopped her. He turned to look at the two women.

"You're right. I don't want them to see me here at the dating service." She picked up the cat and moved down the road toward a fast food place. If she approached from there, it wouldn't lead to any questions. Thank goodness for the cat, and it was a good thing Felicity was otherwise engaged.

THE SPILLED VASE *was a master stroke, if I do say so myself. My daddy would be proud of that maneuver. He was always adept at confusing the bipeds with quick and decisive action. I knew Candy would have to leave the room, and I also knew I'd have that computer file open. Alan Dotsun is someone Tabitha needs to look into. Never doubt the wisdom of a sleek black cat with a penchant for all things British—except maybe the food from across the pond. Americans, especially in the South, have superior cuisine over such British delicacies as kidney pie and blood pudding. That makes my sleek black hair stand on end. No, I prefer the delicately sauced mahi-mahi with a bit of wild rice—seasoned with fresh dill. I'd best stop daydreaming about past repasts and tend to business.*

Now that it appears we're leaving that wretched fast food place,

Tabitha is leading the way to the petrol station across the road. I'll follow her lead without complaint. Felicity sees us coming and concludes her conversation with the lovely blonde in the little blue sports car. The car in question has a lot of zing. It shoots out of the station like a little rocket and the driver waves merrily as if we were best of friends.

Everyone in the Delta does seem to know everyone else. If only the Delta had mass transit, such as London and other hubs of civilization. Both Pluto and I could get along swell. We'd be regular toffs, riding to our destinations. As it is, he's stuck without a ride. His owner, Sarah Booth, and her significant other, the high sheriff, failed to consider the transportation needs of a savvy feline. I'm a bit disappointed I haven't met the Delaney Detective Agency team of Sarah Booth and Tinkie, but our paths haven't crossed. And I'm most interested in making the acquaintance of the spirit that haunts Dahlia House, a bossy haint that goes by Jitty. Pluto has told me some tales about Jitty's shenanigans. I hope to see it with my own eyes before I leave the area.

But now, I need to pretend to be normal—not so difficult to deceive most two-leggers. They simply aren't observant. So many of the bipeds live in the fog of phones, the Internet, and such. While I view those things as tools, I'm simply immune to the addiction that is so common among the humans.

Ah, Felicity is opening the door for my would-be psychic mistress. I presume we'll sojourn to the Long Agricultural business office. But no, Tabitha requests a ride to Long Hall. She says that Roger is waiting for her, a simple statement of fact that triggers a sharp glance from Felicity Montgomery. I wonder if Roger's employee is interested in her boss in a romantic way. I'll have to keep my peepers wide open for any hint of those feelings. Felicity may want more than just a paycheck from Roger Long, and if that's the case, then she should be added to the suspect list. A keen eye on the interplay between Felicity and Tabitha is called for. Trouble is on the case!

. . .

THE TIRES of Roger's truck slung gravel as he circled the drive that fronted Long Hall. He parked, and jumped out with Pluto right behind him. He was aware of the cat, and the way the feline seemed to anticipate his every move. There was something up with the two black cats and the pretty little marmalade that his aunt had fallen in love with. Right now, though, the person in his gun site was his mother. Hannah was brewing up trouble, and he wasn't going to put up with it.

He entered the house and felt the heavy silence fall over him. He wasn't normally sensitive to moods, but the tension in the house was thick. Concern for his uncle Samuel made him take the stairs two at a time. He intended to corner his mother in her quarters and make her understand that Antoine would have no part in running Long Agricultural. Ever. Under any circumstances.

"Mother!" He called out to her as he found himself at her suite of rooms. The door was closed and locked, and he knocked so hard it echoed in the hallway. "Mother, open this door." Pluto was right on his heels, but slipped into a shadow cast by a threshold as he pounded on the oak door.

"I won't put up with your tantrums, Roger. Charline and Samuel have spoiled you, tolerating your oafish conduct."

His mother's voice was prim and proper, a tone she only used when she was afraid of repercussions from some of her bratty behavior. And she was wise to be worried. "You'd better open this door or I will kick it down. And if Antoine is there to protect you, I'll give him a beating he'll never forget." He hit the door with enough force that it shuddered.

"Antoine isn't here. He's gone down to the office to get

some annual report. He has to study the business to assume his role."

Roger realized he had to calm down. He could not use force to break down the door, which would only upset Charline and Samuel even more. "Open the door. We need to talk."

The lock clicked and he pushed the door open. His mother had stepped back several feet—just in case. He smiled at her. "What are you up to, Mother?"

"I'm taking my rightful place in the family business." A bold statement, but she wouldn't meet his gaze.

"Antoine isn't a family member." He struggled to keep his tone civil and easy.

"He will be soon."

"I see. Congratulations on your impending marriage. What is this, five or six?"

"Don't be so cynical," Hannah said. "Antoine has everything I need in a man."

"And you have everything he needs in a bank account."

"You've turned into a bore, just like Samuel." Hannah played a pout.

"Mother, you need to leave Sunflower County. Today. Take that fake man with you."

"I have as much right to a say-so in the company as you and Samuel. I'm an heir, like it or not. I've allowed you both to keep me out of the family business so you could run it however you saw fit. Those days are gone. Samuel and I are equal partners. I have a fifty percent say in what this company does."

Roger had never questioned Samuel about Hannah's stake in Long Agricultural. His uncle had always treated Hannah more than fair. He'd given her money when it wasn't due her.

"What is Antoine's background in large scale farming?"

"Oh, darling, he's run big corporations and taken them public. He has a wealth of financial experience."

"And farming?"

She shrugged. "What's so hard about growing cotton, corn, and soybeans. You put the seed in the ground and the sun and rain do the rest of the work."

His mother's ignorance was so abysmal that Roger didn't comment at all. "So his background is business, not farming."

"Farming is a business. That's what you and Samuel tell me all the time."

Roger only nodded. "I'd like to see Antoine's resume. Maybe check into some of his past jobs. If he's as good as you say, he might be an asset." It took all he could muster not to grin when he saw Hannah's reaction. She hadn't expected capitulation. Or questions about Antoine's abilities. "How long have you been in Mississippi, Mother?"

She waved a hand. "What difference does it make?"

"Oh, if you're both serious about involving yourselves in the farm, then I suspect you've been touring the other plantations and boning up on what's being planted and why."

"It's the same old, same old. Corn, soybeans, and cotton. I can see the plants for myself, Roger. I don't have to ask anyone. You punch the seed into the ground, fertilize, the rains come, and then the sun. How hard is that?" She frowned. "But I understand there's a whole new kind of cotton being planted. Some GMO thing or other. And Antoine tells me you've planted some of it. Now that is exciting. I love the idea of a new cotton. Think how much money that would make."

"New crops are risky. I'm not sure that was a smart move."

"Darling, from what Antoine says, this may be the ticket to the future. How many acres did you plant?"

Inhaling slowly, Roger chose not to answer. "Did Charline

tell you she was in contact with Suellen? Perhaps we should ask Grandmother how she feels about Antoine's involvement and this new cotton crop."

"You think a dead woman is going to influence my decisions."

"No, I don't. But it will be interesting to hear any messages she might have for you, don't you think?"

"Suellen is gone. I'm sorry I was...immature. But I'm trying now, Roger. I want to be a part of the family business. Antoine and I want to know all about this new cotton."

"Trying to put Antoine in the farm management isn't going to work, Mother. But I know you well enough to realize you're going to try, until it becomes too painful to continue. You never learn anything the easy way." As Roger talked, Pluto slipped into Hannah's suite of rooms. Roger said nothing. His mother was not a pet lover of any kind, but Roger had come to trust the basic instincts of the Sunflower County cats.

He heard the front door open and looked down to see Tabitha coming into the foyer with the thinner black cat, Trouble. She smiled up at Roger—a genuine reflection of gladness to see him. His heart lifted and he faced his mother again. "The séance will be at nine o'clock," he said. That would give him time to make the preparations he needed.

"I'm not so certain I want to participate in a séance," Hannah said. "I don't want to be haunted."

"Maybe Suellen will approve of Antoine. Wouldn't that be an interesting twist in the plot?" Roger left the possibility hanging there. "We can talk about this more at dinner. I'm sure Ms. Kingsley will be happy to tell you all about her work and what to expect." He grinned at his mother, a challenge he knew she couldn't resist, before he turned away.

"Roger..."

He turned back to face his mother. "Yes?"

"I'm not the horror that you think I am."

The sadness in her voice almost touched him, but he knew his mother. She could play a role to the hilt. "See you at dinner," he said.

When he went down the stairs, Tabitha was waiting. He pulled her into the library and closed the door for privacy. His impulse was to kiss her, a strong desire he fought back. His feelings for Tabitha had developed so fast, but he wasn't certain how she felt. It would be inappropriate to attempt a kiss before he knew it would be welcomed. "How'd the taping session go?"

"I felt like a fool," she said, but then filled him in on all she'd learned about Trudy and the two men who'd shown an interest in dating her.

He frowned. "I don't like putting you out there as date bait, but if it helps us find your sister, I'm willing to try."

"Speaking of date bait..." Tabitha reached into her pocket and brought out the jewelry Roger had borrowed for her. "Please put this back. I know I came here under false pretenses, but I never really intended to manipulate anyone. And I never intended to steal anything. I just wanted to get inside the dating service and find out about Trudy."

"I'm not accusing you, Tabitha. If we intend to find Trudy, we're going to have to do whatever is necessary. And I'm going to ask you to help me deceive my mother tonight." He held her gaze. "My mother is a wrecking ball. She comes in and starts swinging, and she doesn't care what she takes out or who she hurts. She's on to the concept of GMO cotton and I'm not certain she has a clue about potential environmental damage. This isn't about deception or dishonesty, it's about protecting Charline and Samuel and also my mother. Will you help me?"

Tabitha nodded. "I'll do my best." She looked unsure. "I'll do what you ask."

"Thank you." He heard footsteps and realized Charline was headed their way. When the door opened, he faced his aunt with a wry grin. "We're having a séance tonight at nine. It's going to be exceptional."

"That sounds very exciting." Charline cast him a shrewd look. "You're up to something and I'm not going to ask what. I trust you, Raj. You've always had great instincts." She turned to Tabitha with a warm smile. "Those two black cats are in the kitchen eating like they've never had food before. They have... gourmand tastes." She laughed. "The little Vesta is so dainty beside those big bruisers, but the boys are so deferential to her. It's something to see. Will we need any special preparations?" She asked Tabitha.

Tabitha's cell phone buzzed and she brought it out of her pocket, flashing the screen so that Roger could see that the matchmaking service was calling. "I'll return the call in a moment," she said, tucking the phone away.

"By all means," Roger answered, giving her a wink when he was certain no one would see.

His aunt threw him a knowing look. "Since we're having an event tonight, I'll get with Nancy to be sure we have all we need in the way of refreshments. Is there anything special, Tabitha?"

"The dining room would be a perfect location. Suellen loves that room. And there's a man with her, a handsome young man." Tabitha nodded at Roger, letting him know she was honoring her word. "I don't know this man, but his initials are...I think it's a double initial, or else he has a sibling with the same name. It's hard to tell sometimes." She stared into an empty corner of the room, "I'm getting an...M. Maybe two Ms.

He's pointing upstairs. He has a message for someone upstairs," Tabitha said.

"For Hannah?" Charline's eyes widened, and then sadness touched her face. "Oh, my. I think I know who this may be. Hannah is going to be surprised. Pleasantly, I hope. Micah's death was such a tragedy. I honestly believe Hannah would be a different person if Micah hadn't been killed."

"Tragedy always marks us." Tabitha put a gentle hand on Charline's shoulder. "We really don't need anything but some candlelight, because it's easier for an entity to manifest in a darkened room. Because they're ephemeral, spirits are easier to see in low light."

"I'll have everything to order," Charline promised. "Now let me get busy." She left them with a quick, light step.

Roger faced Tabitha. "I never made it to DayZSeed, and I really need to speak with them there. I'll be back in under an hour. Pluto was in Mother's rooms, but he's managed to slip out. A good thing, too. She'd have a conniption if she found him going through her things. Can you keep an eye on those two black cats? They might need some help making an escape." Roger grinned. "I trust you're up to a distraction."

"If it's necessary to save a cat, of course." Tabitha made a solemn face but then smiled. "I feel like I'm performing all the time now."

"It won't be for long. We'll find Trudy and then this will all be over. When I return, I'll help prepare for the evening's events." He touched her shoulder. "I know the dating service was something we agreed on, and I know you have to follow through on whoever contacts you or there's no point. I have to be honest, though. I don't like the idea of you going out with anyone else. Especially someone who could be dangerous. Promise me you'll be careful." Somehow, Tabitha's welfare had become crucially important to him. In such a short time, she'd eased into his life, filling a blank spot he hadn't even been aware of. He had plenty of lady friends in the Delta, and he enjoyed their company. Tabitha was different, though. She'd touched him deeply, making him protective of her. It was a feeling that made him both anxious and happy.

CHAPTER TWELVE

*R*oger headed back to the seed company, driving faster than normal. He went to the main desk. A pall seemed to hang over the whole reception area. No doubt they'd been notified of Lisa's death. "Who's taking Lisa's position?" he asked. "I need to speak with the sales rep for my crops."

"That would be Boyd Moffett," the receptionist said. She dialed a phone and spoke softly into it. In a moment, she waved Roger through into the private office area behind a thick closed door. He knew where Lisa's office had been and assumed Boyd Moffett had taken her office as well as her clientele.

The door was cracked, and Roger was about to push it open when the sound of hushed voices stopped him.

"You'd better make this right, Boyd. And you'd better do it now," another man said. "We can't afford an investigation. We have too much riding on the outcome of the new seed. Grundle will cut us off if we have any kind of scandal. I'm under a lot of pressure from the top."

"Yes, sir," was the answer.

The receptionist turned the corner of the hallway and saw Roger standing there. She was surprised to see him so clearly eavesdropping. Roger had to think fast. "Mr. Moffett's with someone. Should I interrupt?" At her nod, he tapped softly on the door. "May I come in?" he asked, avoiding glancing back at the receptionist. He couldn't afford to look guilty.

"Please do." The voice was pleasant and non-stressed. "Thanks for stopping by, Mr. Connor. I'll make sure everything goes smoothly."

"You do that." Mason Connor, owner of DayZSeed, stepped past Roger. "Mr. Long," he said. "How's that cotton coming up?"

"Bigger and better than any of the other plantings."

"That's what I want to hear," Mason said before he strode down the hallway, turned a corner, and disappeared.

Roger entered the office of Boyd Moffett. He sat at the desk Lisa East had occupied only a few short days before.

"I meant to come around to introduce myself," Boyd said, standing and holding out his hand. "Lisa's death...well, we didn't know what had happened to her until very recently. I was just told today to take over her clients, so please excuse me for not being up to speed on things."

"Not a problem. I really came here to find out who was taking Lisa's accounts and also if there are any leads in her murder."

Boyd shook his head. "We haven't heard anything. I can't imagine who would harm Lisa. She was outgoing and friendly and a terrific employee."

"I liked her a lot," Roger said truthfully. "One of my employees, a friend of Lisa's, is missing. I hoped maybe someone here might have some idea where she'd gone. You know how young girls make those spur-of-the-minute plans. I wouldn't give it another thought, except for what happened to Lisa." He played it casual.

Boyd frowned. "You're talking about Trudy Wells. Yeah, she was supposed to be by here several days ago and she didn't show or call. I thought that was strange. She was meticulous about keeping her appointments."

"That's the young woman." Roger shook his head. "Hell of an employee. I mean if she found a job with a bigger salary, I can't blame her, but I just want to know for sure she's okay." He stared directly into Boyd's eyes.

Boyd's gaze never wavered. "I hear you, man. I haven't heard anything, but then again, we've been working double shifts filling in for Lisa. We thought something had come up in her life and she'd be back so everyone was chipping in to make sure her job was done. Connor didn't want to replace her..." He sighed. "I guess that's all a moot issue now."

"It's a shame," Roger said. "No one here suspected anything was amiss in Lisa's life?" Roger spiced his question with a hint of incredulity. "DayZSeed has always seemed like such a close-knit family."

"Lisa kept her private life away from work. She and Trudy Wells were very close, always going out." He drummed his fingers on the desk. "It concerns me that Trudy is missing." He hesitated, looking through the open door into the hall as if he wanted to make sure no one was passing by. "You know Trudy was seeing Dirk Cotwell. That's one of the worst kept secrets in the Delta. I like Dirk, but he seems to think he can have his fiancée and his girls on the side. His fiancée's family couldn't have been too keen on him putting a ring on their daughter's hand and still going out with Trudy. I've only met Lily on a few occasions, but I wouldn't want to cross the Kennedy family.

She's her daddy's little princess, and the shame of it is, she'd make a good farmer. That's just not the role her daddy wants her to have."

"No doubt Lily is capable." Roger shrugged. "Gender roles are still a big part of Delta life, it seems. Those young women, Lisa and Trudy, they were breaking out of that."

He nodded. "Lisa was also dating one of the sales reps from Grundle. Alan Dotsun is his name. Trudy and Lisa double dated sometimes."

This was news to Roger, and it was helpful. "Thanks, Boyd. Do you know anything about this Dotsun?"

"Good looking. He's been in the area for the past couple of weeks. He has business here and over in Arkansas across the river. Lots of big planters there. Oh, yeah, he's very close to the Kennedy family. Rumor had it that he'd set his sights on Lily for his own wife."

"Poor Lily. You make her sound like the stuffed bear in a carnival ball pitching contest."

"She's the only daughter of Martin Kennedy. She comes with a lot of assets. If you married her you'd double the holdings of Long Agricultural. That's not a reason to marry a woman, but it sure doesn't hurt."

Roger nodded. Boyd wasn't being mercenary, he was just stating facts. The planter families of the Delta had often considered the merger of two big holdings to be a priority in marriage. Some things never changed.

"If you hear anything about Lisa or Trudy, please let me know. And if you'd ask the other employees to give me a call." He wrote his number on a slip of paper Boyd handed him. "I'd appreciate it."

"Sure thing."

Roger closed the office door. By all rights he should leave, but he wasn't done exploring. Not by a long shot.

TABITHA SLIPPED into her room at Long Hall to return the call to the dating service. She had four queries, and she answered three of them with pleasantries but declined to meet. They were not men who might have appealed to Trudy; Tabitha had no time to waste. A man named Alan Dotsun had requested a date. She knew the name from Trouble's work at the dating service, and as she reviewed his profile, she grew eager. He was a salesman for Grundle Seed Company, a big firm that was on the cutting edge of new technologies in farming. Grundle supplied DayZSeed with some products—Tabitha knew this from talking with Roger. In his profile, Alan mentioned he'd only arrived in Zinnia a few weeks earlier and would be leaving for his Arkansas territory soon. He was the only lead out of the prospective suitors. She returned his call.

"I saw your profile and wondered if you might like to have dinner," Alan said. "I'm in town on business. I come to Zinnia regularly as part of my job."

Tabitha hated to deceive the man, but it was part of what she'd agreed to do to find her sister. "I'd be open to dinner."

"How about tonight?"

"I'm sorry, but I already have plans. Tomorrow night is good."

"There's a little out-of-the-way steakhouse near Drew. Tom's Big Sizzle. Great food, great band, dancing. Only the locals know about it, but it comes highly recommended. I could pick you up at the Prince Albert. When I get a chance, maybe we could fly to Memphis for some great ribs, but my time is jammed right now so a local date is the best I can offer."

"A Delta eatery is probably better than any place else," Tabitha said. "I'm new to the area, so it will be a great opportunity to learn about a restaurant." This was easier than she'd anticipated. She'd already learned he had access to a private plane. Trudy had mentioned something about that, and now Tabitha had begun to wonder if her sister had been spirited away from the Delta by air. "Tell you what, I'll meet you at the restaurant."

"You modern girls always like to have your own wheels. In case the date is a bore."

He said it good-naturedly, but Tabitha was on high alert. "My mama didn't raise a fool," she said brightly. "See you tomorrow night." She hung up.

Feeling a little flushed, she went to the bath that was part of her suite of rooms and put a cool cloth on her face. She'd taken one positive step in her attempts to find Trudy. If Alan Dotsun wasn't a lead, then at least he could be crossed off the list. When she went back to her bedroom, she called the local sheriff's office to see if they'd had any luck with leads on Lisa's murder or Trudy's disappearance. Deputy Dattilo took her call, speaking in a deep voice with a long drawl.

"No, ma'am, we haven't found anything that relates to Trudy Wells. There was something with Lisa East, though. It might be of interest to you and Mr. Long."

"What's that?" Tabitha asked, almost afraid to hear the answer.

"We found DNA under Lisa's fingernails. We don't have a match yet, but we do have something else."

"What?" Now she was a little breathless, feeling the stress.

"Lisa had cotton seeds clutched in her hand. Like she'd

grabbed a handful and most of it had slipped out of her grip, but there was enough to identify the seed. G9-14, some kind of new seed. Does that mean anything to you?"

"Roger will have to call you back," Tabitha said. "That's a crop Trudy was investigating for Long Agricultural. I know Roger will want to speak with you."

"Have him give me a call. Or better yet, I'll ride over to the business office and talk to him in person."

"Thanks, Deputy. If you hear anything about my sister, please let me know." She hung up and sat down on the side of the bed. She'd worked hard not to let worry for Trudy take over. She'd taken action instead of fretting. But now, she couldn't help the tears that welled in her eyes. Where could Trudy be? What had happened to her? She had to keep the faith that her sister was alive.

Trudy's disappearance was connected either with agricultural issues or her crazy dating episodes. Or possible the two had been combined together. Alan Dotsun had a finger in each of those pies. Was he somehow responsible for Trudy's disappearance? She pulled up her phone and googled the name. There was nothing of any real interest that showed. When she typed in G9-14, there was a Grundle company press release that mentioned the "new cotton" and the miracle it would bring to growers. The hype was extensive.

Unable to make any real headway, she went downstairs. She had a few hours to kill until time for the evening's séance and Mama Bettite had always impressed on her the need to be as familiar as possible with her surroundings. Spirits loved the familiar, whether it was a room or a chair or a dress. If Tabitha was going to help Roger with his mother, she needed to be as realistic as she possibly could.

The house was quiet, and she found all three cats in the

front parlor, looking out the window as if they expected company. It was the slenderer black cat, Trouble, that hooked his claws in the bottom of her jeans and urged her to follow him into the parlor. The line of a possible new song came to her—"I'm hooked on trouble and I can't let go." When she found Trudy and returned to her New Orleans life—to the world of writing and music that she'd hardly given a thought to--she'd finish the song. She smiled as she bent down to address the cat.

"What's up, Trouble?" She stroked the cat's sleek black fur and he arched beneath her hand. Tabitha had always loved cats, and she found Trouble to be extraordinary. In fact, all three of the Delta cats were unusually compelling. They behaved as if they had a real understanding of what was happening around them.

Trouble urged her toward the beautiful painting of the Mississippi vista that Asa Redmond had created long ago when the Delta was another world. "You like this painting?" she asked the cat. She didn't expect an answer, so his loud meow made her chuckle. "Not only are you good at finding clues, you're an art critic. Your talents are endless."

He hooked his sharp claws in the hem of her jeans again and moved toward the staircase. The cat's antics diverted her from her worry, and she followed him, willingly going up to the second floor and then the third. She'd seen him up on the third floor and wondered what he was up to. Letting him take the lead, she went into one of the empty third floor rooms and to the windows that opened onto a balcony. The cat was clawing at the window. She opened it for him and he stepped outside into the cold air.

It was a pre-sunset similar to the one in the painting, and she couldn't help but wonder if the cat had discerned this.

How incredible. It gave the feline a whole new level of intelligence. She stood for a moment, drinking in the view. The words of a Jesse Winchester song came to her, and she hummed the melody to "Mississippi You're on my Mind" until Trouble hopped onto the balcony railing, making her anxious that he might fall. When she reached to bring him back to safety, he dodged her hands. "What?" He never avoided being petted or held. He faced the vista that mimicked the painting and cried forlornly.

"Trouble, what are you trying to tell me?" She knew the cat had a message for her. A week before she'd never have believed a cat could or would willingly try to communicate with her. Now she was positive that was exactly what he was doing.

The setting sun came out from behind a cloud and a ray of light struck something metallic far away in one of the cotton fields. It was a momentary beacon that faded with the changing light. But she'd seen it, and she knew what it was. A vehicle was parked in the middle of one of the fields, likely tucked in a brake. She had no proof, but in her heart she feared it was her sister's car.

Heart pounding, she brought out her cell phone and dialed Roger. Her rental car would never make it through the fields. She needed Roger's big truck. And she needed Roger. If Trudy was in the car—she shut that thought down. Trudy wasn't dead in the car. She would have felt it. She would have known if her sister was no longer among the living.

When Roger answered, she didn't procrastinate. "I've found Trudy's car. It's parked in a field behind Long Hall. I saw it from the third-floor window. Trouble showed it to me."

"I'm on the way. Meet me in the drive. Call the sheriff's office. Get Dewayne and Budgie out there with a forensic team. There's no time to waste." He paused. "It's going to be okay, Tabitha. We'll find her. This is not bad news. It's a clue that will set us on her trail."

His reassuring words brought a sob from her, but she fought to control her emotions. "I'll be waiting for you."

The cat hopped down from the balcony and entered the window, calling for Tabitha to follow. In a daze, she walked behind him, shutting the window to keep out the cold. She took a moment to compose herself, remembering not to jump to conclusions. Roger was right. The car could be the lead everyone needed to find Trudy's trail. It could be a good thing, not a bad one. She simply couldn't allow the images of a broken Trudy decomposing in the front seat to settle in her brain.

How long would it take Roger to arrive? She didn't know, but once she was outside the house with Trouble, she called the sheriff's office as Roger had suggested.

"Are you sure it's your sister's car?" Budgie, the shorter of the deputies, had answered her call.

This was no time for hysteria. "I couldn't see clearly," she admitted. "It was a flash of sunlight glinting off something metallic." She realized she might have jumped the gun, but Troubled rubbed against her legs, giving her encouragement. "I'm positive it's Trudy's car. Roger said we would need forensics."

"We're on the way," Budgie said. "I hope this will lead us to your sister, alive and safe."

"Me, too." Once she hung up the phone, there was nothing to do but wait.

CHAPTER THIRTEEN

*B*ipeds come in all shapes, sizes, and mental acuity. With Tabitha Kingsley I hit the top tier. She has an intuitive way of catching my drift, to use a quaint American turn of phrase. And she's no quitter, a real pisser. She's holding herself together by sheer will power alone. And yet she is taking a moment to stroke me and thank me for helping her. She accepts what I did and doesn't try to rationalize it as a coincidence or something of that foolish nature.

A few figure eights around her ankles and she is at least smiling at me, though it's a somewhat tremulous smile. I can feel her anxiety. She has the complexion of a fair, English rose, but now she's a bit pallid. Finding her sister will resolve all of that. The car will give us and the authorities some leads. I know it. Whoever thought I would convey a message through a painting. I have to admit that this episode is a fine example of the positive role art can play in our lives. I went to the third floor to see the vista painted nearly two hundred years ago by Asa Redmond. I was admiring the power of the landscape when I saw the flash of light on the car in the field. I knew then it was a vehicle hidden in the high growth, and it's a logical deduction that it is likely Trudy's car. Thank you, Master Redmond, for the clue.

Now it's time for me to kick into action. I must be on board the truck when Roger and Tabitha go to the car in the field. If there's anything gruesome to be discovered, I can't let Tabitha see it. There are things you simply shouldn't see, and a decomposing loved one falls into that category. While I didn't come to Zinnia to protect and serve our red-haired soothsayer, I've taken on the responsibility and will fulfill it with a stiff upper lip. I won't be a wanker about it either, though I'm not at all fond of viewing dead things. I think back to my bucolic days as a kitling growing up in Wetumpka, Alabama where my biggest concern was slipping around the hedges to spy on the neighbors and flirt with the local feline femme fatales. Now, I'm building a thriving business of solving cases wherever I go, following in dad's enormous pawprints.

And here comes Roger, roaring down the driveway. Tabitha all but leaps off the porch and into the crushed shells of the path. And we are off. Whew! Roger-Dodger hardly slowed enough for me to jump in. Thank goodness Tabitha is as agile and strong as I am. We're aboard the truck, which is something of a land yacht with this huge cab, a long truck bed, dual wheels in the rear, and an engine that sounds like it might be able to fly. And we're off.

ROGER KNEW the road where Trudy's car—if it was her car— had to be parked. It was a little used farm road that wound around the edges of the New Slope field and then dead ended in a thick brake of tupelo gum trees, cypress, and saw-tooth oaks. It was possible Tabitha had merely seen the sun strike an abandoned piece of metal, but his gut told him otherwise. He believed it was Trudy's car, and he was worried about preventing Tabitha from seeing something that would scar her for the rest of her life. Somehow he had to protect her.

Without thinking, he reached across the black cat and put a comforting hand on her arm. "It's going to be okay," he said softly.

"I want to believe that." Her voice was strained with emotion.

"What would you and Trudy be doing if you were in New Orleans?" He sought a conversation where she could find solace. "Tell me about your lives together."

Tabitha shook her head. "I was always the rule follower, the dreamer who wrote poetry and songs. Trudy was the rule breaker. She's been in and out of trouble all of her life, but only one patch of what I consider serious misadventure. In the last five years, she's really grown up and become an...activist. She gets involved in things and she fights for what she believes in. School curriculum, jail reform, prison rehabilitation, animal causes. I admire that about her, because I've always played it safer. I'll write letters, but Trudy will march in the streets. She'll get in people's faces. What's the thing on the news all the time now, 'speak truth to power?' She's courageous."

"I saw some of that with her at the business." He pressed harder on the gas pedal when they were on the open road. As they came to an intersection, he saw Budgie and DeWayne in the patrol car. They pulled in behind him, following. He felt some relief that they were already on the scene.

"Tell me about your writing," he prompted Tabitha, trying to keep her mind occupied.

"I've always loved music. My favorite past time is writing song lyrics, but that's a hard way to pay the bills unless you have a big star who wants your work. Anyway, it was kind of a fluke that I got a job writing a music column for one of the local entertainment magazines. And then the column got picked up by another magazine. Then the local entertainment paper asked me to interview musicians and review new bands. Then a couple of jazz magazines wanted me to work for them." She shrugged. "I love music and musicians and writing. It's the perfect job."

Roger at last came to the rutted field road that disappeared over a slight rise. Beyond that would be the brake and the car. He checked to be sure the deputies were still behind him.

"And Trudy? What is her passion?" He wanted to keep her talking. That way she couldn't think about what they might find.

"Trudy has always been good at science and math, which I'm terrible at. I can't believe we had the same mother because we're different as night and day."

Except in the looks department, Roger wanted to add, but he didn't. Both women were lovely in their differences. Tabitha was fair and red haired. Trudy was dark and mysterious. It was odd because he'd noticed Trudy's physical attributes but never been attracted. Tabitha was a whole different story. He'd been angry at her the first time he laid eyes on her, but beneath the heat of his temper was another sizzle. He could no longer deny that.

As they turned down the rutted road, Tabitha's voice trembled, but she kept talking, forcing herself to stay calm. The black cat crawled into her lap and rubbed his head against her chin, offering his own form of comfort.

"Trudy was always in trouble in school," Tabitha said. The tiniest smile touched the corners of her mouth. "She hated authority. She refused to obey rules unless they made sense to her. She was a challenge. But she is the most loyal friend a person could have. And she has a passion for all living animals and the planet. That was why science interested her. Back in the day, a pet drug company was offering a twenty-five million dollar reward to anyone who could invent an oral contraceptive for cats and dogs that would work and not harm the pets. I honestly thought Trudy might be the person to figure that out."

"I have to agree, she's very smart and has an intuitive ability to understand science." Roger could see the brake in the distance. The car wasn't visible yet, and he didn't know whether to hope it would be there or not. "I was going to promote her into the research department. Lots more money. She was...*is* that good."

Trouble sat up and put his paws on the truck dash. He was eagerly watching the road as they pulled into the shade of the first trees. It took Roger a moment for his eyes to adjust, but then he saw the car pulled down a small incline toward where a creek flowed. It was Trudy's little Honda.

"Oh, no!" Tabitha barely breathed the words. She opened the door but Roger caught her wrist. The cat was out the door and on the ground running toward the car.

"No." He shook his head. "Let me look first. Please."

She swallowed a sob and nodded.

Roger heard the doors on the cruiser slam and DeWayne and Budgie joined him as he walked toward the car.

"There aren't any flies," Budgie said. "That's a good sign."

"You're a comforting devil, aren't you?" DeWayne asked. "The sheriff would be proud of you."

The black cat jumped to the hood of the little car that had obviously been hidden where no one would likely find it. It was a miracle Tabitha had seen the sun striking the metal.

"Me-ow!" The cat clawed at the front glass as if he wanted to get inside the car. Roger noted that the windows were all rolled up, no cracked glass, and there didn't appear to be any damage to the body of the car.

"Please stay back," DeWayne said as he and Budgie took the lead. But Roger didn't need to get any closer. The car was empty. Trudy's body wasn't there. He turned back to face Tabitha with a wide grin and signaled her to join them.

CHAPTER FOURTEEN

*T*abitha stumbled as she started to run down the incline to the car, shedding the awful dread that had held her in a vice grip. Her gait, like her heart, became smoother and freer. Roger opened his arms and she ran into them without a thought. He crushed her against him and she felt the rumble of laughter in his chest. Trudy wasn't dead in the car. There was no body. She could still be alive. That was more than Tabitha had hoped for. So much more. And now the two deputies and the strange black cat were examining the car for evidence. With the worst-case scenario behind her, Tabitha was able to focus on the possibility of the car containing a clue that would lead them to her missing sister.

"Thank you, Roger." She gathered herself and stepped back from the comfort of his arms. He was almost a stranger, but she'd sought his arms when she needed comfort. It was an odd realization. She wasn't the kind of woman to lean on anyone. She'd always been the anchor, the weight that held Trudy to the daily grind of life. It was so odd to find herself needing that same thing from another. But Roger hadn't hesitated. She looked up into his eyes and he brushed a wayward strand of hair from her cheek.

"DeWayne and Budgie are very good at their jobs. We're going to find something that will take us to Trudy. Count on it."

"I hope you're right."

Budgie walked over. "Ms. Kingsley, how tall was your sister?"

Tabitha frowned, but she answered. "Five three. I got all the inches and she got all the science brain—that was our joke."

"Someone else drove this car here. The seat is pushed back to allow a tall person to drive."

Tabitha would never have thought of that. "Anything else?"

"I'd like to have the car towed back to Zinnia. We don't have a fancy crime lab or anything like that, but I have a garage at my house where I can put the car in a clean space so we can really break it down and examine it."

"Please, do whatever you need to do," Tabitha said. She held out her hand for a shake. "Thank you, Deputy. Both of you. Everyone has been so...kind."

"We're just doing our jobs," Budgie said.

"No, it's more than that. You really care. That means a lot. I know you'll do everything you can to find my sister."

"Any new developments in the Lisa East murder?" Roger asked. "We believe the two incidents are linked."

"So do we," Budgie said. "We got a call from the Sheriff last night and we filled him in on everything. Coleman and Sarah Booth will be home soon. If we haven't solved it by then, Coleman and his girlfriend will figure it out."

Tabitha realized he'd dodged the questions about developments, so she rephrased. "Are there any clues as to who shot Lisa or why?"

Budgie glanced over at DeWayne, who nodded. "Keep this to yourselves, but we got a lead on some problems with a batch of experimental cotton seed, something Lisa was selling for DayzSeed. Apparently Trudy was poking around in some of the results of that seed. We did get some DNA from under Lisa's nails, but we haven't hit a match in the system. Indicates that our killer doesn't have a record is all. That makes it harder, until we get a suspect. But once we have some people in our sights, the DNA will make for a positive identification."

"Do you have any suspects?" Roger asked. "You don't have to give us names, just do you have anyone you're looking at strongly."

Budgie nodded. "But we can't scare them. If they do have Trudy then they might harm her if we spook them."

It was a good point and one she was glad the deputy was considering. But if she had a hint, she could pursue it from her angle. The deputy was not about to include her in his investigation, though.

"Thank you for all you're doing. Contact us with any questions or with updates, please." She didn't intend to cry, but she couldn't help that tears welled in her eyes.

"This car will give us more leads," Budgie said. "We'll keep you apprised."

The deputy returned to the car and when a wrecker arrived, he helped hook up the little Honda. Tabitha blinked away tears as she watched her sister's car disappear down the farm road behind the big wrecker and followed by the patrol car.

Roger slipped his arms around her and held her. "Trudy isn't dead. I believe that."

Tabitha nodded. "I do too. I have to." She looked around. "Where is Trouble?"

Roger released her. "He was on the car."

They looked at each other. "That darn cat." They spoke in unison, and Tabitha gave her first real smile in a long time. "He's in the car," she said. "He was dying to get in there and look around, and now he has."

"The deputies are mighty tolerant of Sarah Booth Delaney's animals, but Trouble appears to be a stray."

"I don't think so. I'm pretty sure his owner is staying at the Prince Albert. There are a couple of conferences in town, and one of them involves books, booksellers, and librarians. I'll bet anything Trouble's owner is in that group. While she's at the conference, he's into everything."

"That's a pretty good deduction," Roger said. He drew her to him again, holding her lightly, without any pressure, but the look he gave her was searing.

Tabitha felt her pulse begin to speed up. She wanted Roger to kiss her. It was insane that her sister was missing and she was thinking about how much she needed this man's kiss. When his head dipped toward hers, she met his kiss and allowed herself to think of nothing but this one moment. The timing wasn't great, but her life had never been a smooth ride. With that last thought, she simply yielded to the kiss.

When she opened her eyes, she saw the first glimmer of a star in the deep lavender sky. Roger saw it too.

"I won't ask you what you're wishing for, but I think I'm wishing the same."

"Yeah." She reached up and touched his cheek. "My emotions are a mess."

Roger kissed her forehead. "I know. I felt I might be taking advantage of your vulnerability. We can explore this path when Trudy is safe."

She'd never met a man who could so easily put his own desires and needs behind hers. It was both remarkable and exciting. "Thank you."

"Now let's get after that cat. If Budgie finds him in that car, he may barbecue him." He grinned to show he was kidding.

"And that would not be good for Budgie or the cat." She smiled. "And we have to get back to Long Hall for the séance."

"Thank you for doing this. Mother is being awful, and more than that, dangerous to the farm. I do hate to manipulate her, but she's so damn destructive that I refuse to feel truly guilty. She needs a very romantic message from Micah Malone. Something about the summer they spent together at Big Sur. Micah was a professional surfer, but he was a lot more than that. I think maybe he was the only really good man my mother has ever fallen for. He was killed in a surfing accident."

"Your aunt told me a little about him. That kind of terrible accident would traumatize anyone."

"It hurt Mother, and she changed after that. She was always selfish, but she got worse. And this Antoine, I'm not certain what his game is, but he has no business trying to be an active partner in Long Agricultural."

"I'll see what I can do." Tabitha felt a few qualms, because she hated to deceive people. But sometimes, a gentle nudge was a lot better than a whack upside the head. Roger was about ready to start whacking—she could feel his frustration like an energy around him.

They got in the truck and Roger drove toward Budgie's house where the car would be stored in his garage while the deputies went over it with a fine-tooth comb.

. . .

I'm TRUSTING the bipeds to realize I've hopped a ride in Trudy's car. They'll have to fetch me. I'm normally not one to tamper with evidence at a crime scene, but I know there's something here that will give us a clue to Trudy's whereabouts. I just need time to search, and I'm doing that as the car is being towed. My plan is to wait until they park it and then figure a way out of the vehicle. Without getting caught by the boys in brown. Pluto assures me that Deputies DeWayne and Budgie are good guys, and I believe him, but my Sherlockian training insists that I do this on my own. I trust my abilities more than those of others.

Now to start digging. I haven't had the pleasure of meeting this missing sister, Trudy, but I do believe Tabitha is going to need to print out some instructions on car care for her sibling. If the wrappers on the floorboards are any indication of Trudy's diet, she is well on her way to heart disease. Greasy burgers, fried chicken, something called a break-fast burrito—my eyes are watering from the remaining fumes. Humans will put anything in their mouths and swallow it. This girl needs a food intervention!

Now for the more interesting finds among the rubbish. There's a Google map that indicates a juke joint-slash-eatery here in the Delta. It could be significant. And here's a dried up flower—a zinnia. Perhaps a gift from a lover. It's going to seed, though, so it could be important. Someone has carved a symbol under the dash. It's like the symbol that was on Trudy's calendar. Roger and Tabitha need to see this. And there is something stuck between the driver's seat and the console. A business card. It's wedged in so tightly, the deputy failed to see it. I'm sure with a strong light, Budgie will find it, but not if I have my way. Let me claw it out of there.

Success! I hate to be a clever clog and interfere in the deputies' work, but this card is a clue I can't pass up. Now that I've amassed a pile of relevant materials, I have to figure out how to get this stuff out of the car and into the hands of Tabitha and Roger without getting caught. I'm up to the challenge, because I am Trouble, black cat detective!

CHAPTER FIFTEEN

*R*oger pulled his truck into the little neighborhood where Budgie lived. Sure enough, the wrecker had left Trudy's car parked at the opening to a garage. Budgie could be seen inside, clearing space for the vehicle. Roger slowed and pulled to the side of the road, making certain that a dense hedge blocked Budgie's view of his pickup.

"How do you want to handle this?" Tabitha asked.

"I'm thinking you should go talk to Budgie while I open the car and let the cat out. We'll wait here in the truck for you."

"Talk to him about what?" Tabitha asked.

"Tell him about your date tomorrow. Maybe he could happen into the place while you're dining. I'd feel a lot better if someone was there, watching out for you. And you have to promise you won't leave with anyone—for any reason. I'd be there myself, if it wouldn't blow your cover." More than anything he felt the need to protect Tabitha. But he couldn't lurk around like a jealous suitor, even if that was what he was fast becoming.

Tabitha opened the truck door. "I can handle this. Just be sure you get Trouble out of the car. That cat. He really is trouble."

"I wouldn't be a bit surprised if he didn't find a few clues. He's trouble, but he's extraordinary. I've always appreciated the independence of cats and their ability to survive in tough circumstances. Trouble is so much more than just a cat."

"If he doesn't have an owner, I think he'd make a swell New Orleans kitty."

"Or a Delta cat," Roger said, and for a moment he allowed himself the fantasy of Tabitha and the cat, with him, in their own place. He loved Long Hall, but if he should ever marry, he would want a place to build a life, his life. Long Hall was where Charline and Samuel lived.

"We're not going to have a custody battle for Trouble, are we?" Tabitha teased.

"Nope. We'll have a negotiated settlement." He put a hand on her shoulder. "Budgie is a good guy, but he's a stickler for the rules. He won't be happy if he knows the cat is in the car. He'll be worried about contaminating the evidence."

"Got it. I'll get Budgie to go inside long enough for you to free the kitty." She slipped out and walked over to where Budgie was stacking boxes.

"Deputy, I need to tell you about something I've set in motion. I may need your help, but it could lead to whoever has my sister." She continued to talk as Budgie led her to his back door and showed her inside.

The minute the door closed against the cold night, Roger was sneaking across the lawn to Trudy's car. He opened the door and Trouble jumped on the back seat where he had a pile of things—papers and a business card.

"Let's go." Roger picked up the cat who frantically tried to grasp the things he'd collected. "Hold your horses, I'll get that stuff." He put the cat down to retrieve the things and Trouble jumped to the front seat and began pawing at the dash area. Roger checked to be sure Budgie was still inside, and then used his phone light to check what the cat was after. The strange symbol that he'd seen on Trudy's calendar had been scratched into the bottom of the dash. Trouble bounced to the back seat and again pawed at the items he'd collected. Roger snapped a photo of the symbol, picked up the items and the cat and eased the car door closed. He hurried back to the pickup with the cat in his arms. "Mission accomplished," he said as he closed the truck door.

"Me-ow!" Trouble pawed at the paper. "Me-ow!" His cry was insistent.

"Simmer down," Roger said as he unfolded the paper. The Google map gave directions to Tom's Big Sizzle, a local restaurant and bar in Drew, Mississippi. Tabitha had said she was meeting her date in Drew. This was the place, and Trudy had been there. He felt the net closing around the people involved in Trudy's disappearance.

Beside the map was a dead flower—he had no clue if it was important, but the cat seemed to think so. And the last thing he picked up was a business card. Expensive. Financial planning. And the initials T&S. "Fighting for a clean earth."

While he was waiting for Tabitha to return to the truck, he used his phone to google T&S. A list of possibilities came up, but it was T&S Financials that caught his eye. His mother had said something about Antoine working in finance. Antoine and Hannah had been in the Delta for several weeks. Had they run up on Trudy somewhere? A much darker thought took hold of him. Were his mother and her lover involved, somehow, in Trudy's disappearance? His mother was selfish and unprincipled, but he'd never considered she might harm another human being. He gripped the steering wheel and tried to figure out the best way to tell all of this to Tabitha. If there was a good way.

He didn't have long to think about it. Budgie's front door opened and Tabitha stepped outside, followed by the deputy. Roger was again struck by her easy grace, and the sincere way she shook the deputy's hand, thanking him for his help. Budgie watched her as she walked to the truck and got in. The deputy went back to his work at the garage.

"I see you found the cat." Tabitha stroked Trouble's fur, smiling and shaking her head. "He is truly a source of trouble."

"Me-ow!" Trouble arched his back under her hand. He nudged the map, the card, and flower toward her, then tapped Roger's cell phone on the front seat.

"So this is the stash he found in the car?" Tabitha began to examine it. "I'm impressed."

Trouble pushed the phone toward her. She picked it up and asked, "Is there something on the phone?"

Roger unlocked it and went to the photos. "This was on the dash, just under the driver's side. Someone scratched it into the leather."

"That's the same symbol on Trudy's calendar."

"I know." Roger set the truck in motion. "We have to find out what this is."

"But how?" Tabitha asked.

"Maybe Budgie can help. He's a genius at research. We can send him the symbol in an email or message and maybe he can figure out what it is. I'll try to avoid saying how we got the photo." Roger sent the email and then pulled away from the deputy's neighborhood and was about to head back to Long

Hall, but Trouble indicated he should head in the opposite direction, toward Zinnia.

"I'm telling you, his person is staying in town," Tabitha said. "Let's have a coffee or a drink at the Prince Albert. Trouble will show us who he belongs to. I'm willing to bet you a martini on it."

Tabitha looked wrung out. Roger could only imagine her emotions with her sister still missing. He nodded. "And we can talk about these clues. Just remember, we have to be back at the house for dinner and the séance."

"I need to pick up a few things in town," Tabitha said. "Paper, pens, a chalk board. I learned a few tricks in the French Quarter and tonight I think it might be the best opportunity to use them."

"Medium tricks?" Roger asked. He liked the idea that Tabitha was all in for helping him with his mother. He had a fleeting moment of guilt that he was about to manipulate Hannah, but it passed quickly. His plan was to make sure his mother—and Charline and Samuel—came out on the best end of things.

"Not really tricks, but opportunities for any spirits to communicate. If the spirits are there and willing to connect, this gives them tools."

"I trust whatever you decide to do." They'd arrived in town and he pulled into the parking lot of the Prince Albert. As soon as Tabitha opened the truck door, the black cat shot out, ran across the lot, and was waiting for them to let him into the hotel.

"He sure makes himself at home," Roger said, but he was impressed with Trouble.

"Let's follow him."

. . .

TABITHA LET the black cat lead her through the lobby toward the hotel bar where several groups of people were drinking, laughing, and chatting. Trouble headed straight into one group and jumped into the arms of a pretty red-haired woman who caught the cat and gave him a big hug and kiss.

"What in the world have you been up to?" she asked the cat.

He gave his signature me-ow and leaped from her arms, going back to Tabitha and Roger. It was clear to Tabitha that the cat intended to introduce them. She followed him to the woman and held out her hand, making introductions. "So Trouble is your kitty," she said. "I was afraid he belonged to someone."

"Yes, he's here with me for a booksellers' convention. I'm Tammy Lynn of Wetumpka, Alabama."

Roger ordered a round of drinks and brought them to the small table where Trouble had jumped into Tammy's lap.

"Tell me what Trouble has been up to," Tammy said. "He's something of an amateur sleuth, and yes, I know how preposterous that sounds," she added. "I knew he was busy with a case, so fill me in."

For twenty minutes, the three chatted, sharing stories of Trouble's remarkable abilities to communicate with people.

"He's helping me find my sister," Tabitha finally confessed. "Could we possibly borrow him for another day or so?"

Tammy picked up the cat and stared into his green eyes. After a long moment, she nodded. "You can keep him until Sunday, but then I have to head back to Wetumpka. I have a business there."

"We'll deliver him back to you no later than Sunday morning at ten," Roger said. "If that's agreeable."

Trouble hopped down and ran to the door of the restaurant. He let out a long, plaintive meow. Tammy sighed and shook her head. "He's ready to go with you. I've learned not to fight him when he's working a case. If anyone can help you find your sister, it's Trouble. He has an uncanny ability to solve mysteries."

"So we've discovered," Roger said. He stood and Tabitha rose with him.

"Thank you," Tabitha said, shaking Tammy's hand warmly. "We'll take care of him and he'll be ready to travel Sunday morning if not before."

Tammy put a hand on her shoulder. "Take care. Trouble manages to evade danger, but there are cruel and mean people in the world. Keep yourselves safe, and always listen to Trouble."

"That's an easy prescription to follow," Tabitha said.

CHAPTER SIXTEEN

*L*ong Hall glimmered in the darkening night as they returned to the plantation. Vesta and Pluto came out to greet them, and Charline swept them in the front door tut-tutting at the cold weather. "Come inside and have something warm to drink before dinner," she said. "Samuel is making some Irish coffees." She leaned closer to Tabitha. "All is in readiness for the séance."

"Thank you." Tabitha took the bags filled with colored pencils, paper, chalk and other drawing supplies to the dining room and left them on the table. "When we need these, they'll be ready."

Tabitha was intensely aware of the ticking of the grandfather clock in the foyer as she sipped her coffee and studied the other people in the room. Samuel and Charline, she'd grown fond of. Antoine studied those around him with quick glances, never a direct, confrontational stare. Tabitha couldn't account for it, but there was an air of introspection about him. Whenever the spotlight hit him, he responded as a greedy gadfly, but in moments when he thought he was unobserved, he seemed almost...reluctant to be there.

Hannah was busy playing the victim or the flirt. Yet she kept one eye on her son, and his scowl seemed to tone her down. She ignored Charline and Samuel, which was probably for the best. Roger, well, he was a force of energy, a man's man but one with tenderness. He kept a watchful eye on her, and she was surprised at how much comfort it gave her. She would get through the evening, and she would accomplish her given task of bringing up a dead beau from Hannah's past.

The dinner hour arrived, and they moved to the dining room for the meal, which was a delicious dish of quail gumbo. "The cats were extremely happy with their dinner," Charline said as she supervised the serving of the meal. Nancy had brought in two young helpers to serve the wine and decadent amaretto cheesecake dessert. The minutes sped by, counted by the old grandfather clock. There was something to the timepiece. Tabitha didn't know how she knew it, but somehow the clock would play into the events of the evening.

When the meal was cleared and the candles lit in the dining room, Tabitha laid out the ground rules for the séance.

"If someone or something, like a pet, comes through for you, please don't break the circle. There's nothing to be afraid of. There are several spirits here who wish to be heard. Suellen is here, for Samuel and Roger. And there's a young woman here." She hesitated. She hadn't planned on saying that, but she did have the strongest sense that a young woman was eager to connect with someone in the Long family. She smiled. "Suellen loves this room. And the morning room. The younger spirit is more...adrift. I have the sense she's not certain she's dead. There's confusion all around her."

Roger stiffened, but he said nothing. He cast a look at

Tabitha as if he questioned what she was about. She only smiled and looked into a far corner of the room.

"And there's a gentleman here, though he isn't too pleased with the term gentleman. He's wilder, more free, and he's proud of his independence. He is indeed a very handsome young man, and he says..." She laughed out loud. "It doesn't make any sense, but he says, 'Hang ten.' I have no idea what that means, but he is balancing, arms out..." She imitated the stance of someone surfing. "Exhilarating!"

Hannah had gone completely pale, and she staggered so that Antoine caught her.

"What foolishness is this?" Antoine asked. "Hang ten. What could that possibly mean?"

"You've never caught a wave, have you, Antoine?" Roger said. "It's a surfing term." He looked hard at his mother. "You remember that summer at Big Sur? I've never seen you so happy before or since. I miss that, Mother."

"The past is done, Roger." She hesitated and Tabitha thought she saw a crack in her veneer. "The good and the bad. It's all gone. I've finally come to accept that and to try to let go of the anger."

"That was a lovely summer," Charline threw in. "Samuel and I took Roger to the northern California coast. He was just a tot but he was determined to surf. You met Micah that summer."

"Let's not drag up the distant past," Hannah said, but she lacked the vigor of her usual pronouncements and her pallor was evident to all.

Tabitha meant to move on, but the ticking of the grandfather clock seemed to paralyze her. And then she heard Micah's voice. "Tell her to be careful. She's playing a dangerous game."

Tabitha's gut twisted as the sense of danger flooded over her, passing as quickly as it had come.

Roger was watching her, but he continued to talk to the group. "Micah finally let me surf," Roger said. "He said you were his perfect Gidget, Mother."

"Yes, and then he smashed his brains out on a rock." Hannah had recovered her balance. "Thanks for the memories, Tabitha, but you can move on. I'm not about to fall prey to a little goading from the past. Did Charline or Roger put you up to this?"

Tabitha shook her head. "No one can control the spirits that show up—or don't show up. Not even me. I simply relay messages, and Micah says he's never far and will always love you. He warns you that you're involved in something perilous. Something secret." She did see the young man clearly, amazingly so. If she took a minute to consider what was happening to her—to everyone in the room—she might be freaked out herself. Beneath all that she saw and felt was the ticking of the grandfather clock. "Time is fluid in the land of death," Tabitha said. The words came to her, unbidden. "Micah says he expects great things from you, Hannah. Something about a law degree. And I'm seeing lush, green fields."

Hannah jumped to her feet. The glass of wine slipped from her hand and crashed against the fireplace hearth. "Enough. This is over."

"He's fading away," Tabitha said. "He says to live up to your potential, Hannah. He...He put his hand on his heart and then pointed at you. And he wants you to remove the layers. That's what he's saying. He says to reveal yourself. That others will be...amazed."

Roger spoke. "He did that all the time." He looked at Tabitha. "How did you know that?"

Tabitha felt a cold chill pass over her, and her teeth began to chatter. She wasn't practiced at hosting séances, but the ones she'd attended—or the few she'd performed—had never left her feeling this way. It was almost as if someone whispered in her ear and the words came out of her mouth without effort. "I don't know. I honestly don't. I'm just saying the things that come to me, the images, the messages." She tried to tamp down the fear that assailed her. She was no medium and certainly no psychic. She'd never really seen a ghost in her life, but right now, she clearly saw Micah Malone, a tanned beach boy with a shock of sandy white hair and a ten million kilowatt smile. "I love her," he said before he disappeared. "Make her believe in herself. If she ever really did, she would allow herself to believe in others."

As he faded away, the clock struck ten.

Tabitha was exhausted, but determined to relay the message. "He says he loves you, Hannah. He wants you to believe in yourself." She slumped in her chair, exhausted.

"What foolishness is this?" Antoine demanded. "Hannah has nothing to reveal. Nor do I. Messages from a dead lover don't mean a thing to me or to her."

Looking at Hannah, Tabitha thought differently. The message from Micah meant a great deal to Hannah. Micah Malone's visit had smote Hannah in a place Tabitha didn't believe existed—her heart. She inhaled deeply and continued, hoping she might pick up something from Suellen for Charline and Samuel. If not, she'd make up something that gave them hope and comfort.

"I'd like to try some automatic writing," Tabitha said. "It's a technique I've seen used a lot. You have to understand that I'm not practiced at it, but I have a sense it will be helpful."

"You're going to put yourself into a trance and then let a

spirit take over your hand to write on those blank pages?"
Hannah had recovered from the shock of Micah Malone's
message.

"I've had enough of this foolishness." Antoine stood up. "If
you'll excuse me and Hannah." He reached for her hand but
she pulled back.

"I'm staying. This is the best free entertainment around."

"If you insist." Antoine took his seat but remained worried
and aloof. Tabitha wondered if he was frightened of something
she might reveal.

"Please, dim the lights and let's light the remaining candles.
I need to concentrate on emptying myself, so it would be
helpful if you all focused on the candle in the center of the
table. Try to allow yourself to see and feel whatever sensations
or emotions come over you. Those of you who are sensitive
will pick up on the spirits who are here to give us a message,
and there are plenty here. Yes, Suellen, I will tell them."
Tabitha inhaled slowly. "Suellen wants you all to know she is
happy to have everyone gathered here at Long Hall. It was a
dream for her to see the family united."

"Hogwash," Hannah muttered. "She'd be happier to see me
on the far side of the planet. And the same goes for Roger."

When Roger started to respond, Tabitha lightly stepped on
his foot under the table. "Empty your minds and open yourself
to feelings and emotions."

She tilted her head back and went through the process
Mama Bettite had taught her. She focused on exhaling all negative energy and allowing only white light to enter through her
crown chakra. Calling upon the spirits around her, she
mentally urged them to connect and communicate. Her fingers
found one of the pencils Roger had sharpened for her and she
put her hand on the page he held and began to let her hand

circle. When the lead in the pencil snapped, Roger put another one in her hand. She filled the page with large, looping circles. Roger removed it, and she continued on a clean page.

The only sound in the room was that of the pencil on the page, a light scratching. Tabitha forgot herself. She forgot the room and the people in it. She was lost in a floating sensation.

Beside her Roger stiffened, but she ignored it. Tension built in the room around her, but she felt it only as if from a great distance. She was aware that she was making a strange sound, a seal-like bark under her breath. Her hand was moving across the page and she had no idea what symbols or words she was creating.

She heard Roger gasp and then she was aware of the young woman who stood in the corner of the room. Cold seeped over Tabitha, and her breath condensed as she exhaled. Not even in the séances led by professionals had she felt such a strong presence. A person manifested in front of her. Lisa East. She knew her, was aware of the bullet hole in her forehead.

"Lisa?" She didn't know if she'd spoken aloud or only in her mind, but the spirit came forward, gliding on the air.

The only sound was the lead of her pencil across the page —and then Tabitha was fully awake and conscious of everything around her. The spirit was gone. Lisa East had vanished. When Tabitha looked down at the pages of writing, she inhaled sharply. In a strange hand were the words, "Danger. Beware. Help her." The symbol she'd found on Trudy's calendar and on the dash of the car was beside the words. In several other pages were the initials T&S and a plus sign.

"Did I write that?" she asked Roger.

He nodded, holding the pages up for others to see.

"The messages are from Lisa East." Tabitha made the pronouncement in a firm voice. When she looked up, Lisa was back in a corner of the dim room, not completely manifested but a shade of herself. She nodded, and in a moment she was replaced by a beautiful older woman in a lavender dress who wore the scent of magnolias. Suellen was in the room now and she came forward, a calming presence filled with peace.

Suellen is speaking. She says, "Watch over Samuel and Charline," Suellen said. "They never want to believe the worst of those they love. Hannah needs to be watched. Danger! Beware of—"

Antoine pushed back from the table. "You may all buy into this chicanery, but I will not. I've had a bellyful of talkative ghosts and spirits. I don't know what you Longs hope to accomplish, but it's not going to work. Hannah is going to claim her birthright and I am going to help her."

The sudden interruption made Tabitha feel unbalanced. She swayed in her seat, but Roger put out a strong hand to hold her.

"Are you okay?" he whispered.

She nodded and faced Antoine. "What happened at T&S Financials?" Tabitha asked softly. "Suellen says there is a story there to be heard."

"You think you're very sly." Antoine leaned down into Tabitha's face. "Accusation by innuendo. Prove it, if you can."

Roger grasped the man by the neck of his shirt and held him in a tight grip as he slowly stood up and pushed him back away from the table. "Easy on, there, Antoine. My aunt and uncle don't much care for fighting in the house, but I'll drag you into the yard if I need to. It's one of my character flaws that I don't let men push women around."

"I don't fall for a set-up when I can smell it from a mile away." Antoine shook free of Roger's grasp. "You'll do whatever you have to do to retain control of Hannah's inheritance. Fair warning here, we'll be married shortly, and when that happens, as her husband, I intend to step into a role in this family business. As her representative, I will fully engage in the decisions to make sure her interests are best served."

Samuel started to stand up from the table, but he stumbled and sat down heavily. The color had drained from his face and his breathing was ragged. Tabitha went to him. He was cold and clammy. The confrontation playing out before him was affecting his heart. "Stop it." She spoke to Roger and Antoine. "Stop it now."

"I have a right to my share of the family business," Antoine said.

"You are not a member of the Long family," Roger pointed out. Both men were too angry to heed Tabitha's warnings.

Out of the corner of her eye, Tabitha saw Trouble jump to the top of a hunt board. The grandfather clock in the foyer began to chime relentlessly. With one delicate nudge, Trouble sent a candelabra tumbling. The hot wax spread across the decorative cloth that had adorned the furniture—and burst into flames.

"Fire!" Charline stood so quickly her chair fell backward. The racket finally penetrated the anger of the two men. Roger leapt into action and used his napkin to beat out the flames. In a moment, it was all over. Trouble leaped gracefully to the floor and went to rub against Charline's shins.

"The cat did that on purpose," Hannah said. She eyed Trouble with a speculative look. "Perhaps he's possessed by the spirit of Suellen. She always hated family brawls."

"I hate to do this," Charline said, "but Hannah, you and Antoine need to leave Long Hall. I don't want you here, upsetting Samuel and everyone else."

"You think you can put me out on the street?" Hannah asked.

Trouble walked over to her, jumped on the table, and hissed in her face. A low growl warned that he was capable of much more than hissing.

"Even the cat hates you," Roger said, adjusting his tie. "I'll carry your bags out, Mother."

"I'm not going anywhere." Hannah took another swallow of her drink. "I find that I like it here at Long Hall." Before she'd even finished her sentence, she leaped up from the table. Pluto was clinging to her calf with all four paws. He rode her as she jumped away from the table and hopped around the room. Finally he sprang free.

"It seems the cats have a different take on the situation," Samuel said. He'd regained some color and a straight back. "Leave or I'll call the sheriff to assist you out the door."

"You're going to regret this," Antoine said as he followed Hannah up the stairs to collect their things.

Tabitha couldn't be certain, but she thought she caught a self-satisfied smile flicker across Antoine's face.

CHAPTER SEVENTEEN

That was one spooky séance, and I'd be willing to bet my sleek black hide that Tabitha was not pretending. I know she came here to con some folks, but there was something utterly sincere about what happened here tonight. Cats do have an affinity for the other side, and I believe Tabitha saw exactly what I saw. The spirits came to her when she called them. People have all sorts of strange beliefs about cats and ghosts. We can see spirits more easily than humans, but we can't always see on command. By the way, dogs see ghosts too, but they are no better at "see on demand" than a cat. All animals are sensitive to the spirit world because we're more sensitive to all stimuli in the physical plane. Bipeds have to wade through belief systems, years of training not to be sensitive, fear, and a host of other issues that blind them to what an animal simply accepts. There are spirits among us, good and bad. Take Suellen, for example. Her love for her family and the land is palpable. That Micah Malone, for whatever his reasons, truly loved Hannah, and he is definitely worried about her. He sees her as the potential victim of danger—which I don't get. Yet. What I do get is that had Micah lived, Hannah might have had a completely different life. He saw good in her. And I learned something else while

watching the séance. Something that Roger will want to know. Micah Malone was more than just a surf bum. A lot more. But that's a revelation for another time. My focus is on Queen Bee Hannah.

The bloodletting is done and the wicked queen and her consort have packed their belongings and are leaving. Antoine has pulled the car up to the front porch, and soon they'll be away down the long drive. Tabitha has taken it upon herself to make tea for Charline and Samuel, who look like they've been in a session of brutal fisticuffs, though not a single blow was landed. At least not physically. The emotional trauma will affect both of them for much longer. Charline and Samuel truly care about Hannah, though she's done all in her power to make them disdain her.

And what is Roger up to? He's sidling out the back door. I follow like the sleek black shadow of a famous cat detective. Roger jumps in his pickup. He's going to follow Hannah and Antoine. Brilliant deduction on his part! Should I go with him or stay to protect my favorite psychic-medium? Pluto and Vesta are here to watch over Tabitha, but still I wish I could leave a note to let them know what's going on. Opposable thumbs. It is the only advantage the bipeds have over me. Perhaps I can train my tail to hold a pen and scribble. If the humanoids can do it, how hard could it be?

The choice is upon me. I leap onto the hood of Roger's truck and startle him, but he opens the door and grabs me to pull me inside. I believe he's just a little happy that I've chosen to surveil with him. A stake-out can be lonely work.

The evil duo seem to be headed to Zinnia. Perhaps they've called for a room at the Prince Albert. I'm curious about their financial state. It's my understanding that Hannah is in Sunflower County for her quarterly allotment of funds from the Long Agricultural business. I also understand she runs through her money quickly, so therefore should be short of funds. Yet she's been lolling about the area, staying in the poshest hotels, dining at the finest restaurants. Zinnia isn't New York

City as far as prices go, but two weeks of vacationing, even in Zinnia, can run into quite a bill. Especially when only the very best will serve. The bog-standard is not for Queen Hannah. So does she have another source of income? A possible lead!

Now Roger is driving intently—and at last calling Tabitha.

"I'm tailing my mother and that man. Trouble is with me— just so you don't worry."

Bless his pea-picking little heart. He's taken care to let Tabitha know I'm safe. And her response is exactly what I anticipated.

"Charline and Samuel are fine now. They've settled down. I'm..."

The last bit was garbled. I couldn't grasp it—and neither could Roger. He's got that frown on his face that means he's worried. He can either turn back or follow the lead he's got. And we're pulling into downtown Zinnia right now. True to form, Hannah and Antoine are headed to the Prince Albert. But wait! Hannah is getting out of the car and Antoine is driving away. Roger is taking care that he isn't spotted as a tail. We have to go forward with our spy mission now. Tabitha is safely at Long Hall. If she will only remain there, all will be well.

Why, then, is my little kitty heart so concerned?

No time to ponder the intricacies of emotion and my preternatural instincts. As Sherlock would say, the case calls for cold, calm, logical calculation, not worry and angst. Roger is following Antoine, who is going to...Lisa East's house? Oh, my, this is beginning to get tricky.

He's pulling to a stop, and Roger is doing the same, about three blocks back. I can see we're going to have to sneak through the darkness to see what Antoine is up to. Why would he be interested in anything at Lisa East's? Soon I'll have my answer or my name isn't Trouble.

TABITHA CLEANED UP THE PAPERS, pencils, and various para- phernalia she'd used at the séance. She made sure each candle was snuffed completely. The last thing anyone needed was another fire. She was at loose ends since Roger—and Trouble—had taken off on a clandestine spying mission. Aside from feeling a little left behind, she realized that Roger had entrusted her with making Charline and Samuel feel safe and secure. She'd done that, brewing chamomile tea for each and making certain they were over the shock of the séance. Samuel had gone to their suite to prepare for bed, but Charline was in the kitchen, making another cup of tea.

"I was really glad to hear from Suellen, but Micah Malone was something of a surprise," Charline said as she stirred the hot drink. "Tell me, do you know why Micah came through so strongly. I honestly hadn't thought of him in years. I'd almost forgotten what terrible heartbreak Hannah went through. Instead of grieving, she was the type who went out and got drunk and wrecked a car. When she first learned that Micah was dead...It was possibly the last time I saw her show real emotion, real compassion."

Tabitha had her suspicions, but she wasn't going to open her mouth until she had more evidence. "I don't know," she finally said. "The spirits—time doesn't have any meaning for them on the other side. What takes decades here is a blink to them. And I presume it's the other way around, too." Tabitha was only repeating the things Mama Bettite had taught her. "How did Hannah and Micah meet?"

Charline settled into a kitchen chair, the mug held between both her hands. When she shivered slightly, Tabitha got a throw from the parlor and wrapped it around her. "Thank you," Charline said. "I remember Micah coming up to the beach where Hannah was sunning. He was like a California god. Such a handsome young man, that blond hair, blue eyes, and tan. Hannah was instantly smitten." She paused. "She was never an easy girl. I tried to win her over, to make her like me, but she was so...aloof. But with Micah that protective shell fell away and she smiled and laughed and...I was so happy for her. Micah was more than just a beach bum. He was going to law school. He had his eye on environmental law. That summer Hannah started to talk about pursuing a career in law or maybe urban planning. They would work together to create communities that used the land wisely. She genuinely cared about what humans were doing to the planet and finding alternatives."

Charline looked so sad that Tabitha put a hand on her forearm. "I'm sorry. I didn't mean to make you upset."

"No, it was good. Micah adored Roger. He was the only man Hannah dated who treated Roger like anything more than an inconvenience. Things would have been different for everyone if Micah had lived."

"Was he killed instantly when he hit the rocks while he was surfing?"

"Yes. He was on a wave or whatever they call it. He was further north up the coastline. The surf was bad that day. He shouldn't have gone in the water. A wave caught him and he was smashed into some rocks. Luckily Hannah and Roger weren't with him that day. They'd gone into town with me to buy groceries. We'd planned on staying at Big Sur until the fall semester started, but as soon as the funeral was over, we packed up and came back to Mississippi. Hannah never recovered. She went back to college and left Roger with me. When she showed up at Christmas, she was horrible. Suellen and Big Sam tried. They really tried."

"How old was Roger at that time?" Tabitha calculated that Charline herself must have been a young bride, new to the Long family. She'd taken each member as her own blood.

"Two or so." She cleared her throat. "Micah gave him a

sense of belonging, of being a son. It was a tragedy for every-one. Hannah dropped out of school and began her life as a girl-friend of wealthy men. She's been at it a while now, and to be frank her looks won't hold much longer. Antoine may be her last fling, which is why she's considering marriage."

"Tragedy marks all of us," Tabitha said. She was thinking of her missing sister. "I suppose I should turn in."

"Yes, Samuel will wonder what happened to me. Thank you for the evening, Tabitha. It was good to hear from Suellen. And Micah. Maybe it will wake Hannah up, make her remember what could have been."

Charline put her mug in the sink and left the kitchen. The house fell still and silent around Tabitha. She had one more thing to do before bed—search Hannah and Antoine's room for any clues. It was unlikely they'd left anything telling behind, but now was the time to look.

She waited until she was certain the Longs were asleep, and then she crept up the stairs past her own door to Hannah's rooms. She eased the door open and almost screamed when a black cat jumped from the bed to the floor and came to circle her ankles.

"Pluto, what are you doing here?"

The cat head-bumped her shin, then disappeared under the big four poster bed that Hannah had left in complete disarray. The entire room looked as if a cyclone had gone through it twice. Tabitha shook out the sheets and was rewarded with the clink of something hitting the floor. She found a heavy broach that looked like it had been crafted in the 1890s. It was a work of art, and the emeralds in it looked real. She put it on the dresser so that if Hannah came back for it she could find it.

"She's mighty careless with her things," Tabitha said to the cat, who darted back under the bed. She searched the room, finding only empty drawers and closets. Hannah had left a mess, with dirty towels scattered everywhere, but she'd gathered up all the paperwork she might have had with her. There was nothing that tied Hannah or Antoine to any nefarious plots.

Pluto poked his head out from under the bed and stared at her. In a moment he came out, crying softly. He blinked his big green eyes, and Tabitha knelt to draw him out from under the bed. She couldn't leave him shut up in the room. There were no litter boxes. "Come on, big guy. I'll find you something to eat in the kitchen."

Pluto inched back under the bed, just out of reach.

"Come on," she pleaded. She was tired and worried about what Roger and Trouble might get into. She also needed to get out of the bedroom before she was caught snooping. She reached under the bed from him, and something cold and hard clattered across the floor and into her hand. Pluto had swept it with his paw like it was a hockey puck going into the net for a goal.

Tabitha grasped it and brought it out for an examination. It was a cufflink. The initials T&S—just like the business card--were embossed in black jet in the gold background. Antoine. He was somehow involved in Trudy's disappearance. She had no doubt of it now. Her heart pounded at the realization.

ROGER HAD PARKED two blocks from Lisa's little bungalow and he and Trouble darted from shrub to shrub in the darkness, hurrying to get to Lisa's to see what Antoine was up to. While they'd been watching, another car pulled down the street. It was too far away for Roger to get a model and too dark to get a color, but it was a sleek design, something like the car Antoine was driving. Expensive.

A tall, slender person got out of the car and jogged toward Antoine's vehicle. There was a brief confab, and then the person left. Antoine got out of his vehicle and began working the lock of Lisa's bungalow, clearly intent on getting inside.

Roger eased closer to the little cottage and stopped beside a large, dense shrub. The cat followed at his heels. He made it to a thick Indian hawthorn near the back door of the cottage. As Roger watched, Antoine passed in front of the back windows. He was doing something in the house, but Roger couldn't tell what.

Trouble let out a low growl. The cat was unhappy with the turn of events.

"Easy, boy. We can't just bust up in there. We're going to have to wait and watch. Nothing more."

Roger waited a few minutes and when he saw nothing, he eased closer to the little house. If he could get a look in the window, he might figure out what Antoine was up to. Trouble clawed at his pants leg, as if to drag him back into the shrubbery. The cat was very bossy. When he ignored Trouble and ran to the side of the house to actually peer inside, the cat kept trying to drag him back, though he never made a sound, which was unusual for a cranky cat.

Antoine had disappeared from sight, but as soon as Roger got up to the cabin, he realized what his mother's boy toy had been up to. The smell of gasoline was thick around the back of the cottage. Antoine had been soaking the old wooden structure in gas. He was going to burn the place down.

Roger reached for his phone just as a shadow moved across the white wood of the house. He started to turn, but too late. He heard Trouble's wild hiss and screech just as something very hard came down on his head. He dropped to his knees and was struck a second time, sliding into unconsciousness on the ground right beside the house.

ONLY MY QUICK reflexes save me from the same fate as Roger. I couldn't get to Roger quickly enough to save him, and I don't have a clear idea who the person who struck Roger is. Antoine was the last person I saw, but this figure, even bundled in a coat, doesn't appear to be Antoine. And there's the sound of a car starting on the street. And the rental car Antoine was driving is leaving! But someone is still in the house.

Pox! Roger's phone is on the ground. The probability is that the phone no longer works, but at least the villain leaves it. And he also leaves Roger lying in the dirt beside a house he is setting on fire. If he doesn't move, Roger will burn to death! Now the attacker is running like the cowardly criminal he is.

I have to get that phone—and dial Budgie or DeWayne. They have to come. A lucky break for me, the phone still works. Budgie is answering, and he is none too pleased. But he can hear the panic in my cry, and the sound of the fire is growing in volume.

"I don't know where you are, Roger, or what's going on with that yowling cat, but I can GPS your phone. I'm on the way!"

Thank goodness for a deputy with good common sense. And now for me to use the old sandpaper tongue to bring Roger to consciousness. I'm much rather lick Tabitha, but I don't have that option. I have to make Roger move or he's going to become toast. The flames are building in the center of the house, but soon they'll be back here and I don't want a barbecued farmer. Time to lick those eyelids, one of the most tender spots on the human body. Yep, he is moaning and trying to push me away. More licking, and he is opening his eyes. He's beginning to feel the heat—and so am I. Time to move! He gets it and crawls awkwardly away from the house, which is quickly becoming a furnace. And here come sirens. Police, fire, I'll take whatever arrives to help!

Here! We're over here! Budgie to the rescue, and from the looks of him he's as upset by the arson as I am. The fire trucks are containing the flames, thank goodness. What could have been a total loss will be minimal. I just hope he doesn't think Roger started it.

CHAPTER EIGHTEEN

Tabitha was pacing the well-appointed Long kitchen, the cufflink clutched in her hand, when her cell phone rang. She stepped outside the house to take the call, not wanting to awaken Charline or Samuel. To her surprise, it was the Sunflower County Sheriff's Department. She recognized Budgie's voice.

"Ms. Kingsley, there's been a fire. Roger Long has been taken to the hospital. He was asking for you. It might be best to notify his aunt and uncle, too."

"Is he hurt?"

"Not seriously, but he could have been."

"I'm on my way to the hospital." She hung up and ran to her car. Whatever was going on, she had to make certain that Roger was okay before she terrified Charline and Samuel. If they were needed at the hospital, she would come back and drive them herself.

Pluto the black cat was waiting for her beside her rented car, and when she opened the door, he leaped into the passenger seat. "Let's hit it, Pluto." She knew it was crazy, but she felt better while talking to the cat as she drove madly to the hospital. "Roger has to be okay. He has to be." Pluto was not as vocal as Trouble, but he seemed to nod his head in agreement, and then he rubbed against her side, purring his comfort to her.

She'd lost everyone in her life that she'd ever cared about—except Roger. And Trudy. Trudy wasn't dead. She and Roger would find Trudy. Because Roger was going to be fine. She hadn't been willing to admit it, not even to herself, but Tabitha cared about Roger. In such a short time, he'd become an anchor for her, someone she'd begun to count on. Trudy was missing, her parents were gone, Roger had to be okay.

She ran into the hospital, stopping at the ER desk. She was asking about him when she saw him, standing near the far wall, coughing a little, but standing tall and on his own. He held Trouble in his arms.

"Roger!" She ran to him and put her arms around him, kissing him without a second thought. Life didn't give a lot of second chances, and she wasn't about to miss this one. Trouble jumped to the ground and went to the door, asking to be let out. A nurse, eyebrows raised, obliged. Tabitha just had a glimpse of Trouble and Pluto standing nose to nose. They seemed to consult for a moment and then both dashed away.

"Let's get out of here," Roger said. "Those cats are up to something."

"I saw." She glanced around. No one seemed to want to detain them. "You sure you're okay to leave."

"Just a goose egg on my head where someone hit me and a little smoke inhalation. Trouble saved my life. And Budgie too."

"You know, I never really believed in ghosts or spirits until I saw them here in the Delta. All those years hanging out with the psychics and card readers in New Orleans, and deep down, I always thought they were basically kind people who offered something like grief counseling to their clients. You know most people really just want to believe that their loved ones are safe and happy." She touched Roger's face. "I'm seeing things a little differently. I would never have believed that a cat could help solve mysteries, but now I know it's true." She started to add that she would never have considered allowing herself to be vulnerable to love, but she stopped. When Trudy was found, that would be the time to explore her feelings for Roger. "This Delta excursion is changing my entire belief system."

Roger stared down at her and something in his gaze made her heart want to flip. "Mine too. About a lot more than ghosts and cats. Now let's find Antoine. That bastard knocked me out."

Tabitha brought the cufflink out of her pocket where she'd stashed it. "Pluto found this in your mother's bedroom."

Roger took the cufflink and examined it carefully. "T&S. Like the financial company. I knew Antoine was involved. Now we have concrete proof."

"The question is, what are we going to do with it?"

Roger's body tensed. "We're going to find Antoine and make him tell us where Trudy is."

Tabitha nodded. It was time for action. They didn't have enough evidence to go to the sheriff about Antoine, but it was enough for her to consider making him talk. "What about your mother?"

"She's at the Prince Albert. We'll start there." He hesitated. "I saw a slender woman talk to Antoine before he set the fire. It wasn't my mother." He swallowed. "I know this sounds like I'm defending my mother, but it's possible she's being played.

Hearing from Micah Malone at the séance reminded me how much Mother once cared for the earth and her interest in sustainable communities and crops. She may need our help."

"And she'll fight us from helping her every step of the way," Tabitha said with weariness.

They slipped out of the emergency room and into the night where the two cats sat on the ambulance ramp waiting for them. They loaded up in Roger's truck and sped toward downtown Zinnia and the hotel.

Tabitha couldn't help but notice the emptiness of the town as they drove through. Even Millie's Café, the local hangout that Trudy had raved about, was closed. Both Trouble and Pluto gave the darkened diner a long look, but they seemed to accept that a snack was not in the picture.

Roger parked in the back of the hotel lot and they left the cats in the truck as they went inside. Roger picked up the house phone on a table by the elevator. When the desk clerk answered, he asked for his mother's room." Tabitha held the elevator at the ready. Per their plans, she was going up to Hannah's room before Roger in an attempt to reason with Hannah.

"She's checked out?" Roger spoke aloud. He signaled Tabitha over and she stepped away from the open elevator. "Thank you. Did she say where she was going?" There was a pause. "Was there a man with her?" He nodded. "Thank you."

He hung up the phone and shook his head. "They left. Antoine must have come here and alerted her as soon as he tried to burn me to death. They're on the run."

"Your mother would never condone that behavior, Roger. She may be greedy and a criminal, but she would not want you hurt. I believe that." Funny, when she spoke the words she did believe them. Maybe because the alternative would be a pain that Roger would have to carry the rest of his life. No matter how awful a mother Hannah was, Tabitha refused to believe she'd go along with Roger's murder. Hannah had to retain some love for her son, even if they were often at loggerheads.

"Where do you think they went?" Tabitha finally asked.

"Wherever they're holding Trudy. I feel strongly that Trudy is alive."

"What are we going to do?" She felt helpless, and even worse, she was beginning to lose her faith that Trudy would ever be found.

"My mother's driving a rental car. An expensive one. Let's go to the courthouse. I hate to roust Budgie and DeWayne again, but I believe they can track the GPS on that rental car. If they can locate the car, they'll find Mother and Antoine."

Tabitha sighed long and deep. "Thank you, Roger. I'd never have thought of that."

"It may not work but it's worth a try."

He left the hotel parking lot and drove the short distance to the courthouse. A dispatcher was on the desk, but as soon as Roger explained what he needed, she radioed both deputies to come in.

"On the way," Budgie said, a sentiment echoed by DeWayne.

Fifteen minutes later, both lawmen walked into the sheriff's office. DeWayne's hair was damp from being freshly combed and Budgie still smelled of the fire. Roger thanked the deputy profusely for saving his life.

"You should be thanking that cat. If you didn't place the call to me, it had to be him. And just so you know, the fire dispatch received an anonymous call. That's how they got there so fast."

"Probably a neighbor. I am gaining more and more respect

for Trouble and his sidekick, Pluto," Roger admitted. "But I need your help with tracking my mother and Antoine."

Budgie was frowning. "And I need to show you something." He waved them over to a computer and pulled up the snapshot of the symbol Roger had emailed to him. "This has significance, but until I knew where to look, I can't find it. I've checked chemical tables, trademarks, you name it. And I know you somehow photographed it from the dash of Trudy's car." He rolled his eyes at DeWayne. "I don't even want to know how you did it. But I think Trudy Wells was trying to leave a message for us."

Tabitha's gaze locked with Roger's. He spoke first. "Trudy may have been trying to tell us something about an experimental cotton seed called G9-14. She had a lot of reservations about planting it. When it's daylight, we need to get testing done on my field where it's planted."

Tabitha controlled the rush of fear that swept through her. If Trudy had truly found that the seed was dangerous, someone very well may have taken her to silence her. "We have to find where Antoine and Hannah have gone," she said. "Please. If my sister is alive, they may be on the way to kill her."

DeWayne clapped Budgie on the shoulder. "Budgie is our own private little On Star. Find that car!"

Budgie began clicking and clacking at the computer while Trouble hopped on the desk to watch him. Pluto remained on the floor, looking up at Budgie's screen as if he could comprehend it.

In a moment, Budgie signaled them over. "This doesn't make any sense. The car is near an abandoned cotton gin in Lula. What would take them to a dying town near Moon Lake?"

Roger's eyes were flinty. "Cotton. This is all about cotton. Who owns that property?"

DeWayne picked up a phone and spoke briefly to someone on the other end. When he hung up, he looked at Roger and Tabitha. "Dirk Cotwell owns the old gin now. I just called Ainsley Thimes, the tax assessor. He knows every piece of property in the state. Dirk bought that last year from Martin Kennedy. Ainsley said Dirk was talking about turning it into a research facility for some new kind of cotton. A controlled environment."

"Lula is out of our jurisdiction," DeWayne said slowly. "We have no legal authority there. We could call the local sheriff--"

"No! If they are holding Trudy and they get wind we know where they are, they could kill her. Besides, I don't need legal authority. I just need to find my mother and I am going to wring the truth of her." Roger's expression was grim.

Budgie hit a button on the computer and a printer whirred to life. He picked up the page and handed it to Tabitha. "Here's the map. It should take you exactly to where the car is parked. Remember, a lot of folks don't take kindly to strangers poking around on their property. I don't have any authority to act, but I'll keep an eye on things here, with the tracker. If the car moves, I'll call you and send an updated map. DeWayne's going to check on Dirk."

"Thank you," Tabitha said. She grasped Budgie's hand and squeezed it. "Thank you both. For saving Roger. For everything."

THE VAST DELTA night was nothing but inky black fields and a sky that throbbed with starlight. Roger was acutely aware of Tabitha beside him in the truck. She had a striking profile, and he loved the way her red hair curled in, hugging her jawline and emphasizing her slender, elegant neck. She was a study in contrasts. Her tapered fingers, graceful wrists, and willowy body implied she was a delicate woman, but there was tensile strength in her and a will that a pro linebacker couldn't match. She was also kind-hearted, but she could do what was necessary, as she'd proven when she came into his household pretending to be something she wasn't.

She glanced at him and instinctively reached over and caught his hand. "You okay?"

"I'm good. Are you?"

She shook her head. "I'm praying Trudy is at the old gin, and yet I'm hoping that she isn't. What if she's...dead?"

"Mother and Antoine wouldn't risk going there if she was dead. They'd be headed for Atlanta and a flight to a country that doesn't have extradition." He gave her fingers a gentle squeeze. "They're going there because she is alive. We have to get there to make sure she stays alive. I think I can reason with my mother. I know she's greedy and awful, but at the séance, I caught a glimpse of the mother who cared about me. I think she's still there and I can reach her."

He was already doing ninety on the straight, empty roads, but he pressed a little harder on the gas and the powerful truck leaped forward. Trouble and Pluto looked at him, and he wondered if they were judging his driving. The idea was ridiculous, but he didn't dismiss it. The last few days had upended a whole lot of what he believed about his family, cats, and women.

Tabitha tensed in the front seat, and the cats put their paws on the dash as he slowed and killed his lights. Half a mile in the distance was the outline of the old gin. The building was a black void against a spangled sky, and had he not been looking for it, he might have missed it until he was right on top of it.

"How are we going to do this?" Tabitha asked.

"You're going to stay with the cats while I slip inside and take a look around. If it's safe, I'll call you to come in. If it's not safe, I'll send you a text and you can call the local law. And Budgie and DeWayne." He could tell she didn't like the idea of waiting in the truck, but she wasn't going to argue. She was smart. "If it's safe to come inside, I'll text a 7. If I'm in danger, I'll text a 9."

"Okay." She leaned across the cats and kissed him softly. "Be careful."

"Always." He got out and started walking on the side of the dirt path, his breath frosting in front of him. It was bitter cold, and he geared up into a jog. The dark, rusted tin building had once housed a miracle machine that pulled the seeds from the long fibers of the cotton in the first steps of preparation for it to be woven into cloth. Eli Whitney's cotton gin had revolutionized the production of cotton cloth, and now that 'technology' was passé. The old gin was a place of tin, rust, and abandoned history.

Wind cut across the wide-open Delta and rattled the tin, making it whine. In front of him, the building seemed to rise out of the darkness.

The open metal doors looked like the entrance to eternity, and Roger hesitated. He didn't have a weapon or a light, and while he was physically superior to Antoine, a gun would make all the difference. He slipped inside, allowing his eyes to adjust to the inky interior. From far at the end of the building came a tiny beam of light. Candle? Small flashlight? He couldn't say. He eased forward, using one hand to feel for anything that might trip him up. Voices carried to him from the back of the huge building.

"You couldn't leave well enough alone. We're in trouble, and part of it is because you kept poking into things."

It was Hannah's voice, and Roger felt a rush of relief. Hannah had to be talking to Trudy. She was berating her for poking into the cotton. Which meant that Antoine had likely invested a substantial amount of Hannah's potential inheritance in the experimental cotton. So what was it Hannah didn't want him to find out? What had Trudy suspected?

He crept forward. His mother's voice grew louder, and soon he could make out the shape of a room or office. The light and sound came from there. He crept toward the cracked doorway and was reaching for the knob when something heavy cracked his head. He dropped to his knees and toppled sideways, aware that he'd been caught unawares yet again—twice in one evening—and he was unable to do anything about it.

CHAPTER NINETEEN

*T*abitha *certainly has a stiff upper lip, but I can tell she's suffering. She's about to jump out of her skin, and I'm with her on that. Where is Roger? What's happened to him. It's been half an hour.*

But now there's a ringy-dingy on Miss Long Legs' phone. Whew! Relief. It must be him. No one else would be calling in the wee hours of the morning.

"Roger! Are you okay?"

Tabitha is almost breathless in her anticipation. And I can see from her face that this isn't good news. Oh, dear! What has transpired?

"I want to know that Roger is okay. And my sister. Do you have her too?"

Tabitha is fighting back tears, this isn't good. So now I must avail myself of a plan of action I should have taken thirty minutes ago. I love bipeds and they are remarkably accomplished at many things, but sneaking into a building undetected is not really their forte. Me and Pluto, on the other hand, we were born for spy missions. I give my companion the nod and he is right with me. A little pawing at the window and Tabitha is distracted and rolls it down. We are out of the truck and running down the road. I can only hope whoever she is talking to on the phone can convince her to stay out of the old gin.

Pluto concurs with me that we take whatever action is necessary. I'm more of a lover than a fighter, but when pushed into a corner, I come out swatting and clawing. Few villains are prepared for the wrath of a truly angry feline. It's like trying to grab a spinning ball of knives.

We're at the old gin and I have the strangest sense that the building is empty. This I am not prepared for. In the short time we've been waiting—well, thirty minutes is time enough for the villains to depart, I suppose. It would seem that whoever was here has gone and taken Roger with them.

Pluto and I split up and I head to the back of the gin where Roger's scent still lingers. He was here, but he is most definitely gone. And someone else was here too. Trudy? Perhaps, but Hannah was definitely here. That musky perfume she loves lingers long after she's gone. That woman deserves the Cruella Deville award. What mother would harm her own child? I have to find Pluto and get Tabitha to come and examine the area. She should call the coppers, or as they are called here in the South, the po-po. DeWayne and Budgie may not have any jurisdiction, but they do have fingerprint dust and the know-how to find out who else has been held in this little room. I'll bet Trudy has been here in the past.

Pluto agrees with me. We need to get Tabitha, and right away.

TABITHA SIGHED as she put the phone on the truck seat. Budgie had called to tell her that Hannah's car was on the move. And Roger had never called—which meant he was likely in serious trouble. The two cats had hauled it to check out the old gin, and she was left in the truck waiting. She felt like she'd been there a hundred years, almost paralyzed by her worry.

Now, though, she had to take action. Budgie and DeWayne had urged her to stay in the truck until they arrived, but she had to find Roger. What if he was injured? Or worse.

She drove slowly to the old gin and aimed the truck lights into the open doorway. The place reminded her of the maw of a whale. If she went inside would she be swallowed? She didn't care. If Roger was in there, she was going to find him and her sister.

Pluto and Trouble came running out of the building, meowing in the way she'd learned meant they had something to show her. She got out of the truck, taking an iron pipe she found in the bed of the truck with her. It wasn't much of a weapon but it was better than nothing.

Inside the building she paused to listen, but there was only silence. The building felt empty. She moved forward, slipping around old machinery and pieces of equipment highlighted by the truck's bright headlights. The cats scampered ahead of her, crying. She knew then there was no one else around. The cats would never display such carelessness if there was danger. They'd try to protect her. She followed them to a back room. A small pool of blood stopped her. It looked as if someone had been dragged.

She stepped in the room and realized there was a battery-operated storm lantern on the table. She turned it on and carefully glanced about the enclosed area. In the corner was a cot piled high with quilts and blankets. Someone had been kept in the room. It would have been bitterly cold, even with blankets. She moved toward the cot and noticed long, dark hairs on the pillow. It could be Trudy's hair. Had her sister been here?

The two cats jumped on the makeshift bed and began burrowing beneath the covers. Tabitha knew they weren't cold —they were looking for something. Evidence. She pulled off the top layers of bedding. A small ring fell to the floor and rolled.

She recognized it even before she picked it up. It was a Claddagh with a princess-cut emerald set in the center. Trudy's ring. She never took it off. Their mother had given it to Trudy when she was a small girl. She'd worn it on a necklace until her hands were big enough for the ring to fit. Trudy had left it for a message.

Tabitha felt both relief and apprehension. Trudy had to be alive to have left the ring, but she was nowhere in sight, and now Roger was missing too. There was no choice left. She had to come clean with the deputies about the cufflink and the business card, her suspicions about Antoine and Hannah, and the fact that Trudy's ring had been found in the old gin building, not to mention the hair that had been left on the pillow. DNA would prove whether her sister had been held in that cold little room or not. She didn't know what else to do but call the deputies and wait.

When DeWayne and the local deputies arrived, Tabitha was standing in the headlights from the truck so he could clearly see her. "Budgie is tracking Hannah's car," he said. "He'll check in with me, but if they have Roger or Trudy, he'll run them to ground and we'll get the help we need to bring them to justice. I couldn't find Dirk Cotwell, which is another concern." He looked down at the cufflink and ring she'd given him. "You should have told me about the cufflink sooner. We could have arrested Hannah and Antoine and held them, at least for a little while."

"I know." She sighed. "I was worried if they were holding

Trudy, they might let her starve or freeze." She decided to be completely honest. "And at first, I thought my sister might have gotten involved in something...not completely legal. She's been part of an environmental activist group. Green World. I didn't know what they might have planned."

He nodded. "I've got a kid brother of my own. The local deputies are going to go over this place with a fine-tooth comb. If there's a lead here, they'll find it. It's freezing out here. You should go home."

More than freezing, Tabitha dreaded having to tell Charline and Sam that Roger was missing, and that Hannah likely had taken him prisoner. Antoine had already proven that he would allow Roger to die in a fire. Could she really hope they'd keep him alive? It wasn't the news she wanted to deliver, but it had to be done. "Thanks, DeWayne."

She opened the truck door and the cats sprang inside. She was about to pull away when DeWayne signaled her to stop. She rolled down her window.

"I thought you'd want to know that Dirk Cotwell did own this gin, but just three weeks ago he sold the property to Antoine Fresca and a financial group. Budgie is on it, but it looks pretty shady. It's a front for someone or something."

The implications of that tidbit were far reaching. "Thanks for telling me."

"I know Hannah is Roger's mother. But that doesn't mean she won't hurt him or you."

"She's not a very nice person." That was an understatement.

DeWayne tapped the truck door twice. "Just be careful. Are you still going to meet that man for dinner? Budgie or I will be at the restaurant as your backup."

"Thank you." Tabitha nodded. "I have to carry forward. I don't know what else to do."

DeWayne gave her a sympathetic smile. "That's all you can do. One of us will be there early and keep an eye on things. Just remember, don't leave with him no matter what he says. And as soon as we have results on that hair, I'll let you know."

"I can't thank you enough." She waved and backed out. Day was breaking on the horizon. She had a lot to do, and she intended to keep her date with the man from the seed company, Alan Dotsun. Somehow, the experimental cotton played into everything that was going on. Things were getting very complicated, but she was determined to find out exactly how G9-14 figured into her sister and Roger's abduction. And she would bring both of them safely home. She had the cats to help her, and the Sunflower County deputies. And she had something she'd never expected—a sense that the world around her was not just the here and now, but that there was much more to the shadowy realm of death.

The big truck responded to her slightest touch, but she still felt uncomfortable driving Roger's vehicle. She had to get back to Long Hall, though, and it was the only transportation she had.

The sun was up and warming the fields when she pulled into Long Hall. She did her best to be quiet, but Charline was awake and waiting for her. She handed Tabitha a cup of strong, hot coffee and motioned her into a chair at the kitchen table. "Where's Roger?"

Tabitha told her everything, including her own role and how she'd come to Sunflower County under false pretenses. "I would never have done anything to harm your family."

"You believe Hannah and Antoine have taken Roger?" Charline's normally generous mouth was a thin line of anger.

"Yes. They have him and probably my sister."

"To what end?" Charline asked.

"It's something to do with the cotton. I don't know what, exactly. But there's money tied up in the experimental crop, and my sister was looking into it. She's part of a group of environmental activists. Roger didn't know this." Her voice broke, but she pulled herself together. "Roger went to talk to Hannah and Antoine, and now he's gone. He didn't just vanish."

"If they hurt him..."

Tabitha leaned forward. "You can't think that. Roger is her son. Despite her greed, surely she wouldn't harm her own child."

"I thought I knew Hannah." Charline's clear gaze pierced Tabitha and held her. "And I thought I knew you. I guess you both fooled me. You're not a psychic medium. You just used that to get close to us."

Tabitha couldn't undo the damage she'd created, but she had to try to make Charline understand. "Never with the intention of causing harm. I only wanted a chance to find my sister. I didn't know who to trust. It was complicated, and I did what I thought would cause no harm and yet allow me to hunt for Trudy."

"So everything you said about Suellen was just...a lie?"

Tabitha knew she'd face this question, and yet she wasn't completely prepared. "I didn't make up the things I said about Suellen or Micah Malone. Those images and emotions came to me as clearly as if I was experiencing them in the moment. I knew I was supposed to tell you. I realize you have every reason to doubt me, but please don't. Not about Suellen. She is here. She loves you and Samuel and Roger. She is distressed by Hannah and her behavior. She's afraid for her. I can't tell you how I know this, but it's all true."

"How did you know about Micah Malone? Did Roger tell you?"

Tabitha shook her head. "No, not really much more than you told me. He said that Micah was someone Hannah had once cared about. He hoped mentioning Micah would make his mother remember a time when she was...caring." Tabitha grasped Charline's hand and held it. "I felt what Micah felt, and Suellen, and Lisa. It was strange, but I don't doubt the truth of it. I can't prove it, but I believe Micah is Roger's father."

Charline's face reflected surprise, and then acceptance. "That makes perfect sense. Hannah was head over heels for Micah the first time he showed up on the beach. I thought it was love at first sight, but the way Micah spent time with Roger, the love he showed him. It all makes perfect sense."

"Do you think Roger is aware?"

Charline thought about it. "No. But he should be. And if this is true, Hannah should have told him long ago. Roger never says anything about being fatherless. He's never asked me if I know who his father is, and Hannah has used that knowledge like a cudgel. Samuel and I both are done with her. We'll put her share of the inheritance in a trust. Samuel says he and Roger can buy her out and be done with it."

Tabitha wasn't certain it would be that easy to do. Hannah had a plan, and she and Antoine had already initiated it. Taking Roger hostage was only one in a long line of bad acts. Antoine and Hannah obviously saw a big pay out—and they wouldn't settle for less. "Let's just get Roger and Trudy back and make sure they're safe."

"Samuel is going to talk to Mac MacKinney this morning to draw up the paperwork to freeze Hannah's portion of the trust. Hannah will sign it or we'll starve her out. She's already several months ahead of her monthly stipend. We can hold all funds for six months, at least. She can't last longer than six weeks."

Tabitha was surprised—and pleased—to see the steel in Charline's spine. Hannah was not going to get away with her behavior. "Do you have any idea where they might take Roger?"

Charline thought a moment. "We have a cabin at Moon Lake. I can call the caretaker and see if anyone has been up there."

"That would be a great help. Is there anything I can do to assist you?"

Charline shook her head. "I'm going with Samuel to see the lawyer, but I'll be back this afternoon. If you hear from Roger, please call."

"I will." Tabitha grasped Charline's hand. "I'm sorry for tricking you."

"You only told me good things. If you'd been trying to harm me, you could have said something else that would have disturbed me." She shrugged. "I wish Suellen were here. She'd know how to handle Hannah."

Before Charline even finished speaking, the bottom door of the sideboard cracked open and a skein of embroidery thread fell to the floor. The thread was a beautiful purple color. Charline picked it up and held it. "Suellen loved to embroider. She was working on a bread basket cloth with purple forget-me-nots." She bit her lip. "There is no way you could have made that happen."

"I didn't have a thing to do with it, but I believe Suellen wants you to finish that cloth if you feel up to it."

Charline nodded. "That I can do. As soon as we have our missing people back and Hannah and Antoine punished for their role in all of this." She put the thread in the pocket of her skirt and hurried out of the room. Tabitha was left sitting with the three cats, who lounged about the room. As soon as she stood, they all rose to attention. It was clear she wasn't going anywhere without them.

CHAPTER TWENTY

*R*oger came to full consciousness in the trunk of a car. The wheels hummed and he knew he was traveling over asphalt. It was a long, flat stretch of road. Too bad he couldn't determine how long he'd been knocked out. As he shifted his position, he realized that his hands were restrained behind his back, and he had a serious headache. Otherwise, he was unharmed. And being taken hostage could work to his advantage. He'd gambled on the fact that his mother wouldn't kill him outright—or let Antoine have the honor. He didn't know how long he could count on her "maternal" instinct, though. If she truly felt threatened by him, she would sacrifice him without a backward glance. In the meantime, he felt certain he would be taken to wherever they were holding Trudy Wells. It had cost him another knot on his head, but this was the quickest route to finding Tabitha's sister. The sooner he found her, the better her chances of survival.

As the car whirred down the asphalt, Roger assessed the damage to his body. His head throbbed and he was slightly nauseated, but nothing serious. As Charline had always teased him about his hard head, he had to admit she was right. He'd been struck from behind twice. And left to burn to death once. While his mother was a conniving witch, Antoine was an apparent murderer. The dapper con artist would have let Roger burn to death. Roger felt certain his mother's acknowledged fiancé was involved, if not the trigger man, in Lisa East's death. The arson at Lisa East's cottage had to be to destroy evidence.

The car turned off the highway and bumped down a rough dirt road. Roger felt every pothole and struggled to loosen the bonds on his wrists. Antoine was good with blunt force to the head, but not so good with ropes and knots. As Roger wiggled his bonds so that they loosened, he took satisfaction in thinking that when he got out of the car, he was going to make someone pay.

They traveled for another twenty minutes or so before the car stopped. Roger had freed his hands and he prepared himself for the confrontation, going limp and turning his head so that he was as concealed as possible. The latch popped and the trunk opened to a flood of light. He'd been in the luggage area of the car long enough for day to arrive. Tabitha would be fit to be tied.

He heard Antoine's voice outside the car, but he couldn't tell if his mother was present. Antoine was clearly annoyed.

"What are we supposed to do with him?" Antoine asked. "He's put himself in real danger. He knows too much. Him and that nosy psychic. She's no more a psychic than I'm an astronaut."

"Calm down, Antoine." Hannah's voice was like the crack of a whip. "You knew going into this it could get dicey. We can't turn back now. We almost have what we need. Roger isn't hurt. Not yet. And he'll be out of trouble here. There's a lot more riding on this than a few bumps on Roger's head, though you didn't have to hit him so hard."

"I took action because you failed to rein in your son. Had you done what you were supposed to do, we'd be sitting pretty now instead of worrying about what to do with...bodies."

All refinement was gone from Antoine's voice. The hint of culture and continental influences had been replaced by a flat accent. Roger realized the man wasn't even from Europe. He sounded more like he had ties to the Bronx. Roger forced himself to go limp when rough hands pulled him into a sitting position.

"Snap out of it." Antoine shook Roger. "Get out and walk. We don't have time for this. We could just leave him in the trunk."

"Don't be a fool," Hannah said. "Get him in the house. Make sure he's tied up good."

"Maybe you should help me. He's your flesh and blood."

Footsteps crunched in the shells of a driveway. "Listen, Antoine, we can use Roger to our advantage. So far, we've played our roles perfectly. Yes, this is a tight spot, but Lisa East is the only person who's dead, and we couldn't have prevented that. Let's get Roger inside."

Footsteps crunched away, and Roger felt strong hands pulling him out of the trunk. He moaned softly and rolled his head, looking all around. He saw a dark building set among trees. It was a cabin in the woods, a retreat. And he knew it. Big Samuel Long had built the cabin back in the 1940s as a get-away. Roger had hosted a few high school parties there. He and his buddies had followed the worn path to hangovers and regret that most teenagers traveled. They'd pretended to be all grown up and drank and told stories, played cards, talked about girls. The cabin had been a big part of high school summers.

Since he'd assumed the mantel of running Long Agricultural, he'd almost forgotten the place existed. It was the perfect hideaway, nestled in dense woods with access to Moon Lake and no neighbors. Not far away was a small, isolated little island that he'd loved as a boy. Moon Lake had once been a part of the Mississippi River, but over time, the river had changed course, and this bend had been cut off, leaving a deep lake.

Having a sense of where he was gave him a semblance of control. He'd also deduced that there was only Antoine and Hannah with him. But Antoine and his mother seemed worried about someone else.

"Wake up. Come on, Roger, we have things to finish." Antoine lifted Roger's upper body out of the trunk.

Roger had loosened the rope around his wrists, but he knew if he intended to take any action, his timing had to be perfect. He lolled forward, seeming to bang his head on the trunk lid.

"Come on, stay on your feet," Antoine ordered as he roughly grasped Roger's upper arm.

Roger made his move. He used his left leg to kick at Antoine's ankles, sending the man sprawling into the shells of the drive. When Antoine was down, Roger didn't hesitate. He stomped hard on his chest with all of his weight. The air left Antoine in a whoosh. Roger finished him off with a kick to the head.

"Stay down," Roger said. It took him another moment to work his hands free. He used the rope to secure Antoine and dragged him to the side of the driveway. He also recovered his cell phone from Antoine's pocket. To his disgust, the phone was completely dead. He dropped it into his pocket and jogged toward the cabin.

He'd moved Antoine out of sight in the weeds, but Hannah would be looking for him any minute. He knew his mother. She gave a command and expected instant obedience. Well, he had a surprise for her. At the thought of it, a tight smile crept over his face as he hurried to the cabin and silently climbed the steps.

He listened for a moment at the front door, but no sounds came from inside. Without waiting, he kicked the door as hard as he could, sending it crashing from the frame. He stepped into the large den where Hannah stood. She was frozen in place, a kettle of water in her hand.

"Hello, Mother," he said.

She hurled the kettle at him and took off for the back of the house, but he was quicker. "I don't think so," he said. "There's a very inviting car trunk waiting for you. It might be a little crowded with Antoine in there too."

"How did you get loose? Listen, you have to stay here at the cabin," she said. "I don't have time to explain. Where's Antoine?"

"He's a little indisposed. Now you can make this easy, or you can make it hard, but either way, I'm going to tie you up."

To her credit, Hannah didn't resist him. In a few moments, he had her tied to a kitchen chair with the electrical cord from a lamp. "Now where is Trudy Wells?"

"I don't know what you mean."

"Mother, now isn't the time to play games."

"I have no idea who you're talking about."

"My employee. The young woman who worked as a receptionist."

Hannah lifted her chin in a classic move that Roger recognized, and couldn't help but admire. Even tied to a chair with retribution staring her in the face, Hannah played it regale. "I don't know where she is. Why should I?"

"Because you and Antoine abducted her. I found his cuff-link in her car, which was hidden in a thick brake on my land. Now spill it. I'll tell the police you helped me find Trudy. I'll ask for leniency."

"Roger, I've been trying to protect you, but you need to let me loose and get Antoine. We don't have long."

Roger's headache intensified. He was so close to finding Trudy. So close. "Sit tight, Mother. Then again, you don't have a choice." He quickly scouted out the rest of the cabin hoping that Trudy was stashed there somewhere. He didn't want to punish his mother, not really. He only wanted to find Trudy and deliver her safety to her worried sister.

Even though he tossed the rooms hurriedly, he found no evidence that Trudy had been held there. No sign that anyone had occupied the cabin. He felt his plan unraveling, and he returned to the kitchen. "Mother, where is Trudy? Let me help you."

"I don't have a clue," she said, staring past him. You always assume the worst of me, and I really don't blame you. This is different, though. Antoine and I--"

"Just stop!" His mother was going to do the thing she always did—find a way to cast herself as the victim. "Tell me now or I'm going to gag you and leave you here while I find that young woman."

"I swear to you, I didn't have anything to do with Lisa East's death or the disappearance of that other young woman. I swear it."

Roger held the gag right at her mouth. He took no pleasure in tormenting his mother but he also didn't believe a word that came out of her mouth. And he didn't trust that she would keep quiet in a pinch. He feared she'd willingly give his position away, given an opportunity. The hard facts were that if Trudy wasn't with Antoine and Hannah, then they were working with someone else. Someone who could show up at the cabin any moment. Someone who might be armed. "Last chance. Where is Trudy?"

"Let me loose and I'll tell you everything I know. She's safe, for the moment. I swear it. Antoine and I, we aren't what you think. We're involved in exploring this new cotton."

"I know. Big financial investment, right. Now where is Trudy?"

"I don't know. I swear to you. Antoine and I don't have her."

A chill traced down Roger's back. Hannah was an extremely good actress, and he couldn't tell if she was pretending to be innocent or not. He faced her. "Look, if what you're saying is true and you didn't have anything to do with Lisa's death or with Trudy's abduction, I'm sure you'll make out just fine with the authorities. Right now, I have to find Trudy and return her safely to her sister." He started to put the gag in place.

"Wait! What are you doing?"

"I'm going to make sure you won't try to warn anyone if your confederates show up here."

"Don't tie me up and leave me here. Please. You don't understand what the consequences will be. For me and for Antoine."

"You presume I care." He had a thought. "Where's your phone?"

She indicated her jacket that hung over the back of a kitchen chair. Roger fished the phone out. He didn't remember Tabitha's number, but Charline's number was programmed into the phone. He made the call.

"Hannah, where are you?" Charline answered, her voice frayed with worry. "Roger is missing. Do you know where he is?"

Roger realized Charline had looked at the caller ID and presumed his mother was calling. "Aunt Charline, it's me, Roger. Mother is here with me. She's...detained. But she's fine. Please tell Tabitha that I'm okay."

"I'm going to put you on speaker," Charline said. "Tabitha is right here with me. Samuel and I have been worried sick about you. Where are you?"

"The cabin on Moon Lake. Mother and Antoine are involved in some bad business, Aunt Charline. Would you call the sheriff's department and ask DeWayne or Budgie to send some Coahoma County deputies to the cabin? I know you can give them directions. Mother and Antoine will be here. Restrained and waiting."

"I'll take care of it." Charline didn't bother with extraneous questions. "Where are you going, Roger?"

"Antoine knows where Trudy Wells is. He's going to tell me. Now."

"Be careful, Roger. Antoine is not what he appears to be. Neither is your mother."

"I've come to that conclusion on my own." Roger chuckled. "Mother is in this up to her neck."

"It grieves me to hear that, Roger. Hannah is difficult, but I've always cared about her. I know deep-down, you do too."

The gut punch hit Roger, and he had to acknowledge it. "I do love her. I'm sorry it's come to this, but she has to answer for what she's done. Is Tabitha okay?"

"She is. She's been worried too. She wants to talk to you."

"Listen, I hear someone driving up." He knew his time was short and he had to get the basic information to Charline. "I'm going to find Trudy."

Charline's voice was choked with emotion. "Remember the nature of a scorpion. They bite because that's what they do. Antoine is a scorpion from everything Tabitha discovered."

"I'll remember that, and I'll call back when I can." Roger had been watching his mother's reaction to his conversation. When a slow smile curled her lips, he knew something was going on. He dodged left just as the front door banged open. Hannah's scream rang out and the phone crashed to the floor, knocked out of Roger's hand by a flying screw driver.

"Don't let Tabitha come here. Whatever you do, keep her away. It's too--" Roger said before the phone went dead.

CHAPTER TWENTY-ONE

abitha froze in the kitchen, her gaze locking with Charline's as the older woman called the Sunflower County sheriff's office. Once DeWayne had promised to assist Roger, Charline sank into a chair. She dropped the phone to her side. "Help is on the way."

"Someone was there, at the cabin," Tabitha said. She'd clearly heard the crashing of a door, though she hadn't been able to decipher Roger's last words.

"Yes, I think someone Roger wasn't expecting arrived." Charline redialed the phone several times but there was no answer.

Tabitha knew that Roger wouldn't respond. Whatever he was caught up in, he couldn't talk on the phone. "Do you know where Roger is? Where is this cabin?"

Charline had gone pasty white. "He doesn't want you there."

"Please." Tabitha thought her chest would crack open from the pressure of her emotions. "I have to help him."

"You can't. If you put yourself in danger, it will only backfire on Roger. He was clear, Tabitha. He said not to allow you to go to him."

"He said Trudy wasn't at the cabin. So where is she?"

Charline shook her head. "Hannah and Antoine were there. He said he allowed them to take him prisoner so he could find Trudy. Apparently, he somehow got the upper hand of them. Until…" She didn't finish.

Tabitha sank into a kitchen chair. "He's put himself at great risk. I can't let him do this alone. She's my sister. He's doing this for me."

"And Trudy is his employee. Don't discount the fact that Hannah is his mother, and it seems she's likely to blame for all of this. Hannah won't hurt Roger. As awful as she is, she won't harm her son." Charline's eyes blazed. "Especially if Roger is, as you suspect, Micah's child. I do believe Micah Malone was the only person Hannah has ever truly loved."

Charline's words allowed Tabitha to get a grip on her emotions. She nodded slowly. "What you say makes sense."

"If you go there and confront Hannah or Antoine, and if Roger is in their power, you may provoke them to harm him. Antoine has no kind feelings toward Roger. I'm sure he views all of us as barriers to what he hopes to achieve—getting his hands on Hannah's money. She's always been a fool about men and their motivations."

"And now Roger is with her."

"If anyone can bring her around, it's Roger. I know how difficult it is, but you have to give him the room to convince her. If anyone can make her see reason, it's him. And he deserves this opportunity. Hannah may end up in prison, but Roger needs to know that he did all he could to help her. Just like you need to know you turned over every rock to find your sister."

Charline was right. As difficult as it was going to be, she had to heed Roger's request. Even if she died a little inside worrying about him and Trudy. She put her palms on the table and tried for a smile. "This is why so many famous songwriters explore the dangers of love. I've never felt such emotional pain."

Charline sighed. "Your feelings for Roger have grown deep and true, it seems."

"I don't know what I really feel, except this all-consuming panic at the idea he might be hurt. The same panic I feel for my sister."

Charline's smile was slow and rueful. "To love is to risk pain. Many songwriters have plowed that field." Her expression was pensive. "Maybe one day soon Samuel, Roger, and I can hear you perform some of the songs you've written."

Tabitha didn't hide her surprise. "I didn't expect that from you. I came here with a lie on my lips. Now you want to encourage my songwriting."

"I know. It doesn't make logical sense, but whatever lies you told, they were told for love. You didn't know if you could trust us to help you or if we might have been behind your sister's disappearance. I understand the subterfuge."

"Thank you." Even though she was still desperately worried about Trudy and Roger, Tabitha felt as if a stone had been lifted from her heart. "I still need to go to that cabin. Please."

"I'm sorry. My nephew asks very little of me. This is one time I intend to make sure I deliver for him. And for you and your sister. You have to put some trust in Roger, in his abilities."

"It's not that I don't trust him, but he isn't the kind of man to shoot another."

"I know. But give him a chance. Why don't you see if you

can find out more about Antoine Fresca? My gut tells me that he's the dangerous element. The more we know, the better prepared we'll be."

"You're right, but I'd rather go to the cabin."

"Let's wait to see what Budgie and DeWayne discover."

It wasn't the plan Tabitha wanted, but she knew Charline was acting in Roger's best interest. "Let me see what else I can find out about Antoine. Maybe he has an Achilles' Heel we can use against him."

"I'll get my laptop for you," Charline offered. "Roger keeps trying to drag me into the information age, but I resist. You can put it to good use."

"Thank you."

Tabitha pushed her reluctant body up the steps and to her room. More than anything she wanted to take action, to go to the cabin where Roger was facing danger alone. Trudy wasn't there, but maybe there was evidence that would lead them to her. Staying at Long plantation, working a keyboard, was the last thing she wanted to do.

When Charline delivered the computer, Tabitha took it and sat at a small table by a window that gave a view of the newly sprouted fields. The whirls of rows created a patchwork of brown and green. Lovely. She took a breath and went to work, checking financial companies, searching for any evidence of Antoine's background.

ROGER CROUCHED in the tall grass behind the cabin. He'd cut his mother's bonds before he darted out the backdoor. No matter what she might have done, she was still his mother. He couldn't leave her tied in a chair when he didn't know who was breaking into the cabin or what they intended to do. He circled around the cabin to the parked rental car. When he got there, he wasn't surprised to find that Antoine was missing. Someone had set him free. The ropes remained in the trampled grass.

"Damn." Roger needed only ten minutes with Antoine to make him talk, and now that had been taken from him. He had to assume that whoever had freed Antoine was working with the dapper crook and Hannah. So his mother would not be harmed. She'd played him yet again. He could release his worry for her and concentrate on finding Trudy.

Hidden behind the car, he scouted the area. The intruder had arrived in a silver sedan he didn't recognize and he was positioned where he couldn't see the license plates. Roger looked in the window of his mother's car and saw the keys dangling from the ignition. Antoine had been in such a hurry, he'd failed to take the keys. It was a slim chance, but Roger had to take it. He opened the door, slid behind the wheel, and drove off. Luckily he knew where he was and could navigate the twists and turns of the lakeside road. He was also aware that there was only one road in and out of the cabin until it joined a paved road—County Road 409. All was not lost.

At the junction of 409, he found a wooded drive that was almost hidden. He took the time to back into it, gritting his teeth at the sound of the branches digging into the paint of the expensive car. There was no help for it. When he was certain he couldn't be seen from the road, he killed the engine. He had a clear, unobstructed view of the only road out of the cabin. And he knew what vehicle would be passing—the silver sedan he'd seen parked at the old cabin.

Soon, he could pick up his mother's trail. She would lead him to Trudy one way or the other. And he would discover who was helping Hannah and Antoine—crucial information.

All he had to do was wait. And fret. Because he knew that Tabitha and his aunt and uncle would be worried sick.

IT TOOK ONLY a few moments for Tabitha to familiarize herself with the laptop. T&S Financials was her first search. The company was only a few years old, and it was headquartered in Switzerland. While there was a website and list of services, the site was strangely empty. That gave Tabitha some concern. She argued with herself that Antoine claimed to be an international player, so it wasn't uncommon to have a business located in Switzerland. But she also understood that a lot of companies hiding things had foreign locations. The more she dug into T&S, the less certain she was that it was a legitimate company at all. It seemed more like a ghost company.

When she checked Antoine's resume, she found he'd been involved with financial organizations in the states and Europe. He also had an impressive background in agricultural investment and development. Which meant he might have more information about the G9-14 cotton that Trudy had been poking into. It lined him up perfectly to be the culprit behind Trudy's disappearance and Lisa East's death.

Tabitha had to wonder if Hannah was aware of the web of lies he'd spun. Perhaps she was complicit or maybe just a dupe. If that were the case, Roger was in terrible danger. Trying to save his mother might cost his own life—if Hannah didn't want to be saved.

For nearly two hours Tabitha worked the Internet to find everything she could on Antoine and Hannah. Where Antoine was found in financial news—all in recent years--Hannah was mentioned in a number of international gossip columns for her party-girl and scandalous ways. She traveled among the upper echelons of international jetsetters. There were photos of her at the opening of plays in London, tennis matches at Wimbledon, and gaming tables in Monaco—always with a handsome man on her arm. She was a very conspicuous society woman. And most recently with Antoine. It was a lifestyle of glitter and lack of substance, as far as Tabitha could tell. For all of her high living, her life seemed terribly empty. Much as Tabitha's heart felt.

At last Charline tapped on her door. When Tabitha answered, she stood in the hallway. "DeWayne is working with the Coahoma County deputies and he went to the cabin. It's empty."

Tabitha felt as if a mule had kicked her in the stomach. "What?"

"There's no one there. But the good news is that there's no sign of foul play. No blood, no indication that anyone was roughed up."

"But we heard someone breach the cabin." Tabitha was confused.

"There is no indication of anything untoward. No sign that anyone was held prisoner there. It was absolutely empty."

"Where is Roger then?"

Charline inhaled deeply. "I don't know. The deputies don't know. They're scouring the place, but DeWayne doesn't think there's anything to find there." She braced against the door frame. "And now I wish I'd listened to you and gone to the cabin. But it's too late for that."

The ringing of the doorbell startled Charline. "Samuel has gone into town to talk with the lawyer and I gave Nancy the day off. Let me get that."

"I'll come with you." Tabitha was eager for any distraction, and with so much going on, she wanted to be sure Charline was safe.

The two women hurried down the stairs and Charline opened the front door. Tabitha recognized the new arrival, the beautiful Lily Kennedy.

"Why, Lily. What brings you to Long Hall?" Charline was surprised and didn't hide it.

"I need to speak with Roger." The tall, slender blonde stepped into the foyer. She smiled at Tabitha and held out her hand as she made introductions. "I'm Lily Kennedy." Tabitha shook hands with the young woman.

"Roger isn't here, Lily. Can I help you?"

"Do you know where he is?" Her smile faltered as she asked. "It's very important that I talk to him."

"He can't be reached right now. Can I help you?" Charline was kind but firm.

Lily shook her head. "No. You're going to think me a complete fool."

"What's going on?" Charline asked. "Maybe Tabitha and I can help."

Lilly looked down and sighed. "I feel like a fool. Dirk is off the radar and I was hoping Roger might know where he is. Dirk has taken to disappearing, and it's gotten under my skin. I know I'm spoiled, but we're planning a wedding. Roger didn't mention... Could you tell me where he is? Maybe he's heard from Dirk."

"Roger's away on business, and we haven't heard from Dirk. Not recently. We haven't seen Dirk in a few weeks. Or at least I haven't. We've missed him." Charline was trying not to show how flustered she was. "Would you like some tea or coffee?"

"No, thank you. And I apologize for just dropping by. I'm afraid I interrupted a psychic reading or something." She gave

Tabitha a knowing look. "I'd really like to have you stop by my parents' place if you have time this week. You have quite the reputation around the county."

"Of course." Tabitha would figure a way out of the session at a later date.

"Are you busy now?" Lily asked. "You could come over now."

"I'm afraid I am busy." Tabitha forced a smile. "Later in the week would be much better."

Lily pulled a card from her purse. "Here's my number. Call me, please. I'm so excited about this. I'm getting married this summer, and I'd love to see what my Grandmother Charlotte has to say about Dirk. She passed away about five years ago, and she was smart as a tack. I'm sure she's watching over me and will have some good advice. And if Roger has any idea where Dirk might be, please ask him to call. That man of mine, it's like trying to put on a cat ballet. We have a date with the wedding planner and I think Dirk has deliberately ditched the meeting. Typical man. He acts like planning the wedding is worse than pulling teeth."

"These Delta men are spoiled," Charline agreed. "They're used to us taking care of all the little details and life just magically happens for them."

"Very true. They don't know how lucky they are." Lily smiled at Tabitha. "We love our men, but they can test our patience. Nice to meet you, Tabitha. I hope you do find time to visit with my family."

"Sure thing."

Lily gave a wave as she left. In a moment she was roaring down the driveway in her cute blue sports car.

"She's a lovely young woman from a sterling family," Charline said, "and she's going to have her hands full with Dirk. I doubt he'll ever settle down completely."

Tabitha didn't know how much Charline knew about Dirk's carousing—and dating her sister—so she said nothing. Roger would handle that situation when he came home and when Trudy was found.

"I'm going to try for a nap," Tabitha said. She had a long night ahead of her, and if she expected to learn anything, she needed to be alert.

"Good idea. If anything changes, I'll wake you." Charline gave her arm a squeeze. "This will work out right in the end. I feel it."

BLAST AND BE DAMNED. I should have stuck with Roger. From all the reports, he's managed to get himself in a pinch with that ogre of a mother and her sidekick. I don't know what Hannah and Antoine are up to, but it can't be good. While Tabitha entered Long Hall under false pretenses, her heart was in the right place. I can't say the same for Hannah and Antoine. There's something very off about those two. They're deep into this cotton business, and what a wall of subterfuge they've thrown up. This doesn't parse. They're always showing up where the next crisis is about to happen. And yet when they had the chance to rid themselves of Roger, they didn't. Maternal tenderness? It hardly seems to fit Hannah.

The lovely Tabitha is distressed about Charline's recent news regarding Roger's disappearance. She's holding it together, and because she has to follow through on her plans tonight to meet her date, she needs to get some shut eye. She's been up far too long—and she'll need her wits about her. Let me see if I can nudge her toward the bed. She's giving me that look—the one that says, yes, I know you are a wise cat but I am stubborn. But yes, she is stretching out on the bed.

I'll wait until she nods off and then I need to run to the agricultural office. I have to find the reports on that cotton. There's something we missed. There has to be. If I can find that, Tabitha will be armed tonight when she meets up with Alan Dotsun. Perhaps he is just a man looking for a dinner date. Or perhaps he's someone who knows more about G9-14. Without Roger here to protect Tabitha, it's all up to me. And Pluto. And we won't let Tabitha down. That's one vow I will make and keep.

CHAPTER TWENTY-TWO

*a*n hour passed before the silver sedan sped past Roger's hideaway. There appeared to be someone in the passenger seat and possibly in the back seat. They'd gone by so fast Roger hadn't been able to see clearly. He waited a moment before he pulled out to tail the car. He had to be very careful. Antoine and Hannah knew he'd taken their rental car —they knew what to look for. He could only hope they'd assumed he'd made a run for it instead of waiting to follow them. Now it was a matter of skill to tail them without being detected.

Once Roger had cleared the back road and turned onto a highway, he was able to follow them with less anxiety. Hannah, Antoine, and whoever else was in the vehicle were clearly heading back to Sunflower County—and he hoped to the place where they were holding Trudy. One of his deepest regrets was that he hadn't been able to make Hannah tell him if Trudy was alive or not. He also regretted he didn't have his cell phone. How much easier it would have been to call DeWayne or Budgie and gotten them to set up roadblocks. The car he was pursuing could have been stopped and the occupants questioned. As it was, he couldn't risk trying to borrow a phone. He might lose their trail.

No, he was stuck following like an old hound dog. But when his prey finally came to rest, he'd have them and he'd have the element of surprise.

Roger checked his watch. The afternoon was slipping away as he rolled down a county highway headed vaguely southeast. Soon Tabitha would be going for her date with the guy from Grundle Seed Company, Alan Dotsun. DeWayne and Budgie had promised that one of them would be in Tom's Big Sizzle to make sure Tabitha was safe, but Roger wanted to be nearby. Just in case. He felt things were coming to a head, and he was afraid for Tabitha. She was so single-minded in her pursuit of her sister. He didn't blame her for that, but he did worry about her.

And he was worried about Trudy. If only he'd been worried sooner.

He went back over their discussions about the G9-14 seed. Trudy had suggested that he take a pass on planting the seed until the company claims had been proven. He would never classify Trudy as a traditionalist—heck, she was more of a rebel and risk taker. Looking back, he should have listened to her. It seemed only Lisa East had been willing to heed Trudy's warning and it had cost Lisa her life.

He also wondered how involved Dirk Cotwell had been in Lisa's death. Dirk had owned the old cotton gin where he felt certain Trudy had been held. And Dirk had ties to Trudy that he might not have wanted exposed. Dirk had a lot to lose. He'd planted a thousand acres in G9-14 and Trudy—his "kind of" girlfriend—could blow the lid off Dirk's engagement to Lily Kennedy.

Roger couldn't help but wonder if Trudy had been working Dirk the whole time, dating him to gather information. That would really make Dirk angry, and Dirk had quite a temper. Had Dirk abducted Trudy? How were Hannah and Antoine involved? He thought he had all the pieces, but he couldn't make them fit together.

He went back over the evidence they'd collected—first off the T&S cufflink proved Antoine was involved in Trudy's disappearance. And Hannah's and Antoine's actions proved they were capable of harming someone. Antoine had knocked him out and left him near a burning house.

But why? Hannah and Antoine wanted money—they wanted to be involved in farming? Why, when his mother had never shown the least interest in what happened at Long Agricultural. Why now the sudden interest?

The thing that had changed in the last four months was that he'd hired Trudy and had planted an experimental cotton seed. Those two things combined had put him in the place he was right now, trailing his mother and her lover as they crossed into Sunflower County. And once he understood how those two things connected with his mother, he would be able to solve the riddle of who had Trudy and where they were holding her. And why.

If he assumed that Lisa East had been killed because of something she knew, then the obvious question was why Trudy had not been killed. And the more time that passed, he felt even more certain Trudy was alive. Sunflower County was very rural, but hiding a body wasn't as easy as it sounded. But neither was hiding a living woman.

If only he had a phone he could check with the deputies and see if they'd turned up any results from their forensic examination of the old cotton gin mill and the Long cabin.

Surely the police had checked it by now, even though Antoine and Hannah had eluded them.

To his surprise, the car he followed headed straight into downtown Zinnia. He dropped back to allow two cars to get between him and his quarry. The vehicle pulled into the back parking lot of the Prince Albert and stopped. Roger parked on the street. Something was very wrong with this. Antoine and Hannah had all but walked into a trap with their eyes wide open.

He walked to the back parking lot, taking care to remain concealed behind some shrubs and other cars, and watched as Dirk Cotwell got out of the silver sedan. Of all the people he'd expected to see, none of them were Dirk. He entered the hotel. After a few minutes, when no one else left the vehicle, Roger eased closer to it. What he'd assumed to be two additional passengers was nothing but piled up clothes. No one else was in the car. He'd been played.

Heat flushed through him and he pivoted on his heel and stalked toward the hotel door. Where in the hell was his mother and Antoine? And then he knew. Dirk had been the bait, the tease that had drawn Roger away so that Hannah and Antoine could make good on their escape. But how? They didn't have a vehicle, or at least not one he'd seen. Obviously, Hannah had hidden a get-away car somewhere nearby. Roger felt his temper flair. Dirk would answer for his role in what was happening.

Roger went into the hotel and it didn't take him long to find Dirk at the bar. The bartender put a Maker's Mark on the rocks in front of him, and Dirk took a healthy swallow.

Roger put a hand on Dirk's shoulder and spun him around, "Where's my mother?"

Dirk shook him off and stood. "At the cabin."

"You left her and Antoine there?" Roger hadn't anticipated that comment.

"They were fine. They said a friend was coming up to visit with them. What's wrong with you? You're acting like I robbed a bank or something."

"Or something. What were you doing there?" Roger asked.

Dirk studied him for a moment before he answered. "I don't know what bee got in your bonnet, but it's clear you're really upset, so I'll tell you. It was really weird, but I got a call from a woman who said that Trudy was waiting for me in the cabin. I've been trying to find her for a couple of weeks." He sighed. "Look, I'm worried about her. I care. I know I don't have a right to care. I know I'm making trouble for myself and my future. But I can't help but worry that dating me has something to do with Trudy's disappearance. Maybe I put her in danger."

That was a revelation Roger hadn't expected. Dirk had put his whole heart into winning Lily Kennedy's hand. She was everything he needed to boost his social and economic aspirations to the moon. Roger didn't know if Dirk loved Lily, but they were a perfect match--they each brought something remarkable to the table. With Lily, it was her family and social standing. Dirk brought great business sense and a willingness to work long and hard. Never had he thought to hear Dirk proclaim feelings for a woman who could upset his carefully laid plans.

"Did you harm Trudy?" He had to ask.

Dirk's shoulders slumped. "No. I would never. I'm as worried about her as you are."

"This woman who called you—do you know who it was?"

"I can't say for certain, and I have no idea why she wanted me to drive to the Long cabin. It doesn't make any sense. Trudy wasn't there. Just your mother and Antoine. They were as shocked to see me as I was them." He frowned. "They were really weird acting and seemed in a rush to get me out of there. I was in a hurry too, so I didn't question it. But I should have. Your mother acted like she was afraid."

Roger didn't know if that was accurate. It seemed Hannah and Antoine had a knack for manipulating people and they knew everyone was looking for Trudy. Maybe they'd used Dirk. "Did you ever notice anyone else watching Trudy?"

Dirk thought for a long moment. "You know, I did see a car near her cottage several times. I didn't think much about it."

Roger swallowed. "Can you tell me anything about it?"

"It was a nondescript car parked down the street. A couple of times there was a woman in the car."

"Could it have been my mother?" Roger was prepared for anything.

"No, this woman was more petite. Short." Dirk shrugged. "I figured she was visiting someone on the road. I didn't give it another thought."

Roger had one more thought. He motioned the bartender for a pen and picked up a napkin. He drew the strange symbol that Trouble had found in Trudy's car and on her calendar. "Does this mean anything to you?"

Dirk nodded. "Not sure what it means, but it looks like a rune. A Celtic divination tool."

"And you know this how?"

"Trudy. She was very interested in runes. She said she had a friend in New Orleans who used them to tell fortunes. She cast the stones a few times for me, but just for fun."

"And how do runes work?" It made sense. Tabitha had friends who'd given her enough schooling in psychic methodology to pass herself off. She'd learned it in the French Quarter where she and Trudy lived.

"The symbols have specific meanings. The stones are cast and the pattern they fall in tells the person reading them answers to questions."

"And this rune?"

"I couldn't say. Look it up on the internet."

"Brilliant! Can I borrow your phone?" Roger asked.

Dirk handed over his cell phone. "Go ahead, man. I'm going to finish this drink and try to figure out how to piece my life back together. You always told me playing around would end up hurting me. I should have listened."

Roger clicked through the screens until he came to a website with illustrated runes. It took only a moment to find the one he recognized. When he did, he felt a cold chill. The rune represented poison. He examined it closely to be sure. There was no mistake. Trudy had been trying to tell them something with the symbol in the car—and it was the same thing that was on her calendar the day she disappeared.

"I'm going to make a few calls," Roger told Dirk.

"Sure. Help yourself." Dirk motioned the bartender for another drink as Roger stepped away from the bar for some privacy.

TABITHA TOOK the call on the first ring. She was parked outside Tom's Big Sizzle, killing time until her "date" with Alan Dotsun. Budgie was there, out of uniform and posing as a typical customer. Everything was perfectly set up—except she didn't know where Roger was or what had happened to him. Beside her, Trouble stared out the window, watching people come and go.

"Roger! Where are you? Are you okay?" The relief she felt was so overwhelming she wanted to cry. It was the release from fear and worry.

"Fine. I'm in Zinnia at the Prince Albert bar with Dirk. Let me tell you what I know."

Tabitha caught a glimpse of a fancy car pulling into the jammed parking lot. Tom's Big Sizzle was a hopping dinner place. Blues throbbed in the night, along with laughter. This was a good place to meet someone she was suspicious of, she thought, watching as a young woman got out of the fancy car —a woman who looked vaguely familiar to Tabitha.

"Make it quick, Roger. I've got five minutes before I need to go inside and start this charade of a date. I'd like to get inside before he arrives so I can watch him." Trouble sat up and put a paw on the window button. The glass rolled down and the cat took off, disappearing into the night.

"The symbol on Trudy's calendar and in her car represents poison. You have to be really careful, Tabitha. I don't understand how everything fits, but I believe Trudy has been investigating the cotton from the beginning. Grundle Seed may be behind all of this. They stand to lose a huge amount of money if that seed is poisonous or doesn't live up to the hype."

"Poison?" That stopped Tabitha.

"I don't know what Trudy may have meant, but I found out from Dirk that the symbol is a rune. Trudy told him that much. Did your sister ever study Celtic runes?"

Tabitha tried to keep an eye on Trouble, but he'd disappeared. "Maybe. She had a lot of the same friends I did in New Orleans. We've always been around tarot cards and other things like that. Runes are just another tool." She hesitated. "I think maybe Trudy had a set of the stones. I seem to remember them."

"Okay, so what role does the poison play?"

Tabitha knew. It was so simple. So absolutely simple. "It's the cotton seed. Trudy was studying it and she must have realized the seed was dangerous. Poisonous. Lisa was clutching seed in her hand when she died, remember?"

"Don't leave that restaurant. I'm on my way," Roger said.

"Budgie and Trouble are here with me. Where are Hannah and Antoine?"

"I don't know and don't really care right now. I just want you to stay safe until I get there. Whatever you do, don't leave the restaurant. Especially not with anyone from Grundle Seed company. You could be in real danger, Tabitha."

"And so could my sister," Tabitha said. She got out of the car and started into the restaurant. "I have to go, Roger." She clicked the phone off, slid it into her purse, and walked into the restaurant with a smile.

Budgie leaned against the bar, sipping a cola, along with four or five other single men. There were plenty of available women there too, and in the dining area, couples watched the band and the action at the bar. Tabitha checked her watch. She was on time, but there was no sign of Alan Dotsun. The dating service had sent her a video profile and she'd studied his features. He simply wasn't at the restaurant.

"Tabitha!" A woman called out to her. She faced Felicity Montgomery, who had taken a table and was waving her over.

"I didn't expect to see you here," Tabitha said. She was a little unnerved to find Roger's employee there, but she realized she shouldn't have been. The Delta was a very social place and music was at the heart of it. Music and good food. And she could smell the delicious aroma of grilling steaks.

Felicity stood to whisper in her ear. "Alan sent me. Something came up. It's about Trudy." Felicity could barely contain her excitement. "I know where she is. Alan asked me to meet you and bring you to her."

Tabitha swallowed. "You know where Trudy is? Is she okay?"

"She is. But you need to come with me. Alan said he could help us negotiate for her freedom. We don't have long. Come on!"

Tabitha glanced back at the bar. She had to alert Budgie. She'd promised she wouldn't leave the bar. To her surprise, the man sitting next to Budgie took a swing at him. The deputy countered the swing, but in a matter of seconds, several people were engaged in the brawl, which seemed to be spreading. "What the hell?"

Felicity laughed. "That's Howdy Howell. He starts a fight somewhere every night. Budgie can handle him. Let's go."

Tabitha looked around for Trouble. She couldn't just leave the cat. "Have you seen that black cat?"

"Yeah, he went out the door. He's smart enough to avoid a bar fight." Felicity lightly grasped her wrist. "Come on. Alan said time was of the essence."

Tabitha left her lingering doubt behind. If Felicity knew where Trudy was, then she had no option but to go with the young woman. Besides, Roger trusted her. She was his employee. "Let's go."

Two minutes later they were tearing out of the parking lot and headed south.

CHAPTER TWENTY-THREE

I can't believe Tabitha ditched me. Left me standing right beside the car. And I don't have a good feeling at all about this. I can still see Felicity's taillights on that long, straight stretch of highway. And thank the gods, Roger is pulling up and he sees me on the edge of the parking lot. He's opening the door and I'm hopping in. All I can do is yowl and hiss and indicate he should drive like a bat out of hell down the road. And he is doing it! All those little training moments when I showed him that I needed to go to the Prince Albert or the offices are now paying off. He is listening to me without hesitation. Felicity's taillights are barely visible, but Roger is making up for lost time. Listen to this fancy car purr. Sounds almost as good as I do. We'll be on them before long, and meanwhile, Roger is calling Budgie.

He is wearing his frowny face, which means Budgie confessed that Tabitha slipped away from him while he was dodging fists. Not really Budgie's fault, but I don't blame Roger for being upset too.

"So are we following Tabitha?" *Roger casts a look at me.*

"Me-ow!" *Which is feline for ab-so-lute-ly. And he gets it. He understands! I have sold this biped short for the last time. He is almost an honorary cat with his keen perception and ability to apply logic*

We've closed the gap on the car in front of us and now Roger is slowing down so that we aren't too obvious. The man has learned much from me in the past few days. His tailing techniques have greatly improved. If I could hang around with him for a month or two, he'd be an excellent detective. Tabitha too. Somehow, I suspect they have other career ambitions.

Now that the pace is less frantic, Roger is calling Tabitha. Her phone is ringing, but there's no answer. She's just in the car ahead of us. There's no reason she shouldn't answer her phone. And now Roger is as worried as I am.

The longer we drive the more I wonder if Felicity really knows where Trudy is being held. I'm not a native of this region, but in checking the stars, I get a sense that we're almost driving without a real destination. I give Roger a little nudge.

"I hear you, Trouble. This is making me concerned. I wish you could tell me why Tabitha isn't answering her cell phone."

Now that's something not even I can answer. But we're going to find out, and soon, I think. Felicity is turning into a dirt lane. She's going too slow, lingering, which puts us too close to her. Felicity knows this rental car. It's been parked at the Long house for several days. If we slow or stop, she'll be sure to take note. And now, I have big questions about who Felicity is and where her loyalties lie.

Felicity moves slowly down the narrow, rutted path, and Roger drives past at a blistering pace. Good. Now he's doing a turn around, and we're headed back. About a hundred yards down the road, Roger finds another lay-by and we park, pushing back into the brush on the side of the road. It's not a great hiding place, but the best we can do. I only hope that we don't have a long, long walk in the dark on rough terrain. But whatever awaits us, it's time to get the show on the road.

FELICITY HAD KEPT up a steady stream of easy conversation as she drove, but when she turned down the narrow, rutted dirt road, she fell silent. Tabitha glanced over at her, feeling a lurch in her stomach at the other woman's concentration. And fear. Felicity was afraid of something.

"Who is with Trudy?" she asked.

"I don't know for certain. Alan wasn't specific. He just said to bring you, that you might be able to convince Trudy to give them what they want."

"What do they want?" she asked, realizing that this was a question she should have asked before she got in the car with Felicity.

"Something about that cotton. Trudy ran some tests or did something and they want her evidence or her proof or whatever. She should just give it to them. Save her own skin."

And now mine too, Tabitha thought, but she didn't say it. She had begun to realize that instead of helping her sister, it was possible she was about to make life a lot more difficult. "Did Alan say what he thought Trudy knew?"

"Nope. He just said there was more money than anyone knew on the line. He set up the date with you so he could have a chance to talk to you."

"You know about the dating service?" Tabitha was a little surprised that Alan would share that information.

"I put that together," Felicity said. "Trudy used that match-making service, and then when I picked you up across the street from it...two plus two equals four. I figured you were going to follow in Trudy's footsteps, see if you could retrace some of her movements. I would do that if I was looking for my sister."

The car slowed and in the distance, Tabitha could make out a large building. "What is this place?"

"It's a research facility that Grundle Seed owns. They do a

lot of testing on crops, particularly cotton, corn, and soybeans."

"Why is it so hidden back here? There weren't any signs or any indication..."

"Research is highly secretive and lots of companies try to steal results and information. Grundle never wanted to have a high profile."

"Is Roger aware of this place?" She suddenly believed he wasn't. The skin on the back of her neck was prickling, and she knew it was fear.

Felicity only laughed. "He's a cotton farmer. He knows that research is the only thing that keeps him in business."

"I should call Roger. He'll be worried about me."

"He does seem to care about you," Felicity said as she continued slowly toward the building. "You'll get all your answers in just a moment. Whatever else, try to convince Trudy to just cooperate. That'll be the best thing for everyone."

Tabitha realized she'd gotten into a car with a woman she barely knew and rushed into what looked like serious trouble. Even stupider, she'd left without the cat. Trouble could have made a big difference for her. And so would a weapon. She reached into her purse for her phone. She was going to call Roger right away.

"Oh, I forgot to tell you. There's no reception here. The seed company blocks out the signal."

Tabitha checked her phone. The 'no service' light was on. She tucked the phone away in her pocket feeling more alone than she'd ever felt in her life. And she had no one to blame but herself. She'd come to believe that Felicity was not her friend, so she stopped asking questions. She didn't expect an honest answer any longer. She was on her own and it was up to her to protect herself. If Trudy was in the research facility, it would all be worth it.

The building was cement, tin, and glass, like an industrial building. When they arrived at the front door, it opened without a key and Felicity held the door for her to step inside. "Where's Trudy?"

"You're almost there." Felicity urged her forward. They crossed an open space that echoed with their footsteps and went to another door. Felicity opened it with a key and ushered Tabitha inside a corridor lined with doors. She could hear voices coming from one of the rooms, and she didn't wait for Felicity but ran toward the sound. Trudy! She had to find Trudy. When she pushed open a metal door, she stopped in her tracks. Antoine and Hannah were seated at a long conference table. But that wasn't what stopped her. To the right of the door, Alan Dotsun lay in a pool of blood. He was very dead.

"Welcome, Tabitha," Hannah said. "We've been waiting for you."

Tabitha turned to Felicity. She hadn't trusted her, but she hadn't expected to be betrayed in this fashion. "What—"

Felicity ducked out backward and slammed the door, shutting Tabitha in with her two enemies and a dead body.

ROGER TRUDGED THROUGH THE DARKNESS, following the black cat. Trouble's keener vision was an asset because Roger didn't know if possible guards had been set around the perimeter. He needed stealth and surprise. Tabitha was in trouble. A lot of trouble.

As if he could read minds, the cat stopped and looked up at him. "Me-ow." His cry was soft and plaintive. Yeah, the cat knew too. Tabitha needed them.

They came upon the building—all tin and cinder block—no windows, Roger tried his cell phone again to call the deputies. He had no signal. The building was large—a warehouse or industrial plant size. He didn't have time to circle it and investigate the exterior. The cat led him to a glass door that gave a view of an empty space. The door was unlocked and opened at his touch.

The cat shot inside ahead of him and headed to a door in the far wall. He clawed at the door, but softly, as if he were aware of the need for stealth. Roger realized he was disadvantaged. He'd come without a weapon or means of communication. He couldn't stop now, though. Tabitha was somewhere inside this building, and he meant to find her.

He opened the door for the cat and was stepping through himself when he heard the front door open and female voices.

"She's here, just like I promised."

"And Dirk? Were you able to get him here?"

"He's on his way," the first woman said. "I've done everything you asked. Now I need to be paid. I've got a ticket for an island far from here."

"Of course, Felicity. I don't have the cash on me." The woman laughed. "But first thing in the morning, stop by Daddy's office. I left an envelope there for you and instructions to give it to you."

"I'm leaving."

"A smart move on your part."

"You're going to let Trudy go, aren't you?" There was worry in the question. "You said you wouldn't hurt her."

"I didn't intend to hurt Lisa East. She rushed me. The gun went off accidentally. All she had to do was tell me where she was meeting Trudy, and she wouldn't. She laughed at me and said I was a 'stupid, jealous, twit.' And then she lunged at me. I pulled the trigger instinctively."

"I don't care. I just want my money and to get out of the country."

Roger recognized the voice then—his employee Felicity Montgomery. She was involved in Trudy's abduction up to her ears—and Lisa's murder too, or so it seemed. But who was the second woman? He cracked the door and peeked. Felicity approached, accompanied by Lily Kennedy, the daughter of the wealthiest man in the region and Dirk Cotwell's fiancée. Of all the people he'd suspected, it had never been Lily.

He heard the footsteps of the two women approaching and he hurried down the hallway and into the first door on his right. The room was a neat office and it was empty. Roger let the cat in just before he heard the women coming down the hallway. When they were past, he realized that while he didn't have phone service, there was a computer on the desk.

With a few clicks of the mouse he had a connection to the local sheriff's office. He sent a message to DeWayne with directions. "Be careful. They have Tabitha and Trudy. It's Felicity Montgomery and Lily Kennedy. My mother and Antoine are also involved. I don't know what's going on—completely—but they're up to their ears in this mess. Please hurry."

He shut down the computer and opened the office door, listening intently. Trouble was out into the hallway before he could stop the cat.

Two doors down, a metal door opened and Roger found himself face to face with his mother. The gun she held looked deadly and it was pointed right at his heart.

CHAPTER TWENTY-FOUR

abitha heard the confrontation between Hannah and Roger. They were just outside the door of the room she was being held in. Alan Dotsun's body remained on the floor, and neither Hannah nor Antoine seemed concerned. They pretended it wasn't there. Hannah had left the room, but Antoine remained, his gun trained on her.

"Where is my sister?" she asked. "Just tell me that Trudy is okay."

"Your sister displays a remarkable stubbornness, just like you. You've put yourself in real danger. Her too. And Roger."

"That's no answer. Is she safe?"

Antoine walked around Tabitha, the barrel of the gun never leaving her. "You would both be a lot better if you'd minded your own business."

Tabitha turned to follow him as he walked around the room. When he was in the far corner, he pointed toward the ceiling. It took Tabitha a minute to realize he was pointing at a camera. The room was bugged—and Antoine was letting her know that. She started to say something and he shook his head and began moving again.

"If only you'd stayed in New Orleans, and your sister too. Both of you would be safe, Roger would be safe, and Hannah and I would be in control of Long Agricultural. That might not be Charline and Samuel's chosen outcome, but no one would be dead. Now look. Lisa East. Alan Dotsun. Perhaps more."

"What is it you want?" Tabitha asked. "Why do all of this? Kill people? Hurt others? Why?"

"You have no concept of how much money is tied up in research for cotton and food, do you?" He laughed at her, an ugly laugh. "G9-14, the cotton seed your nosy little sister couldn't leave alone, has ripple implications that go all through the food chain."

"That seed is poisonous. If the same science is producing corn and soybeans and..." She didn't finish the thought. "You'll kill millions of people. Animals. If that stuff washes into the Gulf it'll be an epic disaster." The big picture was more horrific than she'd ever anticipated. "That was what Lisa and Trudy were trying to stop."

"Bingo. And you see where it got them. This is a global concern. It's bigger than the Mississippi Delta or even the United States."

"And when all of these people are poisoned and dead?"

"Admittedly, that wasn't the goal. We'd hoped for a cotton seed that would blaze a trail for other seeds. One that would allow crops to be grown without the pesticides and fertilizers that are destroying land, rivers, and the oceans."

"But it was a failure, and Trudy and Lisa were the first to document that."

"I have to admit, I never suspected two women without any real training would ferret out the problem. Poor Lisa came to us, tried to warn us. And when she realized we had no intention of stopping production of the seed, she made a fatal mistake. She threatened us. But she was key in luring Trudy to her house so that we could take her."

"Is my sister still alive?"

The door of the room swung open and Roger was thrust inside. Hannah was on his heels, the gun still pointed at her son. He went to Tabitha and pulled her into his arms. "Are you hurt?"

She shook her head. "Antoine was about to tell me if Trudy is still alive."

"She'll be here soon," Hannah said. "But I don't know how much longer any of you have to live."

Tabitha saw Hannah glance at the camera in the ceiling and then signal Antoine with her eyes. What was going on between them? She couldn't begin to guess, but something was definitely up. They were aware of the surveillance and both were not being secretive about it. They wanted Roger and her to know. So that meant someone else was involved. Someone that Antoine and Hannah answered to.

She rushed back into Roger's arms and whispered. "There's a camera. Your mom and Antoine are trying to let us know. Someone is watching all of us."

They didn't have long to wait. The door opened again and Trudy was shoved into the room in front of a slender blond woman. Lily Kennedy. She was the last person Tabitha had expected to see. But suddenly it all made sense. Lily talking to Felicity. Felicity setting her up. Felicity working for Roger and knowing about Lisa's plans for investigating the cotton on her calendar. The whole thing clicked into place—except for Antoine and Hannah.

"I'm fine," Trudy said, rubbing her wrists as she moved

closer to her sister and Roger. "I'm sorry I dragged you into this," she said. "I should have warned you, Tabitha. I should have told you the truth about what I was doing. About Green World and going undercover to stop this poisonous crop from being released. I just knew you'd try to protect me. Roger, I'm sorry."

Roger put a hand on her shoulder. "No apologies necessary." He turned to Lily. "I should be shocked, but I'm not. There was always a...ruthlessness about you. It's one reason I never understood why Dirk would marry you. How deep is Dirk in all of this?"

Lily scoffed. "Dirk is too stupid to be involved. In the world of the Delta, a woman of my position needs a man. Dirk suited me nicely. And he would have been free to do whatever he wished. He just couldn't stay in his own lane. All he had to do was plant the fields like I told him, let the cotton grow, and play the wealthy landowner to my Scarlett. And keep his pants on like a good fiancé. When I realized he was seeing Trudy behind my back, I couldn't let her work him for information."

"You were jealous of Trudy?" Roger asked. "You took pleasure in hurting Dirk."

"It was beautiful to watch. He'd show up for dinner at my home and moon out the window, depressed and worried. I'm going to wait until he gets here before I kill Trudy. You first, Trudy, then your sister. We'll pin the whole thing on Roger. Antoine and Hannah will take over Long Agricultural and we can expedite production of the cotton seed." Lily kept the gun trained on Trudy and pretended to pull the trigger. "Blam, you're dead."

"All your big plans. Dirk never loved you." Trudy got in Lily's face. "You were social status, money, the road to success, but you were never loved by Dirk, though he did try. I know that for a fact. He put his whole heart into trying because he wanted that for both of you. The problem is, you're just an unlovable witch and not even your daddy can love you. He loved Dirk far more than he ever loved you."

"Trudy, stop it!" Tabitha could see that Lily was furious. Any minute she'd pull the trigger and kill Trudy. "Just shut up."

"Listen to your sister," Lily said, her face flushed with anger. "I want to see Dirk suffer, but not as bad as I want to kill you."

"Then do it, you coward!" Trudy hurled the words.

"You little fool!" Lily stepped forward and hit Trudy on the side of the face with the gun butt. In a split second, Roger was flying across the room into Lily. Roger knocked the gun out of Lily's hands and it spun to a stop in front of Hannah. Tabitha went for it, but Hannah was faster. She picked it up and stepped back. Antoine rushed toward Roger and Lily, fighting on the floor. Antoine grabbed Lily's arm and pulled her to her feet. Instead of releasing her, he pushed her against the wall. "Lily Kennedy, you're under arrest."

Roger got slowly to his feet. Tabitha rushed to Trudy's side. "Are you okay?"

"Maybe," she said, "but it's going to be a whopper of a headache."

Tabitha scrambled to her feet. Hannah still held a gun, but it was pointed at the floor. "Drop the gun," Tabitha said. She was unarmed, but she meant to back up her order.

Hannah stuck the gun in a holster. "I'm working with Green World," she said. "Antoine and I have been undercover for months, trying to find out who was actually behind this new seed. And now we have Lily's confession, on tape." She pointed to the camera in the ceiling. "The whole time the cameras were rolling. Now we can drop the charade. We couldn't tell you sooner, because if this had gone the other direction, Antoine and I needed to protect our cover."

For a long moment, no one broke the stunned silence. Then Lily began to curse Hannah and Antoine, and a loud commotion started in the hallway. A cat yowled and a young woman began to scream.

"Trouble!" Roger and Tabitha said at once. They rushed the door to find Felicity cornered in the hallway. She'd been trying to run, but Trouble wasn't about to let her pass. Roger stepped forward and grabbed her by the arm while Tabitha scooped up the cat. She hugged him to her and kissed the top of his head. There were a lot of unanswered questions, but Trudy was safe and Roger wouldn't have to see his mother behind bars. All in all, it was turning into a glorious evening.

ROGER DROVE to the highway where he had cell phone coverage and called Budgie and DeWayne and told them where he was.

"You're a lucky man," DeWayne said. "We're on the way, and Sheriff Peters is with us. He and Sarah Booth just got home, and they have one very upset black cat at Dahlia House."

"We have a black cat of our own, here," Roger said. "I think they both need to be deputized."

"That could happen," DeWayne said. "See you in fifteen."

Roger was still reeling from the revelation that his mother and Antoine were working to capture the bad guys—and that they weren't bad themselves. He owed Hannah and Antoine an apology, and when the time was right, he'd do it on a grand scale. But Lily Kennedy took the cake. He'd known her his whole life. She'd been the golden girl, the girl with the most land and money. She'd had everything and it wasn't enough.

Headlights fell in behind him as he drove back to the research facility. It was too soon to be the deputies. He parked and waited, his mother's gun in his hand. Just in case.

Dirk almost tumbled out of his truck he was in such a hurry. "Lily called me. She said to get here fast. What is this place?"

And Roger had at least one answer. Dirk wasn't involved. He was just another victim left in the wake of Lily Kennedy's greed.

"Trudy is alive, Dirk. She's not hurt." He grasped his friend's shoulder. "I have some bad news about Lily."

"Is she injured?" He was instantly concerned.

"No, not injured. But she'll be going to jail for a long, long time. She abducted Trudy and killed Lisa East. Alan Dotsun too."

"What are you saying?" Dirk stopped.

"That cotton seed, G9-14. There's a problem. A big problem. We'll have to figure that out tomorrow, how we deal with what we've planted. But we can do that. Together. And we will. What's important now is that Trudy and Tabitha are safe. My mother..." He laughed out loud. "My mother works for the good guys. She and Trudy both. She tried to tell me, but I wouldn't listen." He laughed out loud. "Man, oh man, I can't wait to see Samuel's and Charline's faces. They're going to be so surprised."

"Lily was behind all of this?" Dirk almost staggered. "Why?"

"Greed. Simple greed. If Lily had been able to get all of the farmers to plant this new cotton seed before they learned of the consequences, she could have controlled cotton production in a lot of places. But part of it was also to punish you because of your feelings for Trudy."

"I do love her," Dirk said. "I fought it. I didn't want to care. But I do, and I can't pretend with Lily anymore. I didn't mean to hurt her, but Trudy is so...loving and honorable. And Lily...isn't."

Roger and Dirk entered the building and were greeted by one pacing black cat. "Trouble is on the side of the angels," Roger said. He entered the room where Antoine and Hannah kept Felicity and Lily under control. Tabitha and her sister were hugging in a corner.

"Just have a seat and relax," Roger said. "The law is on the way. It's all over now but the crying." He took a seat by the door and Tabitha joined him. The black cat jumped on his lap. "I couldn't have done it without you, Trouble."

THE NIGHT HAS PASSED. *Breakfast—a delicious mahi-mahi in a light sauce—has been consumed. Pluto is safely home with his bipeds, and Trudy is a guest of the Longs. She's been reunited with the charming Miss Vesta, and what a heartwarming scene that was. My work here is almost done, and a good thing, because Tammy will be heading back to Wetumpka in a matter of hours, and I must be with her. While I do my best for the humanoids I work with, in my heart of hearts, Tammy Lynn must come first. Only a few loose ends to tie up.*

How wonderful to see my psychic beauty and Mr. Farmer ogling each other. They are about to catch on fire, which is amusing for me, an old hand in the art of attraction. There is no longer any impediment in the way of their lustful longings. So it has all come round to right. I overheard Tabitha talking with her sister last night, and they're both considering a vacation in the Delta. Roger has invited them to stay in Long Hall. And let me add that Dirk genuinely seems to care about

Trudy. What started for her as an attempt to infiltrate the planters of the area to find out what was happening with the seed and research has turned into an affair of the heart. It looks as if both sisters might find that Cupid's arrow has hit home.

As to the rest of the Long family, I have to admit, Hannah and Antoine had even me fooled. I am normally on top of such pretenders and posers, but those two played me like a cheap fiddle. I'm just so relieved that Roger won't have to visit his mama in jail that I can't even be mad at them.

Antoine's resume was fabricated. His background on the Internet, a total fraud. He's been an agent with the FBI for the past twenty years. When he became involved with agricultural espionage, and he was assigned to follow the development of this "magic" cotton seed, he made it a point to meet Hannah. At first he meant to use her unwittingly, but as he got to know her, he realized what an asset she could be, with her family connections, to follow what was happening with G9-14—and other crop research. Hannah has always been interested in the environment. It only took a nudge from Antoine to bring her on board and her background as a social flibbertigibbet and scandalous woman served her perfectly. Now, at last, Hannah has found a job where she gained the respect she craved, and the ability to do something good. Antoine allowed her to become the woman that Micah Malone fell in love with. The woman who is Roger's mother, and now someone that will be welcomed into the family business—if she chooses to give up her work with Green World. I'm not certain that will happen. Antoine and Hannah make a formidable team. They could take on so many issues. And they do work well together. I also sense that there is much more to that relationship than work. For Hannah's sake, I hope so.

Hannah has even made peace with Charline—and apologized for her rotten behavior in the past. She spent the morning with Samuel, and I don't believe I've ever seen him happier. The same is true for Roger. Now when he looks at his mother, there is a light in his eyes.

Before I head back to Wetumpka, Tammy and I will join the Longs, Dirk, and Trudy at Dahlia House, Pluto's home. We've been invited for brunch—a yummy second breakfast as Bilbo Baggins would assert--to celebrate the capture of those involved in agricultural espionage. Hannah and Antoine will be there and I can't wait to hear about their lives as spies. I'm something of a vagabond and adventurer myself, but I lust for some spy action. Think of it—Trouble, the master spy. And with my British accent, I am perfect. "The name is Bond. James Bond." It just gives me the chills.

This visit to Dahlia House is the perfect opportunity for Trudy to take little Vesta to visit. Pluto will be thrilled. We have to make the bipeds understand that Pluto and Vesta are romantically involved. If Trudy returns to New Orleans she must promise to bring Vesta to the Delta on a regular basis for visits with Pluto. I have to convey that.

The time to depart for Dahlia House has come. I do believe I heard someone mention shrimp stuffed pasta shells. Heaven awaits!

CHAPTER TWENTY-FIVE

$\mathcal{T}$he old plantation house sat atop a slight rise. Sycamore trees, just beginning to show the first tiny green sprouts of leaves, lined the driveway. Dahlia House. It wasn't as large or ostentatious as Long Hall, but it had a charm all its own, Tabitha thought as Roger drove her for the brunch. By all reasoning, she should be headed back to New Orleans, not going to brunch, but Roger had invited her and Trudy to visit for a week or two. She'd found her sister, and Sheriff Coleman Peters and his deputies had arrested Lily Kennedy and several employees of the Kennedy agricultural business. Lily was charged with the murder of Lisa East and Alan Dotsun. Alan had uncovered the seed issues and threatened to go to the USDA, so Lily had shot him.

Even as they drove across the fertile fields, a team of bio-scientists were at the research facility where Alan had been killed. They would determine what Dirk and Roger would do with the fields they'd planted with the G9-14 cotton seed.

"I would never have suspected Lily," Tabitha said. She held

Trouble on her lap. The cat acted like he had ants in his pants. He was talking in little gerbil sounds and spinning in circles.

"I've known her all my life. I never figured her for a murderer, either. I don't think she ever really cared for Dirk. He fit the role for her, but Lily isn't just greedy. She's possessive. Even when it isn't something she really wants, she can't stand for someone else to have it." Roger sighed. "If her father isn't involved, this will break his heart."

"I'm sorry for that."

"Two people are dead and no telling how many more will be hurt. But at least the cotton will be contained."

Roger's anger seemed to have left him. Tabitha put a hand on his arm. "Lily was ruthless and she wasn't used to opposition. Few people in the Delta would go up against the Kennedy family. They had the money and the power to push things their way."

"The way I see it, Dirk was the perfect husband and also the perfect place to try that experimental seed. My land was a bonus for her—until Trudy started asking questions."

"This is hard to accept. Lily was willing to risk the land, the future?" Tabitha still had plenty of questions.

"Seemingly, so. The minute Alan caught on, he was going to call the feds. And DayZSeed was also caught up in this without any malicious intent. Sure, they were eager to have that new, magic seed, but they never intended to produce anything poisonous."

"Alan asked me out on a date so he could find out what I know, didn't he?" Tabitha asked.

"Well, I'm sure he thought you were pretty hot." Roger finally smiled. "If he didn't, he was blind."

"Me-ow!" Trouble added.

They stopped at the front of the house and the door

opened and the tall, handsome sheriff and a dark-haired woman that had to be Sarah Booth Delaney came out of the house to greet them. They were joined by a red tick hound and the plump black cat, Pluto.

Trouble jumped out the open truck window and ran toward Pluto. The two cats did a meet and greet and ran to the end of the porch. Trudy and Dirk, along with Vesta, pulled up and got out of the car. Vesta joined the black cats and they all three ran into the house. Charline and Samuel arrived, with Tammy Lynn in the backseat. Hannah and Antoine were the last to pull up.

"Looks like homecoming week," Roger said as he made the introductions all around.

Coleman pulled Roger and Tabitha aside. "Thanks for helping my deputies put this case to bed."

"Glad we could help," Roger said. "You actually should be thanking those cats."

Coleman nodded. "I know. A lot of folks would be skeptical, but not me." He leaned in a little closer. "I asked Millie from the café to cater this brunch. Sarah Booth tries, but bless her heart, she isn't much of a cook. I'd hate to see y'all survive a kidnapper and murderer only to die of ptomaine poisoning."

"Thanks," Tabitha said. "Do you know what the USDA is going to do with the cotton that was planted?"

"They're going to pull it up and destroy it. That land will have to remain fallow until there's research done to make certain it isn't contaminated. You guys prevented a serious disaster."

"Glad we could help," Tabitha said.

"Let's go inside and eat."

. . .

ROGER COULDN'T HELP GLANCING at his mother and Antoine. He'd already apologized for assuming the worst, and surprisingly, Hannah had been very reasonable and forgiving. Antoine had excused himself, and Roger had had a long conversation with his mother. She'd told him that Micah Malone was his father, and that at long last, she was going to be able to put that loss behind her.

"The bitterness of losing Micah nearly ruined my life. And yours," she'd said. "But I want to make a fresh start, if you can allow that. Antoine and I won't be staying in Sunflower County. We're going to continue our work, Antoine with the FBI and me with Green World. We seem to make a very good team. But I'd like to feel welcome with you and Charline and Samuel."

It had been a happy resolution, and now he smiled at his mother and she blew him a kiss. Dirk and Trudy, too, seemed to have found a groove where they had a shot at some happiness. Roger had gotten over his first impulse to take her to task for not confiding in him. And he still had one unanswered question.

"Trudy, how did you come to work in Sunflower County? How did you know about the experimental seed?"

"I was waiting tables in the French Quarter and I fell in with some young people who were passionate about the environment and politics. They'd heard a rumor about a new seed being developed by a chemical company. The rumors were really bad, and they had a line on the fact that the Mississippi Delta had been targeted as the place to try out the seed. We knew it had to be stopped." She grinned. "Yeah, they were talking about agri-espionage. They needed someone undercover in the business here in Sunflower County. I showed a talent for that kind of science and also for undercover work. I took a few classes and set up to move to Sunflower County. The dating service was their idea, and it worked like a charm. I hooked Dirk." She cast a smoldering look at him.

"She hooked me good," Dirk said. "I think she saved me from a lifetime of woe."

"You don't mean to say you're giving up your womanizing ways," Roger teased him.

"It's time for me to grow up. Lily gave me license to stay forever a juvenile, but I don't want that. I really don't. I want to be someone a woman can be proud of."

Roger raised his eyebrows and squeezed Tabitha's hand. "Wow. The bigger they are, the harder they fall."

His comment drew laughter from everyone around the table.

Roger looked around at his family and realized how lucky he was. He counted Tabitha among his family. He didn't know what the future held for them, but he wanted a chance to get to know her better. New Orleans wasn't that far away. And he had a sneaky suspicion that Trudy intended to spend a lot of time in the Delta. He glanced into the kitchen and saw the three cats chowing down together. Yes, there were many reasons that the two sisters needed to spend a lot of time in the Delta.

TABITHA FINISHED THE BRUNCH, which was delicious. Millie Roberts was highly touted as a local chef and she lived up to the billing. Everyone was engaged in lively conversation, but movement in the kitchen caught Tabitha's eye. She excused herself and stepped into the kitchen. The swinging door shut silently behind her.

"Still hungry?" The striking black woman dressed in a costume from the 1860s stood at the stove.

"Who are you?" Tabitha asked. Her breath condensed in front of her and she felt a sudden bitter cold.

"I'm Jitty. Sarah Booth's haint."

Tabitha realized she was speaking with an apparition, and one that knew she was dead. And she wasn't in the least bit shocked or afraid. "Why do you haunt Sarah Booth?"

"To keep her company. To keep her straight. To give her the advice that only a lovin' family member can give." She shrugged. "To keep her from bein' too lonely about the past."

Tabitha understood completely. "You're her guardian angel."

Jitty scoffed loudly. "She wouldn't see it that way."

"But I do."

"I got a message for your friend, Charline. It's from her ma-in-law."

"Suellen." Tabitha breathed the name.

"That's her. She says to tell Charline to plan a wedding. Not summer, but fall, when the weather is cool and the cotton is comin' in."

Tabitha laughed. "Are you talking about my wedding?"

"Listen, Missy, I'm not askin' you to interpret. Just deliver the message. Tell her Suellen recommends the rose garden on a fine November day. Could be a double wedding if that Dirk Cotwell plays his cards right." The apparition faded slightly. "Maybe you could inspire Sarah Booth to think about makin' a commitment. That girl is gonna end up a spinster if she doesn't get busy."

Before Tabitha could even laugh at the idea, the kitchen door swung open and Roger entered. "You okay?"

"Better than okay," she said, bending down to refill the cat bowls. "Way better than okay." She stood up and put her arms around Roger's neck and kissed him with all of her heart.

I HEAR Tammy Lynn calling my name. I can leave Sunflower County in the capable hands of Pluto and his lady love, Vesta. I even feel a small fondness for the red hound dog snoring by the stove. For a dog, she's smart and non-intrusive.

It's been a fine adventure in the Mississippi Delta. Now it's on to new cases, new scenery, and new black cat fun.

ACKNOWLEDGMENTS

Many hands are involved in the creation of a successful book. I want to thank Priya Bhakta. None of the books we write would exist were it not for her. She designs the interior, formats for the various platforms, creates promotional materials, runs contests, and deals with a million other vital issues. I'd also like to thank Rebecca Barrett, Susan Y. Tanner, Claire Matturro, and Beth Terrell--all members of the Mad Catters for their help and comments on this story. And the efforts of our wonderful Beta readers must be acknowledged. They have saved me from embarrassment more than once! Thank you. A special thanks to Cissy Hartley at www.writerspace.com who creates our covers. If you enjoy this book, please check out the other Trouble books by writers in the coalition. We all share the Sherlockian cat detective, Trouble, but each writer brings her unique gifts to the telling of the story.

ABOUT THE AUTHOR

 **Carolyn Haines** is the *USA Today* bestselling author of over 80 books. In 2020, she was inducted into the Alabama Writers Hall of Fame. She was the recipient of the 2019 Lifetime Achievement Award from the Alabama Library Association and the Mississippi Writer's Guild, the Harper Lee Award for Distinguished Writing, the Richard Wright Award for Literary Excellence, as well as the "Best Amateur Sleuth" award by *Romantic Times*. Haines writes in a number of genres, from cozy mystery to horror and short fiction. She got her start in publishing in romantic mysteries with one savvy black cat detective called Familiar. She's delighted to bring back the first *Familiar* stories—and to introduce Trouble, son of Familiar, in a delightful new Trouble Cat Mysteries series which features a number of talented authors (and cat lovers!)

www.carolynhaines.com

facebook.com/AuthorCarolynHaines

twitter.com/DeltaGalCarolyn

instagram.com/carolynhaines

goodreads.com/CarolynHaines

bookbub.com/profile/carolyn-haines

amazon.com/author/carolynhaines

GAME OF BONES

Sarah Booth Delaney mystery series #20

GAME OF BONES

Chapter 1

*M*arch is the month when hope returns. Even a spirit sorely challenged and worn down finds renewal in a shaft of warm March sunlight or the sight of green pushing through the soil. The new plantings that stretch from horizon to horizon across the vast Mississippi Delta seem to vibrate with a soft green haze that is nothing less than magical.

It's the perfect, crisp morning for a horseback ride, and I've saddled Miss Scrapiron and set off around the western property line with my loyal hound, Sweetie Pie, at my side. The smell of the soil is familiar and calming, as is the motion of my horse. This is a morning of perfect awareness, a feast for the senses. I stop at a brake that bisects a field to take in the tiniest buds on the tupelo gum trees. Miss Scrapiron stamps her foot and snorts, impatient. She is a creature of movement, of elegant maneuvers, speed and agility. She wants to run, and after I bid the spring buds a welcome, I loosen the reins, lean into her neck, and let her sweep me across the land in a rhythm of pounding hooves that is as primal as a heartbeat.

I let her run until her neck is flecked with foam where the

reins touch her, and when she slows of her own accord, I look back to see Sweetie Pie coursing toward us. She, too, is glad of the rest and flops onto the cool earth for a moment. Horse, dog, and human amble over to a small spring-fed creek swollen with February rains. Sweetie Pie unceremoniously leaps into the middle of it, despite the chill, and comes out shaking.

In the stillness of the brake, I listen to the trill of tiny songbirds. They flash yellow and brown through the pale and leafless tree trunks. In another two weeks, the green haze will settle over the trees as winter yields to spring.

I awoke this morning after a troubling dream. Only the fragments remain—a bare-chested man wearing a bear head mask. There are images scrawled across his chest with red, white, and black paints. I wonder if this is a visit from a past dweller on the acreage that comprises my property and home, Dahlia House. Long ago, before the white men came down in wagons to claim the land as their own, the Mississippi Delta was home to numerous indigenous tribes.

At times, most often dusk or dawn, I've seen the spirits of slaves or state prisoners contracted out for labor clearing the land or hoeing the long rows of crops. They are a vision from a long dead past, but I've watched them toil against the purpling sky, hearing the chants of the field hollers that allowed them to work in a steady, unrelenting beat. Those old work songs are the bedrock of the blues.

Today the fields are empty of ghosts. The sun and rain must do the work to bring the tiny plants taller. Humans have no magic for this part of the process. This is Mother Earth's gift to us. The vast acreage of Dahlia House is leased to a local farmer. I have none of the talents—or the love of gambling—that is necessary to put a fortune into a crop of corn, soybeans, or cotton and hope the weather and the market cooperate enough to bring a profit. I've saved out forty acres around Dahlia House for a hay field where the same man who leases the property cares for the Alicia Bermuda grass pasture to make winter hay for my horses. That's risk enough for me.

I turn Miss Scrapiron toward home. I'm meeting Coleman for breakfast. He's cooking and I'm eating, which is a fine arrangement. Last night he worked late so he didn't spend the night with me, but we'll catch up before we both begin our work day. His inclusion in my life has given me, like the land I love, a sense of balance. I'm still terrified of allowing myself to love him with everything in me, but on mornings like this, as I anticipate seeing him pull into the driveway and get out of his cruiser, I feel the shell around my heart softening. No one can protect us from loss or injury. If you love, you risk. I want to risk. I want to abandon my fear, but right now, caution is the only path I can travel.

"Sweetie Pie," I call my dog from the brake where she's gone sniffing the trail of a raccoon or opossum. She's a hunting dog who now seizes on the scents of evil-doers and has more than once saved my skin from bad people. The small furry creatures that roam the land, though a point of curiosity, are safe from her. And from me.

The wind blowing across the wide-open fields has a chill to it, but the sunshine on my back warms me through the light polar riding vest I wear. Miss Scrapiron rocks my hips with her long-legged Thoroughbred stride. I close my eyes and simply enjoy the sensation of sun and movement. My cell phone rings out with "Bad to the Bone."

Tinkie Bellcase Richmond, my partner in the Delaney Detective Agency, is on the horn. Tinkie, aside from being my best friend, is the Queen Bee of all the Delta society ladies. She is bred-in-the-bone Daddy's Girl, the 180-degree opposite of me. She holds teas, cotillions, garden club gatherings, and debutante balls for the social elite. She knows the DG hand-book backward and forward and manages to cram in her social obligations between caring for her husband, Oscar, and helping me solve crimes. Beneath the coiffed hair and haute couture wardrobe she wears beats the heart of a forensic accountant. Tinkie's daddy owns the local bank and her husband is presi-dent. Tinkie comes from money and she knows how to track it, find it, and sort through the many paper trails every crim-inal leaves behind.

"What's shaking?" I asked. I like to sit on my horse and talk on the phone. It could only be better if I had a cigarette. Sadly, those days were behind me.

"What do you know about the archeological dig at Mound Salla?" Tinkie asked.

"Let's see. No one knew the mound was actually a real Indian mound until recently, though it's been in plain sight for at least two centuries. An archeological crew started digging back around Thanksgiving. It's a team of university professors, some students, some archeologists. They believe Mound Salla was a sacred site for the Tunica tribe that once settled all up and down the Mississippi River."

"How did you know all that?" Tinkie asked.

"Mound Salla is not on the Mississippi River but here in Sunflower County. That's why it wasn't really explored or exca-vated until recently. No one knows why the Native Americans decided to build a mound this far from their normal settle-ments. It was hidden until recently. Well, not hidden, but there was a house sitting on top of it. Folks thought the mound was simply an outrageous foundation for the old estate house, but it's more than that. It's a burial ground."

"That doesn't explain why you'd know this." She sounded a

little testy.

"I thought I might go and volunteer to help with the dig so I read up on it," I said. "I love the idea of studying the original people that lived on this land."

"Old pottery shards, arrowheads, and for your trouble you get dirt under your fingernails that takes a professional manicure to clean out. And for what?"

Tinkie had never enjoyed making mud pies—it wasn't her style. She was more the accessorizing kind of girl. I loved finding treasures, even buried ones. "It's exciting to find things that tell the story of the past. Archeological digs show the day-to-day life of people who lived hundreds of years ago. Their struggles and celebrations. Their beliefs. It's fascinating." Okay, so I was a bit of a history geek sometimes. Most Delta society ladies were all over genealogy, doing their damnedest to prove they were descendants of the original Mayflower refugees. Right. My reading of the Pilgrims made them a club I didn't want to join—they were religious fanatics and a rather unpleasant lot. I kept hoping for more exotic DNA. Maybe gypsy!

"Hey, Sarah Booth. Did you hear me?" Tinkie's voice came over the phone. "We need to run out to the dig today. And Coleman said to cancel breakfast plans."

"Why? Why is Coleman cancelling breakfast and why do you want to go to the dig?" Tinkie wasn't about to volunteer as a worker bee. The day was sunny and warming, but the cotton fields were still damp from a recent rain. The gumbo, as the soil was called, was notorious for clinging in thick cakes to the boots of anyone foolish enough to walk through the fields. And Mound Salla was in a large forested area beside two vast plantings of cotton.

"There's been a murder." Tinkie was excited and repelled. I

could hear it in her voice. I was aggravated.

"Tinkie! Why didn't you say that right off?"

"It's not like the dead person is impatient, Sarah Booth. Time means nothing to the dead."

I wasn't so sure that was true. My experiences with the ghost of my great-great-great grandmother Alice's nanny, Jitty, had taught me that dead people were keenly attuned to the passage of time, and the ticking biological clock of my eggs. "Who died?"

"One of the scientists involved with the dig."

"Not Dr. Frank Hafner?" I was shocked at the thought. Hafner was a poster boy for the dedicated scientist who also worked out at the gym. Handsome, charming, and known to be a lady's man, he'd also headed up three of the most successful archeological digs of the past two decades. He was quickly developing almost a cult-like following among serious archeologists.

"No, not Hafner. It's his co-worker, Dr. Sandra Wells."

"A woman died at the dig? What happened?" I had visions of walls caving in or perhaps an accident with a pick ax. Digs were always dangerous because the method of removing the soil also allowed for cave-ins and mistakes.

"Her body was found hanging above an intrusive burial grave. It's this really deep shaft someone—and not someone with the dig—cored out of the mound. They were either going to bury Dr. Wells' body and got interrupted or they were looking for something." Tinkie said. "Oh, yeah, Dr. Wells was tortured."

That was a surprise. "She was murdered?"

"Since she didn't torture herself, so it would seem she's the victim of murder," Tinkie said.

"Thanks for the sarcasm," I said.

"Sorry, it's just that I happened to know Sandra Wells. She was a guest speaker at the Zinnia Historical Society. Prima donna, and she was a piece of work."

In Tinkie's terminology, a "piece of work" was either a conniving woman who trapped men into marriage or someone who pretended to be someone they were not. "How was she killed?"

"Hung upside down and her throat was cut. She bled out into a bowl just discovered in the dig. A ceremonial bowl that the lead archeologist, Frank Hafner, said could possibly have been used for human sacrifice."

"What?" That was way beyond gruesome for my home county. Things like that didn't happen in Zinnia. We had our share of murders, but not ritualistic killings. "The Tunica tribe wasn't known for human sacrifice. They were peaceful, until the whites began claiming all their land."

Tinkie was matter-of-fact. "I'm just reporting what Frank said. By the way, he's our new boss. I took the case. You're always saying how you need money, so he paid the retainer upfront. Now we should hustle over to the dig and see the body before Coleman has it removed. Doc's already there."

I nudged Scrapiron into an easy trot. It was hard to hold the phone, post, and talk, but I managed. "I'll head that way as soon as I get home. Maybe five more minutes."

"I'm going out there. I'll make some photos at the scene and start the interview process. Hafner hasn't been arrested yet, but Coleman told him not to leave the premises."

"If Hafner is innocent, did he have any idea who the murderer might be?"

Tinkie's laughter was clear and contagious. "He thinks it's a spirit guarding the burial grounds, which means he's not pointing the finger at anyone until he has more information.

He has this woo-woo story about the student workers too afraid to stay there after dark because of some spirit plodding around in the woods. But he's smart enough to know he's going to be the first suspect. He and Sandra Wells hated each other."

"Then why was she at his dig?"

"It was sort of *their* dig. She brought a grant that totaled over three-quarters of a million dollars and she bought a lot of specialized equipment with it. That's a lot of money for a dig that isn't likely to yield gold or jewels."

No kidding. Other than pottery shards and a better knowledge of the Native Americans who lived in the region, there wasn't any wealth to be gained. The Tunica tribe that populated the Delta area, adding onto the mounds left by a much earlier people, was not warlike. They'd gotten on well with all the French and Spanish explorers who walked through the land, sharing their food and hunting skills. Trouble began when the white settlers claimed the land as their own. In the Tunica world, the earth belonged to all and was meant to be shared. The concept of fences or property titles didn't exist.

Tinkie cleared her throat. "Hafner has made headlines with some of his finds in the mound." There had been news media, photographers from national magazines, a few international delegates, and some tribal officials on the site. I'd driven by the mound, which had been there for centuries beneath a gracious old plantation house. The Bailey family that owned the house abandoned it years back, and not so long ago the house had burned to the ground. No one thought anything about the high mound—assuming that the people who constructed the house had built it to avoid the flooding that had been a bane of the late 1800s and early 1900s. No one in recent times had considered that the Bailey plantation might sit atop a burial mound. No one except Frank Hafner, and he'd been correct.

Miss Scrapiron clopped down the driveway with a trot that was easy to post, and I hung up so I could unsaddle and hurry to meet Tinkie. My single desire was to grab a cup of coffee and slap some make-up on my face more to avoid getting chapped in the windy sunshine than for glamour reasons. When Miss Scrapiron was running free in the pasture with her buddies, I hurried to the back door. Someone stood in my kitchen window.

I stopped dead in my tracks to study the strong profile of the woman in my kitchen. She wore her hair braided and pulled back in a deer skin sheath decorated with beads. Her blouse was of woven fabric. Whoever she was, she was striking and fearsome.

In the back of my mind, I suspected that Jitty was at work, and I had to wonder about my dream of the masked person and the sudden murder at a dig excavating a Native American burial area. Now a bronzed warrior goddess was standing in my kitchen.

When I opened the back door, she turned to face me and I heard the rattle of a snake and the low, throaty tones of a Native American flute.

"There is danger around you." She lifted one hand, palm outward, and made a motion that seemed to encompass the space around me. "The grandfathers are unhappy. The grand-mothers weep at the destruction of their rest."

"Who are you?" I asked. I knew it was Jitty, taking on the persona of someone who had come to give me a warning.

"I am Lozen, warrior, medicine woman, and prophet of the Cheyenne Chiricahua Apache. I am the right hand of my brother, Chief Victorio. We shield our people in battle. We protect our right to ride free. Though we are gone now, even our resting places are destroyed for the greed of some."

"Is this about the archeological dig?"

"This is about your need to be strong. You will be tested. You, too, must stand and fight for what you believe in."

A chill swept across me. Jitty was forever deviling me with half-cocked theories and advice that would land me in prison for twenty years. But this was something different. This was chilling and had the feel of ancient wisdom brought to me from the Great Beyond.

"Don't talk in riddles. Please just tell me."

She lifted a small earthen bowl she held in her right hand. She dipped the fingers of her left hand in the bowl and drew three red marks on each cheek. "Chiricahua for the Red People. For the red clay that is our home. For the right to ride free."

"Jitty." I whispered her name, almost a plea. Lozen was a fierce warrior and she had scared me so badly I found it hard to draw in a full breath.

The features of the warrior began to shift and meld, modeling into the softer features of my beloved haint. "Jitty!" I was so glad to see her I wanted to hug her, but I would clasp only empty air.

When I saw the eye roll that was so typical of my sassy ghost, I exhaled a long sigh. "What in the hell are you trying to do to me? I'm not fond of your impersonations, but sometimes they're at least entertaining. That was downright unpleasant."

"Lozen died of tuberculosis in an Alabama prison camp. Now that's what I would call unpleasant."

She had a point, but I was still glad to see her. "I have to hustle out of here, Tinkie is waiting. If there's a message from Lozen or the Great Beyond, spit it out quick." The whole time I was talking I was walking up stairs to the bathroom to put some foundation on. Jitty followed still in her Indian garb. "Spit it out, Jitty. Time's a'wastin'."

"You want to talk about time wastin', do you? Put a hand on your gut and feel the slow death of those eggs. You want a message from me, get pregnant. You got a good, virile man, at last. He knows his business when he wants to bump uglies. Now get out of your own way and let nature take its course."

More than anything Jitty wanted an heir to haunt. I was the last Delaney so it was up to me to provide for her future—or so she thought. I'd fought too hard for the right to be just me to be considered an incubator by society or Jitty. "I don't have time to reproduce." It was a statement of fact.

"Lozan delivered a baby in the middle of a battlefield while she and her people were retreating."

I wanted to know more about this woman, but not now. Tinkie was waiting, as was Coleman and a dead body. I grabbed a cold biscuit from the bread box and some hot coffee in a thermos. I had to get to the site.

"Be safe," Jitty said. She'd returned to the stoic warrior goddess of the Apache tribe. A wind rippled through the kitchen and the rattle shook. Then Jitty/Lozen was gone.

Chapter Two

PLUTO WAS on the front porch waiting for me when I stepped outside, and I knew there was no hope of leaving him behind. Sweetie Pie magically appeared at the car. I opened the car door for the critters and we were off. I suspected Dr. Hafner would not be happy to see a cat and dog, but when he paid for Delaney Detective Agency, he got all of our resources.

The dig site was only twenty minutes from Dahlia House down a little used dirt road that led to the abandoned estate that had once belonged to a family named Bailey. They'd fallen on hard times, sold the land to an agri-business, and shortly after that, the family had left the area. The house was abandoned for years and had stood sentinel on the high mound until it had mysteriously burned down. No one had lived there, and there were no insurance claims. Rumors were that kids had accidentally set the fire, but lightning was ruled the official cause.

The blackened timbers of the house had been reclaimed by the woods and volunteer trees had sprouted all over the top of the mound, until the archeological crews showed up. When they'd begun excavating, they'd taken out the trees and plants in their way. Now, after a few rains, parking was a mess at the base of Mound Salla and the steep sides of the mound, fitted with large timbers to use as steps, showed recent wear. The site had become a big news item, and along with the officials who had a reason to be there, about four dozen gawkers had arrived. I called them the Tragedy Vultures. Whenever disaster struck, the same people came to see the latest accident or drama. Several locals were filming on cell phones. Budgie, one of Coleman's deputies, had them so far back their little phone cameras would be useless.

Tinkie and her dust mop, Chablis, were waiting for me, and Budgie waved us through. He knew we were on official business. I hadn't been to the mound up close and I was awestruck by the fact that something built hundreds of years before had not eroded. It was a steep incline, and the massive cypress timbers used to make steps had weathered the decades and decay. The Mound Builders had been masters of situating and packing various types of dirt to provide permanence.

It was a vigorous climb up the side of the mound, but Tinkie and I put our glutes into it and made the top where Coleman and Doc Sawyer, the local emergency room attending and county coroner, knelt beside a sheet covered body.

"Sarah Booth, Tinkie," Doc said, nodding a greeting. "Are you tourists or working?"

"Dr. Hafner hired us," Tinkie said.

"And he's going to need you," Coleman said matter-of-factly. "He's my number one suspect."

"You know that already?" Tinkie asked.

"I do. When I'm done here I'll tell you why."

Coleman wasn't a man who rushed to judgement. The evidence against Hafner had to be pretty convincing. But it was Tinkie's and my job to look around and find details that would lend themselves to Hafner's innocence, if he was innocent, and that remained to be seen.

About twenty yards from the sheet-draped body was a tripod of poles that had been lashed together with stout ropes which also held a massive hook. I was reminded of the hooks in slaughter houses, a thought that made me queasy. I stepped over and photographed the rope and knots. It was a primitive hoist, and I knew instantly that Dr. Sandra Wells had been hung from the hook in the center. She'd died on that spot, or if not died, this was where she'd been bled.

The earthen bowl that contained her blood remained on scene. I glanced at the symbols drawn into the clay bowl, ignoring the pool of gore inside. The bowl was huge—and I was amazed that it had survived hundreds of years buried in the ground without a crack or chip.

"Good lord, Sarah Booth, she was hung up like a cow or pig, her throat was cut, and she just...they say exsanguination is painful."

Death was always shocking, but even more so when it was such a brutal murder. I stepped back and looked out over the vista. The flat fields below us, newly planted, stretched for miles to the east, and the dense foliage of a swampy brake extended west. All evidence of the plantation house that had burned had been removed, but in the thicket of trees I saw what had to be a fort made by children. I'd done much the same on the grounds of Dahlia House, taking old boards and scraps of wood, wire, and tin to construct my own secret hideaway. The Bailey family included several children—this had to be their work. For a rural child, a fort was a perfect hideaway.

My father had offered to build a fort for me, but I'd refused. Then it wouldn't be my secret place. I'd created a hut out of old fencing, boards, weeds, and straw. I was happy with my makeshift work. I turned away from the past and faced my partner, who was poking at a dead fire some of the dig crew had left behind. At the base of the mound, the student workers had been herded into a group. They milled around like cattle, looking up at the top of the mound with varying degrees of curiosity, horror, annoyance, or sorrow. Sorrow was definitely in the minority.

Dr. Frank Hafner stood with them, consoling some and giving a pep talk to others. He was a very handsome man. Chiseled jaw, dimple in his chin, blue eyes the color of the March sky, light brown hair that ruffled in the breeze. He wore an expensive jacket that fit his broad shoulders and narrow waist to a T. He didn't have the air of any academic I'd ever hung out with. He was more...super hero. Any minute he might jump in the air and fly off. He'd leave behind a bunch of broken hearts. Almost all the young women working the dig looked up at him like he was Adonis.

"He's a looker," Tinkie said.

"And he knows it," I added.

"Confidence is very sexy. And power. At this dig Frank Hafner has both."

"I wonder if he was willing to kill to retain those things."

"He told me he was innocent." Tinkie arched one eyebrow.

I faced my partner. "Then I assume he has an alibi?" Tinkie had spoken with him, but I had not.

"He was with someone."

Oh, I could see this coming a mile down the road. "But he won't say who because it's a student and he doesn't want to be fired or destroy the young woman's reputation."

Tinkie only grinned. "Bwana pretty smart for a country girl."

I only rolled my eyes. Tinkie had developed a fetish for Alexander Skarsgard as Tarzan. She'd watched the movie at least a dozen times and sometimes when we were riding along a country road, she'd burst out in a Tarzan yell that would almost make me wreck. It was a phase she was going through and it would pass, but not quickly enough for my taste. "Stop calling me bwana."

"Yes, bwana." She grinned and stepped out of my reach. "Frank Hafner kind of reminds me of Alexander, don't you think? Tall, sexy. I wonder what he'd look like in a loin cloth. I'll bet he works out regularly. I can almost see his six pack beneath that cotton pullover."

He did look good. "Call him bwana. He'll love it."

"I suspect you're right." She held out a little finger with a crook in it. "Truce?" "Sure." I hooked her finger with mine and pulled. It was second grade secret pact stuff, but so much a part of our history. "I'm going to see if Doc will give me a view of the body before they move it."

"Someone used an auger to drill deep into the mound.

There are some things down in the hole, but Hafner has ordered everyone to stay clear. Coleman believes they were going to put Dr. Wells in the hole. An intrusion burial. Hafner is pissed about the destruction of the mound, though. Digging fifteen foot holes with an auger is not how an archeological dig is done."

"Great. Talk to Hafner about who knew how to run an auger. That would take some kind of expertise, I would think."

"Correct," Tinkie said. "Hey, Hafner is eyeballing you pretty hard. I think he may have the hots for you."

I could feel his gaze drilling into my back. "Poke him in the eyes, then." I wasn't in the mood. "I'll join you when I finish."

"Take photos. I don't want to look at the body, but we might need the photos."

"Sure thing." She was right about that.

Sweetie Pie and Chablis had taken a watchful stance not far from Dr. Wells' remains, but Pluto was nowhere in sight. If he didn't show in a few moments, I'd begin a search. He was an elusive cat with a nose for trouble—causing it and finding it.

I walked behind Coleman so that my shadow fell across him as he knelt beside the sheet covered corpse.

"Death by exsanguination," Doc Sawyer, who was on the other side of the body, said. "Not the method of death I'd pick. The cut was jagged and irregular, like the blade was rough. Maybe even stone."

"Like a caveman's tool?" Coleman asked.

Doc looked at Coleman and his gaze traveled up to connect with mine. "Yes. Like that. I'm tempted to guess that Dr. Wells was killed with a knife found here at the archeological site."

That put a new spin on the death. And it added to the ritualistic element of the murder. "Are you saying Dr. Wells was...sacrificed?"

"I'm saying no such thing." Doc was more tired than annoyed. "The use of an artifact as a murder weapon indicates this was a spur of the moment murder. Or it could be the complete opposite—that the killer brought such a tool with him because this method of murder, this particular victim, this location means something to him."

"You're sure it's a him?" Coleman asked.

"Yes. Dr. Wells weighs about a hundred and forty pounds. She was alive when she was hoisted up on the hook, and she was likely fighting for her life. I don't believe a female, unless she was exceptionally tall and strong, could have done that."

"Two females?" I asked.

"It's possible, but not likely." Doc waited for Coleman's response.

"I found footprints by the hoist."" Coleman said. "Male, probably size twelve. I'm certain our killer is a male. Dr. Hafner wears a size twelve and the patterns on the soles of his boots match the prints left in the dirt here. The circumstantial evidence is pretty damning."

A few strands of Sandra's hair had escaped the sheet and I could see that they were clotted with blood. I didn't really want to look beneath the sheet, but I asked if I could. Doc held the sheet back and I snapped a few photos to study later. The wound was indeed gruesome. It had not been an easy death for Sandra Wells. She'd once been a beautiful woman. I'd seen her about town with some of the younger students. She seemed to be held in respect by the young people. Now all of that was moot. Death had left her pale and with an anguished expression on her face.

"Any idea about motive?" I asked.

"That's why Hafner is my number one suspect," Coleman said as he rose to stand. He was a tall timber, solid and in his prime. He was a magnet for my affections, though I had more class than to put on a public display.

"I heard rumors around town that they were romantically involved," I said.

"I've heard the same," Coleman said. "And they were great competitors. Dr. Wells brought her own funding to this dig. She intended to amplify her standing as an archeologist. Dr. Hafner had separate funding and sought to control the method of excavation. It was a war from the get-go that included yelling matches and threats."

"Why didn't Hafner just kick her out of the dig?" He'd been on the scene first. He was already established here when Wells showed up with fancy equipment and her students and team. The story had flown all over Zinnia—and several magazines and television channels dedicated to history had made the competition into something of a reality TV show. I'd watched a few of the specials—because it involved my hometown area--and thought that both professors had engaged in the lively match to build ratings, and gather more donors. Typical reality show formula and nothing like controversy to bring in the money.

"Frank Hafner's grant only covered some of the cost. Dr. Wells had the equipment grant, the high tech that Hafner needed to complete the dig without destroying critical aspects of the site." Coleman pointed to the hoist. "That hole is twenty or so feet deep into the mound. Yet no graves appear to be disturbed. Someone knew exactly where to dig. Were they looking for something or looking to bury something?" He led me over to the bowl filled with Dr. Wells' blood.

I snapped a few photos and bent closer to examine the

markings on the bowl. They were strange hieroglyphics of a sort, the same thing one might find in a pyramid. Or on the painted chest or face of a warrior. I remembered the slashes and symbols from the dream that had so disturbed me. "Is this from the dig here?"

"I don't know," Coleman said. "Hafner isn't talking. But he will."

We both glanced down to the bottom of the mound where Hafner still corralled all the student workers. One was missing, though. The attractive brunette I'd seen earlier wearing overalls with a bright red kerchief tying back her hair was missing. And I could clearly see two distinct groups of students. They were all from a Michigan university. Some were Hafner's and some Wells' students. A handful of them, Wells' students I presumed, looked confused and mournful. Two were crying.

Coming toward the mound was a very official looking group of men in suits and women in office attire. "Who is that?" I asked Coleman.

"Those are sponsors of the dig. I don't know which ones, but this dig had some serious backing. The National Science Foundation, the Archeology Institute of America, and one very big private grant from the Americus Cleverdon Foundation run by Elton Cade. That guy with the striped tie is Cade. He's a big philanthropist and scientist."

He looked like any other businessman of means. "Why do people invest big money in these digs?" If artifacts were found, they most often went to a museum or public collection. In the narrow, narrow world of archeology there was some smattering of acclaim, but nothing that would bring in the bucks. "I get unraveling the mystery of the past. It's an exciting bit of detective work. But who has half a million to put toward something like this?"

"Rich people." Coleman helped Doc to his feet and signaled the EMTs to come and remove the body. They would take it to the local hospital so Doc could perform the autopsy. "If I had a lot of money, I'd fund cancer research. That's a mystery, too."

"I'd fund vaccinations for children all over the world." It was good to know that we both had a philanthropic bone, though it wasn't likely to get much exercise based on our current earning power.

"History is important too. If we understand our past, we can better chart our future." Coleman wiped his forehead and gave me a wink. "We can more easily figure out what motivates a person. In crime solving, motivation is ninety percent of the game."

"Well aren't you the philosophic brain today?" I couldn't resist putting my arm around him, just for a moment.

"How about a date tonight? I have body parts that aren't interested in philosophy. I'd like to show them to you."

I laughed, drawing more attention than I wanted. "Perfect. We'll talk later. Those suits are coming up the mound and I need to intercept them and get some answers. If I turn up anything interesting, I'll let you know. As long as it proves my client innocent."

"You do that," Coleman said.

Tinkie approached Elton Cade and as I joined them, I searched through my memory for the tidbits I knew about him. He was from the disappearing town of Hilo, Mississippi, an inventor who'd created a popular action game for children. Instead of selling the toy to a major company, he manufactured and sold it himself. It was the beginning of an empire of toys that included stores all across the nation. His products were safe and healthy and were highly touted by moms and environmental groups. He had the bucks to invest in digging up bones or buying islands or anything else he wanted. He'd married a local girl, had a kid, and lived a quiet life in a house not ten minutes from the clapboard home he'd grown up in.

I was about to introduce myself to Cade when a tall, handsome man with straight black hair worn in a queue came toward us. "This dig must be stopped." He blocked Cade's path, cutting me and Tinkie out of his way.

"What are you talking about?" Cade said. "This will reveal so much about the first settlers of this land. It's a boon for the local economy—hotels are filled and restaurants have catering jobs. Peter, we all benefit from this."

"The first settlers were my people. I'm legal counsel for the Tunica nation. This is sacred ground and all excavation must stop."

I recognized Peter Deerstalker. He'd been in town for a few days too and he hadn't bothered to be discreet about his opposition to the dig. The only thing missing from Deerstalker's speech was a court order. He didn't have one and I could tell by the look on Elton Cade's face he had no intention of stopping the dig. Not for a lawyer—not even for a dead woman.

"You know I love and respect you, Peter, but when you have a court order, then we'll talk," Cade said. "This is an important site. This mound is far off the normal geographic location of the other major mounds and it's been hidden here, untampered with, for all these years. Your people stand to benefit with the rest of the area."

"That's you're assessment. We believe this was a sacred temple site and was removed from the other sites to keep it safe and hidden. And that's how it should remain." Deerstalker stood his ground.

"I'm sorry. You don't have the say-so in that," Cade said. He shook his head slowly. "Look, I understand where you're coming from. But there is so much to be learned, so much that can benefit the Tunica tribe if their history becomes better known. There's not a downside to this for you or your people."

"Except that if this is a temple site with burials, the bones of my ancestors will be disturbed. In my culture, this is a violation, just as it is in the white culture. Imagine if I wanted to dig up a cemetery."

It was a valid point. I looked at Tinkie, whose gaze was on Frank Hafner. The professor was watching the interaction of Deerstalker and Cade with great interest.

"If there was a cemetery that might lead to a better understanding of the white migration to this land, I would say dig it up," Cade said. "The truth is, we know plenty about the spread of white settlements, the brutal tactics used, the way claim was laid to land that rightly belonged to the Native Americans. The predominant religious belief was Christian. The people who came here were often poor and tempted by the concept of owning their own plot of land. There's no mystery here. The Native settlers are far more intriguing. They could have settled anywhere. Why here? They weren't hunters as much as gatherers. Why here? In the most successful tribes, they had a society based on caring for each other. But they could also exhibit great brutality."

"We love the idea that there is great mystery in studying the *savages*." Deerstalker made his point without raising his voice.

"Can we have this conversation somewhere else?" Cade asked. "We can continue this back at the house. There's a dead woman here. The sheriff and Doc Sawyer are ready to carry her down the mound and I'd like to speak with the sheriff."

"I'll see you in Hilo," Deerstalker said.

The men nodded and scattered. Tinkie and I looked at each other. "Who knew a dig could be so controversial and fraught with such drama?"

"Let's talk to some of the students here. I want to find out the relationship between Hafner and Wells. And looks like Hafner has ducked out, or maybe Coleman has taken him."

Tinkie nodded agreement. "I've heard the two competing professors were hostile to each other. Wells made a scene in town a few days ago. She was badmouthing Hafner in Millie's when some of Hafner's students challenged her. Millie had to call the sheriff's office. When Budgie and DeWayne showed up, the students took off."

"That's a lead we need to pursue."

As Coleman had pointed out earlier, motivation was one key in finding a villain. Hafner was handsome and had a reputation for charming his students. Perhaps one of them had taken his defense to the point of homicide.

End of excerpt from *Game of Bones*
by Carolyn Haines
Sarah Booth Delaney mystery series #20

TROUBLE CAT MYSTERIES

Please join our Trouble Cat Mysteries page on Facebook:
fb.me/TroubleCatMysteries

www.troublecatmysteries.com

Familiar Trouble | Carolyn Haines
Trouble in Dixie | Rebecca Barrett
Trouble in Tallahassee | Claire Matturro
Trouble in Summer Valley | Susan Y. Tanner
Small Town Trouble | Laura Benedict
Trouble in Paradise | Rebecca Barrett
Turning for Trouble | Susan Y. Tanner
Trouble's Wedding Caper | Jen Talty

TROUBLE'S DOUBLE CONTEST WINNER
Blackie

This was my beloved cat Blackie. He would follow my husband Jimmy the way a dog would. As you can see in the photo, he enjoyed sitting on top of the back door. Blackie loved laying in the sunshine. I enjoyed watching him look out into the backyard where he'd stare at the birds and squirrels.

One quirky thing that Blackie would do was burrow his head and nap inside of a leather shoe, warmed by someone's feet. He also tried to fit his head in flip flops as well! I miss him so much. He would snuggle up against my side or back when I was sleeping. When he was a little kitten, he preferred to sleep on top of the bathroom sink.

You know what I miss a lot? When I'd be at my desk playing computer games, Blackie would get right in front of the monitor and chase the cursor with his paw.

Another of my precious memories would be our daily morning hide-and-seek game. When I got up, he'd run and hide behind the sofa. Then when I entered the living room, he'd run behind me and tap my leg. I'm thankful for all the memories I have of my dear Blackie.

— CAROLYN HUDDLESTON

Made in the USA
Las Vegas, NV
18 November 2022

59737664R00173